Praise for Fay Robinson's debut novel, *A Man Like Mac*.

"Without a doubt, Fay Robinson is publishing's newest, brightest shining light. She did the impossible—she made me fall in love with a most unlikely hero. *A Man Like Mac* will leave a lasting impression engraved on the heart of anyone lucky enough to read this book. Well-done, Ms. Robinson."
> —*New York Times* bestselling author Fern Michaels (*Finders Keepers* and *Yesterday*)

"A new writing star is born! Fay Robinson is an author of incredible depth and breadth. *A Man Like Mac* is an earthy, sensual and compassionate book overflowing with wonderful characterization and a plot with twists to keep any reader turning the pages to find out what happens next. I predict that Fay will very quickly become a favorite writer with romance readers the world over."
> —Lindsay McKenna, bestselling author of *Morgan's Mercenaries, Untamed Hunter* and the upcoming *Heart of the Warrior* (Silhouette, August 2000)

"What makes Fay Robinson's novel a must-read is the author's ability to escort her readers inside the hearts and souls of her characters…. Fans who enjoy a delicate but potent contemporary romance starring enchanting characters who will steal your heart will relish *A Man Like Mac*."
> —Harriet Klausner, reviewer

"Powerful, poignant, a story to remember."
> —Stella Cameron, bestselling author of *All Smiles* (MIRA Books)

Dear Reader,

I've always wondered what a musician would do if he or she couldn't play. Or a dancer who couldn't dance. What would *anyone* do if fate tried to take away his or her one special gift? Especially if that person mistakenly believed this gift defined him or her as a person.

In *A Man Like Mac*, I've created John "Mac" McCandless, who must heal the physical and emotional wounds of a woman from his past, even though it means he might lose her a second time. Mac has experienced tragedy and survived. He knows what it's like to have a dream taken away.

When Keely Wilson comes back into his life after a seven-year absence, he must use all his strength and patience to help her face the devastating injuries threatening the career she loves.

This story is about hope and courage, about an extraordinary man and the woman whose life he changes.

I hope you enjoy it.

Sincerely,

Fay Robinson

A MAN LIKE MAC
Fay Robinson

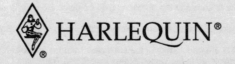

HARLEQUIN®

TORONTO • NEW YORK • LONDON
AMSTERDAM • PARIS • SYDNEY • HAMBURG
STOCKHOLM • ATHENS • TOKYO • MILAN • MADRID
PRAGUE • WARSAW • BUDAPEST • AUCKLAND

ISBN 0-373-70911-0

A MAN LIKE MAC

Copyright © 2000 by Carmel Thomaston.

This edition published by arrangement with Harlequin Books S.A.

Visit us at www.eHarlequin.com

Printed in U.S.A.

ABOUT THE AUTHOR

Fay Robinson believes in love at first sight and happily-ever-after. And she believes that some hearts are simply destined to be together. How could she not? Her English mother and American father were married by transatlantic phone six months after their first and only date. Fay had her own rendezvous with destiny while doing a story on a firefighter for her local newspaper. That night she told her best friend, "Today I met the man I'm going to marry." Fay and her firefighter will celebrate their twenty-fifth wedding anniversary this year.

Fay lives in Alabama within one hundred miles of the place where her paternal grandparents settled in the early 1800s. She spends her spare time canning vegetables from her husband's garden and researching her family history. You can write Fay at P.O. Box 240, Waverly, Alabama 36879-0240. And she invites you to visit her web site at http://www.fayrobinson.com. You can also check out the Friends and Links section at http://www.eHarlequin.com.

For my mother, who was fearless

And for Tom Woodward and the late Robert Mount, who taught me that heroes sometimes come with wheels.

Acknowledgment

My deepest appreciation to Paralympics gold-medal winner Shawn Meredith, respiratory therapist Steve Patton and rehabilitation specialist Lynn Carpenter-Harrington for their help with research. Any errors are mine and not theirs. Thanks also to the many disabled people and their spouses who were willing to answer questions. And to the staff at East Alabama Medical Center in Opelika, Alabama, for the guided tour of the trauma center and the smelling salts.

PROLOGUE

September 27

''TELL ME YOUR NAME!''

The demanding voice lurked at the edge of her consciousness, an intruder who prevented her from slipping into the welcome comfort of a pain-free sleep.

She struggled to keep her eyes open. She wanted to see the annoying person attached to the voice, but her eyelids felt heavy, too heavy to lift for more than a few seconds, and the enormous sun that hung in the air a few feet above her face blinded her.

Impossible. Her muddled mind tried to make sense of it. The sun couldn't be so large or so close, yet it was there each time she opened her eyes. Dark figures danced around it to a music that was eerie and frightening, that pulsed in rhythm to the fiery pain in her right side.

What were they doing to her? Who were these people whose hands roamed her body? They hurt her. They made her cry out as they poked her chest and stomach, as they slid their hands downward along her legs.

''Tell me your name!''

A man's voice? She licked her cracked lips and

tasted blood. The smell of antiseptic fouled the air and stung her nose and throat.

"Hurts," she cried.

"Where does it hurt?"

"Everywhere."

The voice pressed closer, just above her face. "Do you know your name?" This time she was certain the voice belonged to a man, but what man hated her so much to inflict this kind of pain? She opened her eyes and saw him, a green shroud covering his body and bloody bandages on his hands.

"Please...no more. Don't hurt me anymore."

"Honey, it's okay," said a soothing female voice at her ear. "You're in the emergency room. We're going to help you."

Emergency room? Images floated through her head, but they were indistinct, as if she were looking at them through frosted glass.

Hands moved along her legs and feet, touching and squeezing, sending pain shooting through her whole body. She screamed in protest.

"Stabilize and splint that leg," the man said. "That's all we can do for now." He leaned down. "My name is Dr. Tatum. Can you tell me yours?"

She tried. The name was so close she could almost touch it, but it toyed with her memory, scooting away just when she thought she had it.

She concentrated as hard as she could to clear her mind. The name revealed itself first. Then a flood of childhood memories poured out to overwhelm her. Her father. Her mother. Euphoria and pain. Love and anger.

"Keely. My name is...Keely Wilson."

"Keely Wilson, the runner?"

She nodded before he even had a chance to finish, an automatic response to a question she had answered thousands of times. *The runner.* The phrase defined not only *what* she was, but *who* she was. Over the years people had referred to her that way so often, the words were no longer a description but an extension of her name. Keely Wilson, *the runner.*

The doctor told a nurse, "Call Dr. Vanoy back and tell him the patient is an Olympic runner with a serious orthopedic injury. And make sure the pulmonologist knows she has a pneumo."

Serious orthopedic injury? Panic seized her. Details of the accident suddenly hit her. She'd been in the third hour of a slow run in midtown Atlanta. A car hadn't stopped at a red light and struck her as she crossed an intersection.

"Do you have family we can call?" the doctor asked.

She was an only child. Her mother lived a few miles away in Buckhead, but Keely hadn't seen her in months. Since the divorce seven years ago that had caused her father's fatal heart attack, she and her mother hadn't had much to say to each other.

What was there to say? With her betrayal, Liz Wilson had destroyed their family and caused the death of the most important person in Keely's life. Never would she forgive her mother for that.

"No, no one. I have no one."

The doctor pulled down his mask and took off his visor. She guessed he was in his late fifties or early sixties, nice-looking for an older man, but his face was much too grim.

"Will I be able to run again?" she asked.

"I don't know. Let's wait and see what happens."

His words held a glimmer of hope but his expression told her the dark truth. Not only didn't he believe she would run again, he didn't believe she would live.

She closed her eyes. Reaching deep inside herself, she grabbed hold of the strength that had seen her through more than one tragedy. Maybe this thing she possessed wasn't strength at all but pure stubbornness. Hardheadedness, her mother called it. An inability to ever give in, even when the odds were against her.

Not once in her amateur or professional career had she quit a race. Now she faced the toughest one of all—a race against death.

Calm replaced fear. Determination replaced sorrow. For twenty years she had struggled to become one of the world's elite athletes. While she might be worthless at everything else, racing was something she knew how to do.

And there was something else she knew how to do, something that, despite the grim line of the doctor's mouth and the sorrow she saw in his eyes, told her everything was going to be okay.

Keely Wilson knew how to win.

CHAPTER ONE

April

I NEED YOU.

No, Mac corrected himself. That wasn't what she'd told him. Old fool that he was, he had allowed his heart to trick him into hearing what he longed to hear, instead of what she'd really said.

I need your help.

Yes, that was it. She needed his *help*. Nothing more than that.

He'd been so overwhelmed at hearing from Keely after all these years he had let old feelings eclipse reason. Her sultry voice on the telephone, her soft pleading that he help with her rehabilitation, had distracted him. When she'd broken down and cried, his normal good sense had crumbled. He'd been willing to promise her anything just to make her feel better.

Had he been rational, he would never have agreed to this meeting, but he'd hesitated just long enough to wonder what it would be like to see her again in the flesh, rather than having to be satisfied with her photo on a magazine cover. That hesitation had done him in.

Now, he realized, and with deep regret, they would both pay a high price for his weakness, because he couldn't give her the thing she wanted most—to run again. No one could. And telling her in person was going to be ten times harder than doing it over the phone.

He shifted and did a few more lateral raises on the exercise machine, feeling the tautness of stress in his shoulders and back with every movement. A touch of vanity and a choking dose of insecurity had brought him to the athletic department's weight room to meet her, rather than having her sent to his office.

Normally he was neither vain nor insecure about his looks. Having had thirty-nine years to reflect on them, he considered himself in that gray area between handsome and ugly, somewhere around "passable." But today, for this woman, "passable" was inadequate, especially considering how much he'd changed in the six years since she'd graduated from college and they'd last seen each other.

With nervous fingers, he combed through his hair. He started to wipe the sweat from his face and put on his shirt, then thought better of it and tossed away the towel. He wanted to look like he was working out, instead of sitting here, waiting for her.

Although it galled him to admit it, he wanted her to see him without his shirt. The rest of him might be questionable, but he had put hundreds of hours into building the muscles in his chest, arms and shoulders. If he was going to give in to his stupid vanity, it only made sense to show off his assets. His defects were glaringly obvious.

The crowd in the weight room had thinned with the ringing of the eleven-o'clock bell, but twenty or so faculty members and students without a class the next period had lingered to work out, making Mac suddenly question the wisdom of this location for his meeting with Keely. He hadn't considered her feelings. She might not want anyone to know she'd asked him for help.

"McCandless, you're an idiot," he mumbled to himself.

Now it was too late to correct his error. She entered the room surrounded by student admirers she'd collected on her way up to the second floor. They bombarded her with questions.

"Are you recovered?"

"Are you competing in the Sydney Olympics?"

She answered the questions patiently, but the tightness around her mouth told him she was fighting pain. Her left leg appeared unstable, although seven months had passed since her accident. She favored the leg when she walked, favored her entire left side, and that worried him.

The beautiful skin he remembered as bronze from outdoor roadwork was sallow, a visible reminder of the trauma she'd sustained from the accident and the months away from training. The huge blue eyes, once so bright and full of life, reflected her weariness.

No way was she as far along in her recovery as she'd led him to believe.

"Hi, Coach," she said, smiling softly. "I'm so glad to see you." The hand she extended felt weak when he shook it. He could have pulled her off her feet with a simple tug.

"I'm glad to see you, too, Keely."

Her gaze left his face to creep with excruciating

slowness across his upper body, then slid downward. Feminine admiration lit her eyes and left him feeling almost dizzy.

"You look terrific." Her words seemed genuine. "Fit. More handsome than ever."

"And you're still beautiful."

"Well...older."

"So how come it doesn't show?"

Her smile widened, showing her dimples, making his heart constrict.

"I should have come much sooner, Coach. I'd forgotten how charming you can be."

"Call me Mac." He was twelve years older, and while that had probably seemed like a lot to her at seventeen, he hoped it didn't seem like much to her now at twenty-seven.

"Okay...Mac."

The young people had crowded closer and were grinning, obviously enjoying the exchange between their coach and his famous former student. Mac cleared his throat; it was enough to make them scurry out the door to class.

He motioned to the other end of the padded bench. "Do you want to talk here or would you rather go to my office for privacy and some quiet?" The noise of machines and the grunts of bodies straining for perfection surrounded them. The air, he suddenly noticed, also reeked with the smell of sweat.

She eased without hesitation onto the weight bench facing him.

"Here's fine. Feels like home to me. Besides, I've found it's impossible to keep anything private anymore. Ten minutes from now I'm sure some sports reporter will have discovered I'm here. Figuring out why will take about another two seconds.''

He nodded, understanding.

''The receptionist told me on my way in that you're now the athletic director. From assistant coach to A.D. in such a short time? I'm very impressed. Do you still teach?''

''Oh, sure. Sport Management and also undergraduate classes in Adaptive Physical Education. At a small university like this, it's not practical for me not to teach. And I like teaching. I still coach, too, although my duties have changed.''

''I can't believe how out of touch I am. I've been meaning to visit, but my schedule's so tight it's hard to even get home to Atlanta more than once or twice a year. Still, I feel bad that I've let so much time go by without dropping in. The drive from my mother's house to Courtland only took a couple of hours.''

''Hey, don't worry about it.''

''I'm glad I have the chance to thank you in person for the flowers you sent while I was in the hospital and your sweet note. Hearing from you meant a lot to me. I was feeling pretty low at the time with the rehab and the pain, and the doctors so discouraging about my future th-that hearing...''

Her voice cracked and her bottom lip trembled. An awkward silence descended between them as she struggled not to cry. She fingered the car keys in her lap, looking at them, instead of him.

Watching her, Mac struggled with his own emotions. The ache inside him, the one he'd carefully controlled since meeting this woman ten years ago, threatened to overwhelm him now and make him do something foolish. He could imagine his arms reaching out to hold her, his face against her own as he reassured her everything was going to be all right.

But he couldn't tell her everything was going to be all right because it wasn't. And he couldn't hold her, because if he did—even once—he would never be able to let her go.

"I'm sorry," she said in a near whisper, finally looking at him. "I detest weepy women, but I seem to be one of them lately. I'm fine and then without warning I feel like I'm going to fall apart."

"You sustained terrible injuries. Your emotions need to heal just like the rest of you."

"People keep telling me that, but everything's taking so long."

"Like your rehab? I can see you weren't straight with me about that when you called."

"Yes, like my rehab. I shouldn't have lied and I'm sorry, but I thought if I could only talk to you in person I could convince you things aren't as bad as you might have heard. I'm not healed, but I really am feeling much stronger physically. A few weeks ago I couldn't walk without crutches. Now, I'm getting around fine."

Mac bit back his comment. She was fooling herself.

"I understand I have a long way to go before I can run again or get back to a level where I can compete, but with you coaching me and supervising the rest of my rehab, I can do it. I know I can."

She sounded so certain that Mac wanted to believe

it, too, but what she wanted was impossible. The thick package of medical records, X rays and progress reports he'd insisted she have her doctors send him told the horror story. He had read and reread them, praying for something that would back up Keely's claim. He never found it. She *might* run for pleasure, but she'd never be able to compete again at a national or international level. Her career was over.

"Your doctors don't seem to think it's physically possible for you to run again," he reminded her.

"Those doctors don't know what they're talking about! They didn't think I'd live, but I did. Then they told me I'd never walk again, but you notice I walked in here without any trouble. So I have no reason to believe they're right when they say I can't run."

"And your current trainer? What does he think?"

"Former trainer," she corrected. "We had a difference of opinion about my chances for a full recovery so I fired him."

"I see."

She leaned forward, her face taut with determination. "Mac, no one understands me the way you do. You know what I'm like when I set my mind to something, how relentless I can be. You know I'll give this everything I've got."

Yes, he knew. She had more heart and talent than any student he'd ever coached, had always put running ahead of everything else, including her personal life. She would focus every breath, every hope, every moment on getting back her career. And when she failed…she would have nothing left.

Unless *he* gave her something.

"What will you do if you try your best and it's not enough?"

"That won't happen."

"Keely, you have to consider the possibility. All the grit in the world won't matter if your body's physically unable to do what you're asking it to do. Believe me, I know."

"Are you saying I can't ever run again?"

Well, there it was. He had prayed she wouldn't put it to him quite so bluntly. He didn't want to give her false hope, but he didn't want to crush her faith, either. She would need that faith, and much more, to get through the long months ahead. Her rehabilitation had only just begun.

"I didn't say you couldn't," he answered, hedging. "If it turns out, though, that you can't get back to the same level as before your accident, you need to be able to accept it and go on with your life."

"If I can't run I don't have a life, and that car might as well have killed me."

"You don't mean that."

"I *do* mean that. Mac, being a runner isn't just something I do, it's what I am. I get up in the morning so I can run. I go to bed at night so I'll feel rested enough to run. I eat only what I know will help me run faster and longer. These legs—" she grabbed her good thigh with one hand for emphasis "—are what make me Keely Wilson. They're all I have."

"Keely, life is more than running, and you're more than just a set of legs. You're bright. You're a hard worker. You could retire and—"

"I'm not retiring! I'm going to run again and I'll do whatever it takes to make that happen."

Mac rubbed the back of his neck in growing frustration. She was determined to try this, and no argument he could make was going to change her mind.

Her iron will was a curse, as well as a blessing. She couldn't accept that she had a permanent physical problem, wouldn't accept that her career was over until she exhausted every chance to save it. In doing that, she'd push herself to the limit. She could end up even more severely injured unless a qualified trainer guided her.

The reality was, *he* was the most qualified for the job and they both knew it. His credentials in rehabilitation were as good as anyone's in the country. He had also coached Keely during her four years in college. He knew her strengths and weaknesses.

"Please, Mac, don't say no. Maybe the doctors are right and it will take a miracle, but all I'm certain of is...without you I don't have any chance at all. Please. I *need* you."

He groaned, knowing now what he should have known the instant she walked into the room. It didn't matter if she didn't have a chance of ever running another race, much less winning one. It didn't matter if she couldn't run three feet without falling on her face. He was going to help her, anyway.

"All right, Keely, I'll oversee the remainder of your rehabilitation. If, after that, I think you can do any serious training, I'll help you. But I have a major condition you'll have to agree to, or the deal's off."

She let out a breath in relief. "Oh, anything. I'll

agree to any condition you make. Thank you. You won't regret this.''

''I hope you're right about that. Let's go to my office and work out the details. I need access to a telephone.''

She stood to follow him. He grabbed his towel and slung it around his neck, then reached out and grabbed his wheelchair, pulling it closer. He started to transfer but Keely shrieked, attracting not only Mac's attention but the attention of everyone working out around them.

He froze at her expression of horror.

''My God! What happened to you? Why are you in a *wheelchair?*''

Exercise machines around the room were turned off one by one. Conversation stopped. Silence wrapped itself around them, and he felt its smothering embrace. He prayed for a giant hole to open up and swallow him, but nothing happened.

Everyone waited for his response. He could feel their eyes boring into him.

Finally he found his voice. ''I assumed you knew. There was an accident and I can't use my legs anymore. I'm paralyzed.''

SHE WAS GOING to throw up. The nausea was moving up her throat, and Keely fought it with every bit of strength she had left.

She hung her head over the sink in the women's washroom and commanded her stomach to stop its roiling. Already she had humiliated Mac in front of his students and some of the staff of the athletic department. Getting sick would be another insult to him. She couldn't do it. Wouldn't do it.

But as she thought about him, about his useless legs, misery overwhelmed her. She hobbled to the small couch against the back wall and put her head between her knees.

Paralyzed! How? When?

Next to her late father, she admired Mac Mc-Candless more than any man she'd ever known. At one time she'd even imagined herself a little in love with him, as most of his female students probably had. That rugged face, those eyes the color of expensive chocolate, had driven her to distraction whenever she was close to him. As a coach, he was as gifted as anyone in the business.

Now he was paralyzed. Dear God!

The door to the rest room opened and a woman walked in. Keely straightened. "Hey, hon, are you gonna be okay?" the woman asked. "Mac's about to go crazy outside worrying about you."

"I'm okay. I just needed a minute to myself."

"Do you want me to get you some water? A cold drink?"

She shook her head. The woman plopped down on the edge of the couch facing her. She was shaped like a basketball, and Keely had to turn sideways and slide all the way to the back to give her room.

"I heard what just happened. The story's all over the building."

"Oh, no!" Keely put her hand to her stomach as another wave of nausea hit her.

"Name's Miriam Ethridge. I've been Mac's secretary for the last five years."

"Did he send you in here to check on me?"

"Yep, he's pretty frantic. You scared him when you nearly passed out in the weight room."

"The shock of seeing him…you know, like that."

The horrible moment flashed back to her. Oh, no, she'd screamed! She'd seen the wheelchair, realized it was his and let out a loud awful scream, as if suddenly confronted by a monster.

"Mac will never forgive me for this. I humiliated him in front of all those people."

"Honey, what that man's been through the last few years would've killed anyone else, but he hasn't let it beat him, so I don't think a bit of insensitivity from you is gonna be lethal. As soon as he could get around after he got hurt, he was right back at work as if nothing was wrong, showing people that he was still the same man. And he *is* the same man. They don't come any better than John Patrick McCandless, in or out of a wheelchair."

Keely wanted to ask what had happened to him, how Mac had been injured, but she didn't know this woman. She already felt uncomfortable discussing Mac with a stranger.

Miriam patted her on the arm with a chubby hand. "Pull yourself together and come on out. He's not as patient as he likes people to think. I won't be able to keep him out of here much longer."

"I can't go back out. I don't know what to say to him."

"Oh, I think you do. You just have to find the courage to say it."

COURAGE. SHE DIDN'T HAVE much of that lately. Her courage was in a constant battle with self-pity, and more often self-pity won. But Miriam had stood and walked to the door, leaving Keely no choice but to gather what little courage she had left, ease off the couch and follow.

Mac was in the hall in his wheelchair. His demeanor was calm and his complexion was no longer flushed from embarrassment, but those dark expressive eyes of his told her he was in pain. Regret, as sharp as the blade of a knife and just as deadly, pierced her heart.

"Feeling okay now?" he asked.

"Y-yes." The quaver in her voice made her statement seem false and ridiculous.

"Maybe you should lie down aga—"

"No, I'm okay." *Please,* she wanted to shout, *don't fuss over me! Don't be nice to me!* His concern only made her feel worse, because she knew she didn't deserve it.

With extreme effort she tried not to look at his legs or the black and chrome wheelchair, but a force stronger than her willpower *made* her look. The chair was bad enough, frightening, but seeing him in it put a horrible pain in the center of her chest.

She had come here expecting to find the Mac McCandless she remembered, the man who liked to run with his students, the man who had so loved to dance that at the graduation party for her class he spent the entire night whirling one partner after another around the floor. A physically perfect Mac.

Confronted with *this* Mac, she didn't know how to act or what to say.

Miriam coughed, breaking the silence. Keely's eyes snapped upward. She turned scarlet, realizing she'd been staring at his legs, trying to detect any change in them. Were they misshapen under those sweatpants? Scarred like hers because of some horrible accident?

"If you don't need me anymore, I've got errands," Miriam said, giving Keely a warning look as she walked away.

Mac suggested they go to his office. Once there, he cleared off a place on his couch and told her she could lie down if she needed.

"No, I'm fine now. Mac, I'm so sorry about everything, about coming here today without understanding...the situation. I feel terrible about what I did, how I reacted."

"Don't. I'm as much to blame as you. I assumed when you called you knew. I should have made sure."

"What happened to you? Why are you in a wheelchair?"

"I got shot a few years back. The bullet hit my spinal cord."

"Shot? Who? How?"

"I walked into the middle of an argument between a man and his girlfriend, not realizing the guy had a gun. We struggled, the gun went off, and I got hit right below the waist."

"When was this?"

"Four years ago this fall."

She thought back to that time, remembering where she'd been: France, Spain, England. Four major marathons and a string of personal appearances had kept her out of the country. She'd hardly had time to read an international newspaper, much less keep up with the Georgia news. But that was no excuse. Had she stayed in better touch with Mac after graduation as she'd intended, he could have told her about the shooting himself.

"Can you walk at all?"

"No, and I never will."

The thought was too horrible to even contemplate. "I'm so sorry."

"I've accepted it. Things could have been worse."

He ran his hand roughly through his hair. The strands of gray at his temple hadn't been there six years ago, and the deepened lines around his mouth and eyes added a maturity that was also new.

"Keely." He shifted in his chair. "After this... misunderstanding, it might not be a bad idea for us to rethink our coaching arrangement."

Slowly, she nodded in agreement, but depression overwhelmed her. Hope drained away.

When she'd had her accident and the doctors told her she wouldn't run again, a solitary idea had planted itself in her brain and refused to leave—Mac McCandless could help her. She'd fed on that notion, using it to sustain her during the agony of physical therapy. She had called it up and clung to it at night, when the pain had gotten unbearable and hopelessness had nearly defeated her.

But now... What was left for her now? Mac wasn't going to help her. She had nowhere else to turn.

"I can't blame you for not wanting to coach me anymore," she told him, determined not to make him feel bad about it. "I've acted like an idiot today."

"I don't remember saying I wouldn't coach you."

Her pulse quickened. "Are you saying you might still be willing?"

He hesitated. "Before I decide that, I think the bigger question is, are *you* willing? You had a pretty strong reaction to my disability. Given what you've been through the last several months, it was understandable. But—and this is a pretty big but—my paralysis isn't going to change. A month from now, six months from now, I'll still be in this chair. Can you handle being around a paraplegic?"

"Yes."

"Don't be so quick to answer. If you can't keep yourself from getting sick or feeling like you're going to pass out every time you look at me, the days'll get pretty long."

"Mac, I'm sure," she countered, desperation rather than confidence guiding her answer. "Please, will you help me?"

AS HE SAT ON HIS PATIO late that night, polishing off another beer, Mac wondered how he'd talked himself into taking on a project that was doomed before it started. Keely was hoping for a miracle, and he didn't believe in miracles. After nearly four years of asking for one every night and waking up every morning still paralyzed, he'd finally gotten the message and stopped asking.

No, miracles weren't his department. He couldn't deliver. Knowing that, knowing that if he did this she'd probably blame him or even hate him when she failed to get her career back, he'd still been stupid enough to agree to coach her.

He was crazy. Hell, they were both crazy. A runner who couldn't accept that she would never run again and her gimp coach stupid enough to help her try. The problems were enormous. She couldn't even look at him below the waist without turning green.

Where was he going to find the time to coach her? He was already overworked.

How could he keep her from hurting herself? She had no patience.

But the biggest question, the one that had been consuming him since that first telephone call: *How could he keep himself from falling in love with her again?*

CHAPTER TWO

May

LIZ WILSON WATCHED as her daughter stuffed clothes into a suitcase. "I can't believe you're going through with this," she said, no longer able to keep quiet.

Keely sighed and latched the bag. "Mother, please don't give me a hard time. You promised."

"At least wait until you're feeling better. Surely six months won't make any difference. In the fall, when you're more completely healed, then you can move to Courtland."

"I can't afford to lose the training time. I'm already deconditioned."

"But—"

"No, it's settled. I've rented a house. I've already enrolled in graduate school. Support my decision, please."

"Sweetheart, you know I support you. I'm thrilled you're going back to school, but you don't have to move halfway across the state to do that. You can stay here."

"Getting out of the city where the air is cleaner will help me recover faster. You know the smog bothers my lungs. Besides, Coach McCandless is there."

True, Liz thought, somewhat consoled. A nice

young man that John McCandless. Polite. Responsible. Liz was sorry to hear he was now in a wheelchair.

Keely opened another suitcase and limped to the dresser to begin emptying it. Liz doubted she'd ever walk normally again.

"What about the commercials you're doing? Didn't Ross Hewitt negotiate some new ones for you? I don't understand why you don't wait until after you've completed those."

"I'm not doing any new commercials. The sportswear company dropped me as their spokesperson."

"Dropped you? Why?"

"I guess they decided no one wants to wear gear endorsed by an injured runner with ugly scars all over her arms and legs. I don't make a pretty picture anymore."

"Don't be ridiculous! You're as beautiful as ever."

"And you're slightly biased, I think."

"What about your contract? They can't simply cancel it, can they?"

"Ross made them pay it off. He bought me a company with the money."

Liz couldn't have been more shocked. When had this happened? Keely had never mentioned it. "You own a company?"

"Uh-huh. Coxwell Industries in Miami." She crammed shorts into another suitcase and threw running shoes in on top of them.

"What does it do?"

"Makes custom linens for hospitals and nursing homes."

"A big company?"

''No, more like a small business. Only fifteen employees.''

''But textiles? Why?''

''Because I have a patent for a fabric I developed a few years ago while trying to come up with racing clothes I could wear in extreme weather.''

This was news to Liz as well. ''And...? she prompted, wanting to know the rest of the story.

''And...it turns out the finished fabric also makes a perfect covering for trauma victims because it helps regulate body temperature and reduces shock.''

''Sweetheart, that's wonderful!''

''It's no big deal, Mother. The lab I hired did most of the work because I didn't have the skills. And the medical application thing...I only stumbled on that by accident.''

''But it was still your idea.''

''Yeah, but Ross is the one who saw the potential for using it outside sports. He's convinced me to go into limited production with the stuff and test the market.''

''When did you make this decision?''

''I don't know. Two, three months ago.''

''And you didn't tell me?''

Keely shrugged as if she hadn't thought of it or, worse, hadn't considered her mother important enough to be told.

Wounded, Liz sat on the bed and busied herself by trying to straighten out the chaos created by her daughter's haphazard method of packing. Communication between them had been minimal for years, at times nonexistent, but Liz had worked hard since

Keely's accident to correct that. Insisting she come home to recuperate had helped.

Liz believed she was making progress, as much progress as Keely allowed her to make. Her daughter's pain over the divorce was so deep-rooted Liz didn't know if she'd ever be able to overcome it.

"Will you let me visit you?" she ventured to ask.

Keely stilled momentarily, obviously surprised by the request, then recovered sufficiently to counter Liz's attempt to get close to her. "You'll be too busy with what's-his-name to do much visiting, won't you?"

Touché, Liz thought, but she wasn't going to let her daughter beat her that easily. "I'm sure I can find the time. Perhaps I can bring Everett with me. I'd like the two of you to know each other better."

"One big happy family," Keely said sarcastically.

"Everett is a good man, and I care about him. I wish you'd make an effort to get along with him for my sake."

"Please, don't start this. Not today."

"Not today. Not yesterday. Not tomorrow. When?"

"Mother, if we talk about this we'll only argue, and I don't want to start arguing ten minutes before I leave."

"Neither do I, but I'd rather argue than have you push me away. You don't talk to me or share your life with me. You refuse to share in mine. We're becoming strangers. Is that what you want?"

"No, of course not."

"Then why can't you at least try to be tolerant of my relationship with Everett?"

"I'll say goodbye here. No need for you to come out to the car."

"Keely, don't do this."

"I have to. I appreciate your letting me stay here these past few months and everything you've done to help me get back on my feet. I really do. But I have to go on with my life now."

"You could have a life in Atlanta with me."

Keely stared at her in disbelief. "That wouldn't work and you know it. We'd be at each other's throats all the time, yelling and fighting like..." She looked away.

"Like your father and I did? That's what you were going to say, wasn't it?"

"Yes. And I couldn't go through that. Not again."

She made her way slowly to the window and called to the gardener to come inside for the last two suitcases, then picked up her billfold and keys and limped to the door.

"Please, Keely! It's been seven years," Liz cried in desperation. "How can you continue to hate me for divorcing your father when you know it was better for all of us?"

She hesitated, then turned. "Mother, don't say that or even think it. I don't hate you. I know you had some problems, some differences of opinion, but I can't understand how you could kick Daddy out. I certainly don't hate you for it, though."

"You act like it sometimes. You've put up a wall between us, and no matter what I do, I can't seem to get past it. Little by little you've shut me out of every part of your life, as if you're trying to…to punish me.''

''I haven't.''

''Yes, you have. At least admit it to yourself, if not to me.''

Keely stood quietly for a moment. ''I'm sorry. I don't mean to shut you out, but I'm not sure I know how *not* to.''

''You might start by forgiving me.''

''I want to, it's just…'' She shook her head. ''I can't help wishing things could have been different between you and Daddy—that you'd somehow worked things out so the last months of his life could've been happy. You claim to have loved him. But when you love people, you don't give up on them.''

Her daughter's words cut deeply. For seven years Liz had allowed herself to shoulder the blame for the breakup and she longed to tell Keely what had really happened.

But to do so would destroy the only thing her daughter had left of the father she adored—good memories. And she couldn't do that to Keely or even to Spence, not with him dead and unable to defend himself.

So instead of telling her the truth as she wanted to, Liz kept silent. Keely would never believe her, anyway.

Liz watched from the window as Keely somberly walked to her car with the aid of a cane and climbed in. ''You're right,'' she whispered, saying to herself what she wished she could openly say to her daughter.

"When you love people, you don't give up on them. And I'm not giving up on you."

KEELY WAITED until she was a safe distance from the house before she let the tears flow freely. She pulled over to the side of the tree-lined street, turned off the engine and wept until there were no tears left to shed. The purging was long overdue. The pain had been festering for years, just waiting for the right time to come spewing out. The intensity of the release, however, surprised even her.

Her father had meant everything to her. He'd been her first coach, but most importantly, her best friend. The divorce, then his death from a heart attack less than two months later, had ripped a hole in her life, and that hole kept getting bigger, no matter how many times she attempted to repair it.

In truth, the hole had almost always been there; it had started as a tiny crack one winter night when she was five and had awoken in the dark to the frightening sound of her parents' raised voices in the next room. The words were unclear, but their tone was unmistakably angry.

After that, many more arguments had followed to widen the crack.

"Why do you and Mother fight?" Keely had asked her father one day with a child's innocence.

"Because your mother likes things her way."

For a child who worshiped her father and had little in common with her mother, that had been sufficient explanation.

Later it was clear they fought for exactly the reason

her father had said. Her mother liked to be in charge. When she wasn't, the people around her suffered.

But knowing the reason for the unhappiness in her family had done nothing to alleviate the pain Keely felt every time her parents screamed at each other. Only running had done that. What had started as a way to escape the house during their verbal wars quickly changed to a lifeline for her, a means of self-therapy that could help her endure.

She used to convince herself that if she made it around the block without stopping, everything would be all right when she got back home. When around the block wasn't enough, she ran a mile, then five, then more. The silly superstitious ritual had given her some sense of control over a situation that was beyond her control.

Her parents stayed together twenty-three years, until their differences finally tore them apart. How it had worked that long, Keely didn't know. They were terribly mismatched. Her mother liked expensive clothes, fine wine and elegant dinners. She came from old money and was a patron of the Atlanta Symphony Orchestra and the Alliance Theater Company.

Her father had been a simple insurance salesman, happy in a pair of shorts from Wal-Mart. He'd loved beer, hot dogs and sports of all kinds. The Braves hadn't played at home without his being in the stands.

Different politics, different friends, different interests. Her parents were as far apart as two people could be. Keely wished they'd called it quits long before they did, although the breakup, when it had finally come, had been terrible. Her father's death on the heels of it had devastated her.

Her mother was to blame for the divorce. To her father's credit, he had at least tried to find some common ground. Her mother had refused to give an inch.

Your mother likes things her way.

Her father's words explained everything.

THE HOUSE SHE'D RENTED in Courtland was larger than she really wanted, but size hadn't been her first priority. She had needed something in an area with quiet streets, a house with no steps or difficult areas to trip her up since she was walking no better than a child in her first pair of shoes.

With Mac's help she'd found a great house in an older neighborhood about three miles from campus. Airy, with plenty of glass to let in the sunlight, it had a big tub in the master bathroom. The pool, though, had sold her on the place. Anytime she felt like taking a swim, she could step out the back door.

Well, almost anytime. Mac had given her specific instructions about the use of the pool and threatened her with unspecified consequences if she disobeyed. The man could be downright dictatorial at times.

And he could be a saint. When she arrived, several burly young men had been lounging on her steps, saying "Coach" had given them orders to unload her car and carry everything into the house. What little furniture she owned, in storage since the accident, had also arrived, and she supervised its placement.

Now it was dark and after eight, and she sat at the kitchen table making a list of things she needed to do this week. Picking up the portable phone, she dialed Mac's number again to thank him for the help, but as with the previous calls, there was no answer. She quickly hung up before the machine clicked on. One message was enough.

Was he out with friends? With a woman? Even men in wheelchairs dated on Saturday night, she supposed. She guessed they even got married, although she was pretty sure Mac hadn't.

Did he have someone special in his life?

"No, Keely, don't start this," she warned herself out loud. Mac's personal life was none of her business.

A WOMAN WASN'T KEEPING Mac's body occupied but definitely his mind, as he raced lap after lap around the track. He was desperate, and exercising to exhaustion was the only antidote he could think of.

It wasn't working. The desire to drive to Keely's house was as overwhelming now as it had been hours ago. The last month had been hard, waiting for her to move to town some of the worst agony he had endured. But it was nothing compared to what he was going through now that she was here and he was trying to stay away from her.

Ever since three o'clock had rolled around—when she was due to arrive—he'd fought the urge to stop by or call her. He wanted to see her, talk to her, hear her laugh. He wanted to say something witty so she'd smile really wide, and her dimples would appear.

Maybe he should go over there just to make sure she got moved in okay. No, that was a bad idea.

He hit the push rings on his racing wheelchair with

a hard even stroke. Her training and school would throw them together enough hours; he didn't need to invent reasons to be with her.

Finally having achieved the exhaustion he'd been seeking, he gave up and drove home. The light on the answering machine blinked, indicating three messages. The first and second were from women he dated occasionally. Both wanted to know where he'd been the last month and why he hadn't called. The third was from the object of his misery.

"Mac, it's Keely. Sorry I missed you. Just wanted to thank you for sending over the help this afternoon. I really appreciate it. You're sweet. Bye."

The last of his resolve drained away at the sound of her voice. He took out the piece of paper in his wallet where he'd written her new number and dialed it. She answered on the second ring.

"Hi, it's Mac. Sorry it took me so long to get back to you."

"That's okay. I really didn't expect you to call me tonight."

She sounded strange, so he asked, "Did I wake you?"

"No, I was up. I'm trying out my big bathtub. Mmm, it's wonderful."

He hung his head as his mind created the picture: Keely naked, that incredible body slick with soap.

"Did you get moved in?"

"Uh-huh. Thanks to you. I can't thank you enough for providing all the help."

He could hear her moving in the water, and he closed his eyes in an attempt to block out the image the sound created. He could almost see the droplets beaded on her breasts, her face flushed from the heat, her hand moving across her skin.

"Are you feeling okay?" he managed to croak out.

"I'm feeling fine. Better emotionally than I've felt in months, as a matter of fact. Can we start on a light exercise program this week?"

"Don't push it. We need to do a full evaluation of your condition first. Get settled in with classes next week. After that, I'll work out a program with your doctors."

"Oh, all right."

"Hey, cheer up. I've got something to keep you busy. I'm doing roadwork with a few of our wheelers tomorrow afternoon, and I could use your help."

"You want me to help with wheelchair racers?" He could hear the tension in her voice, could almost hear her mind clicking away, trying to find an excuse to get out of it. "I don't know anything about wheelers."

"You don't need to. I only need another pair of hands. You're on my way, so I'll pick you up at about a quarter to two."

"But I'll be useless."

"No, you won't. And this will be good experience for you. As Coach Stewart's teaching assistant, you're going to have to work with all the athletes, even the disabled ones, so you might as well jump in and get your feet wet."

"Okay, then. I'll try my best."

After they hung up and Mac started to think about what he'd done, his smile of triumph faded. This was only her first day in town and already he'd found an excuse to call her. And to spend tomorrow with her. He glanced at his watch. Actually he hadn't lasted a whole day. Only about six hours.

He sighed deeply and shook his head. He was never going to make it through the next few months.

CHAPTER THREE

"WHO ELSE NEEDS sunscreen?"

Male hands shot upward at Keely's question. Mac groaned and his best friend, Alan Sizemore, who sat next to him on the track, chuckled.

"I may be wrong, but I think she's already put sunscreen on half those jokers with their hands up," Alan said unnecessarily, just to needle him.

"Sizemore..." Mac warned under his breath, but he doubted it would do any good. He should never have told Alan he'd once had feelings for Keely. His second mistake was inviting her to come here this afternoon, when he knew Alan planned to train with them. Never one to miss an opportunity to taunt him, Alan had been in rare form from the moment they'd gotten out of the van.

"Who's next?" Keely asked the students, oblivious to the turmoil she was about to create.

Wheels clashed and elbows jabbed as the six young men scrambled in their racers for the front position. Ben, a senior from Athens, pushed forward with amazing agility to crowd out his teammates; he was moving faster than he had in any race. Mac and Alan watched the drama from several feet away, Alan with an amused look, Mac with an uncharacteristic scowl.

Watching the guys hit on her didn't bother Mac. He'd expected that. But watching her touch them was driving him nuts.

What was going on? When she looked at *him* in his wheelchair, she got sick to her stomach. So how come she could slather lotion on *these* guys in wheelchairs—guys she'd never met before—and not so much as blink an eye?

"Here you go," she said, leaning over to offer Ben the bottle of lotion.

She had dressed in loose-fitting blue shorts cut high on her thighs and a matching top that was little more than a couple of straps and a swatch of cotton across her breasts. It was a typical running outfit, worn for comfort and not to entice, but on Keely's perfect body, enticing as all get-out. From their low vantage point in the three-wheeled racers, the men were treated to a constant view of those incredible legs of hers. Long, supple and perfectly formed, they seemed to go all the way up to her throat.

"Man, oh, man," Alan muttered as the back of her shorts rose to expose even more of her legs.

Five heads cocked so five sets of eyes could get a better look at her backside.

Ben asked Keely to help him with the lotion. "My hands aren't working right today," he complained. "Always takes them a while to loosen up."

"Are you telling me the truth?"

"Really, I can't do it by myself." After the lie he gave her his "poor cripple" look, the one they'd probably all used a hundred times to get attention from women, the one Mac had used himself more than once.

The other guys exchanged grins behind her back.

"Seems to me that someone with enough dexterity to race a wheelchair ought to be able to put sunscreen on himself," Keely told him. Squeezing some into her palm, she smoothed it across Ben's shoulders and down his arms while every man there watched with undisguised longing.

"You suppose that guy's as sensitive on his upper body as you are?" Alan wondered out loud. Then he added with a devilish twist, "Probably more sensitive. Yeah, I bet he is. If she rubs him just right, she's liable to make that old dead pecker of his stand up and salute."

Mac could only growl a response.

Keely had finished applying lotion to the last man and was carefully making her way over to them with the help of the cane Mac had insisted she use for a while.

"Oh, goodie," Alan said. "Here she comes."

"Embarrass me in front of her, and I'll beat the crap out of you."

Alan just grinned.

Keely stopped in front of them. "Hi."

"Hi, beautiful," Alan said. "Any fatalities over there when you started rubbing on sunscreen? Do we need the paramedics?"

"Did they really need help or am I just exceptionally gullible?"

"You're exceptionally gullible," Alan told her.

"But don't feel bad. Guys in wheelchairs are experts at hitting on women, so you never had a chance."

"I was afraid they were conning me, but I wasn't sure."

"That's standard operating procedure. The first things you learn in rehab are how to hit on women and how to get laid. We call it Rehab 101."

She reddened, but she laughed. "Oh, Alan, you're terrible. I don't know when to believe you."

"That's easy," Mac said. "Never believe a word he says."

He called to the students to put on their helmets and gloves, then picked up his own.

"Is there anything else I can do?" Keely asked him.

"No, not right now. We'll pull out in a minute." He told himself not to bring it up, but he couldn't help himself. "You seem to be getting along okay with the guys. No queasy stomach?"

"No. Funny, isn't it? I feel comfortable with everyone out here."

"Not everyone."

The smile left her face and her eyes filled with regret. "No, not everyone."

"Why do you think that is?"

"I can't explain it. Maybe because I knew you before you got hurt. I'm not sure."

Alan looked at Mac, then at Keely, then at Mac again. "I think I missed something here."

"Never mind," Mac told him.

"Is the university funding this program?" Keely asked, deftly changing the subject.

"The university provides minimal training, but

nothing for racing, since it's not a recognized sport here. I'm working on corporate sponsorship, but right now we sponsor ourselves. You have to understand that a bunch of crippled guys racing wheelchairs isn't exactly what businesses want when they hire an athlete to represent them.''

"I do understand. Aztec couldn't wait to drop my sportswear contract after my accident.''

"I'm sorry.''

"Oh, don't be. I was never comfortable with it, anyway. Now I can concentrate on getting back in shape and not be distracted.''

"Your shape seems fine from where I'm sitting, doll,'' Alan said, wiggling his eyebrows, ''but don't tell my wife I was looking at it.''

"Is this one of the lines you learned in Rehab 101?''

"Absolutely. But it's Rehab 102 I really want to excel in.''

"Oh, and what's Rehab 102?''

"Get Mac to show you,'' he said slyly with a wink. "He teaches the class.''

THE ROUTE TOOK the wheelers through the oldest part of campus, where the buildings predated the Civil War and sat among the magnolia trees like graceful elderly ladies. Keely rode in the front seat of the van, while graduate student Dean Averhardt, Mac's teaching assistant, drove.

Ahead of them, Mac led the men in a tight line. His arms flexed as he worked the wheels, and his body stretched forward until every muscle in his back showed, a truly awesome sight. Watching him, Keely had to keep reminding herself to breathe.

He was wearing only a black spandex unitard that left most of his upper body uncovered, black gloves and a black helmet that allowed a glimpse of his hair on the sides and back where it was cropped close.

His muscles were taut. His skin had the patina of rich polished wood, and like the surface of a finely made table, it tempted you to reach out and run your fingers across it. How was it possible to be physically attracted to a man, yet repulsed by his physical condition? She had struggled with the answer all day.

"He's really good, isn't he?" she said to Dean. He knew immediately that she was talking about Mac. No one else came close to having his endurance or speed. While the others labored, Mac seemed to race effortlessly.

Dean answered without taking his attention from the road. "People have started calling him the Terminator because, when he races, he dresses all in black and he wipes out the competition. He's unbeatable in the shorter distances. Nobody can touch him when he wants to win. Just wish we could get him to want to win more often."

"Why doesn't he?"

"He didn't tell me this, but I think he feels bad competing against his own students in road races."

"When does he turn forty? He can race as a master then and be out of their division."

"November, I think."

They passed through an intersection that marked a change between city and country, where smooth asphalt turned into coarse gravel pavement, and condominiums gave way to thickets of pine and pastures of green spring grass. Cows the color of the red Georgia clay lifted their heads to stare or call out an occasional greeting as the athletes streaked by.

"Do you like working with the wheelers?" Keely asked.

"To be honest, I hated the idea at first, but Mac can be pretty persuasive when he thinks you ought to do something. Part of my graduate study is adaptive sports for the temporarily and permanently disabled, so Mac felt this would be good practical experience. And it is. I'm glad he convinced me to do it."

"Will you teach me about the physical needs of the students?" Keely asked. "If I'm going to help out, I want to learn as much as I can so I don't do something stupid."

Dean snickered. When he glanced at her his pale eyebrows were lifted in amusement.

"Uh-oh," she said with dread. "I've already done something stupid, haven't I?"

"Not stupid, just funny. And the guys are to blame for tricking you into it, so you shouldn't be embarrassed about it."

"Tell me, Dean."

"Well, a couple of them have said they're supersensitive on their shoulders and chests since their accidents, and apparently that's common among people with spinal-cord injuries. Areas not affected by the paralysis become almost like sexual organs. And when you stroke them—"

Keely held up her hand to stop him. "I get the picture."

"It's really kind of funny when you think about it."

"Oh, hysterical," she said dryly. "I don't know when I've heard anything quite so funny."

CHAPTER FOUR

BY THE TIME they returned to the track, Mac's hair was lank and oily and his body was covered with enough dust and road grit to fill the bed of a pickup. The sweaty odor wafting from him wasn't something he wanted Keely to have to deal with, so he transferred from his racer to his wheelchair and pushed up the hill with the rest of the guys to the athletic complex. He took a quick shower while Keely waited in his office talking to Dean.

He was in the dressing room trying to get his feet into some old loafers when Alan rolled up and popped him in the head with a towel. "Bring Keely over to the house tonight and we'll throw something on the grill. You know Vicki's going to freak when I tell her about you two. She'll want to check Keely out—make sure she's good enough for you."

Mac looked around to see if anyone had overheard. Thankfully the others were still in the shower or getting dressed on the other side of the wall in the student area. "There's nothing to tell about me and Keely. We're not involved like that, Alan." Giving up on the shoes, he tossed them back in the locker.

"Okay, there's nothing to tell, but you know I'm going to tell it, anyway, so you might as well bring her to the house to meet Vicki and get it over with. C'mon, buddy. We can grill some steaks or chops.''

''I'll pass. Having Vicki interrogate her and embarrass me isn't my idea of a pleasant evening.''

''She won't if I tell her not to.''

''Yeah, right.'' Asking Alan's wife to mind her own business was like asking Alan to keep a confidence. Both were impossible. The minute Alan told her about Keely, Vicki was going to be all over him asking him personal questions and wanting to know if he was involved with Keely romantically.

He closed the locker and patted his pocket for a comb, belatedly realizing it was in the storage compartment of his van with his wallet. He ran a hand through his wet hair to get it off his face, but dark strands fell in his eyes each time he raked them back.

''If you won't come to the house, then invite Keely over to your place,'' Alan suggested. ''Vicki and I will leave you alone so you can have some privacy. Fix dinner, open a bottle of wine, light a few candles and,'' he added just to goad him, ''show Keely your tattoo.''

''Very funny.''

Why Alan got so much pleasure from reminding him about his stupidity, Mac didn't know. Getting a tattoo was just one of several outrageous things he had done after his injury, but it was the most permanent. The shock of suddenly finding himself unable to walk or maintain an erection had pushed him over the edge.

He had gone a little crazy, drinking too much and trying to prove his manhood in a variety of insane ways: skydiving, white-water canoeing, orally satisfying Courtland's female population. That last one had earned him a nickname that three years later still had women leaving messages on his answering machine for "Mouth" McCandless.

The ultimate insanity had occurred one night when he and Alan had driven to Columbus, Georgia, to a grimy little place called the Hole in the Wall near the Army's Fort Benning. Countless beers later, the party moved to a tattoo parlor and they'd both come away with souvenirs of their foolishness. Fortunately the tattoos were small and located where they couldn't be seen by just anybody. Born to Raise Hell, Alan's groin proclaimed. Mac had a hissing coiled snake about two inches long on his hip.

Alan, with his usual irreverence for everything, thought the experience amusing, but Mac cursed the tattoo every time he took off his pants.

"So, are you going to ask her to your place tonight?" Alan's question drew him back into the conversation.

"I already have." Alan's delighted grin faded to a scowl when Mac added, "I'm working out a conditioning schedule for her, and we plan to go over it."

"Ah, man, are you nuts? You don't invite a beautiful woman you're crazy about to your house and then talk business. And I *know* you're crazy about her, regardless of what you say. When she's around, you're like a hungry dog with his eyes on a T-bone."

"Alan, she needs a friend right now, not a relationship."

"How do you know that? Maybe a relationship with you is exactly what she needs."

Mac dismissed the idea immediately. "She came to me because she needs a coach, not a man in her bed. Besides, she isn't attracted to me. The sight of me turns her off."

Alan rolled his eyes in disbelief. "I don't buy that for a minute."

"I'm not kidding. My disability freaks her out. That's what we were talking about on the track earlier. She's uncomfortable with my chair and me. Didn't you notice how she avoids looking at my legs or even touching my chair?"

"I was too busy looking at *her* legs to catch it. She admits she's turned off?"

"Not in those words, but yes."

"So, use a little of that McCandless charm. Spend some time with her when it isn't part of her training. Romance her."

"No. She's struggling through a tough time because of her injury, and the last thing she needs is me hitting on her."

Alan popped him hard with the towel again, doing more damage to his hair. "There you go, getting into your self-sacrificing mode. You always worry about what everyone else needs. What do *you* need? Do you ever think about that?"

Yeah, he thought about it, but he was afraid to think about it very seriously. What he needed and what he could have were too far apart.

Now, what he *wanted*—that was an entirely different matter. Immediately his mind drew her picture: blond hair, big blue eyes, coltish legs. He had a weakness for women, but Keely Wilson made him weak to the point of near-helplessness.

His heart had been in jeopardy from the instant he'd first laid eyes on her more than ten years ago. Telling himself it was just an older man's infatuation with a younger woman, or a strong case of lust, hadn't done a thing to lessen the ache.

Now as then, he had to keep his feelings in check. She was emotionally vulnerable; she trusted him to help her, and he wasn't going to betray that trust by doing something stupid, like making a move on her.

"I've got to go. She's waiting for me." He bundled his dirty unitard and jock together and put them in the net sling under his chair, then pushed toward the door.

"Hey," Alan called. Mac stopped and turned the chair to look back. "How much of a chance does she have for a comeback?"

"No chance at all."

"You're kidding. Then why did you agree to coach her?"

"When the doctor walked in that day and said you'd never walk again, do you remember what you did?"

Alan chuckled. "That wasn't one of my better days."

"You called him a few choice names and threw a water pitcher at him. The minute he left the room you tried to get out of the bed and walk. You fell on your ugly face."

"We both did, my friend. Remember our great escape attempt? We decided we were gonna blow that place, but neither one of us could even get our underwear on, much less escape.''

"We had to fall on our faces a thousand times before we finally accepted that we wouldn't walk again.''

Alan nodded slowly, understanding what Mac was getting at. ''And letting Keely fall on her face is the only way she's going to really accept not running again.''

"I think so. If she doesn't take her best shot at a comeback, she'll spend the rest of her life wondering if the doctors were wrong and maybe she just gave up too soon. I care about her. I don't want her to have any regrets.''

Alan pushed over, looked at him squarely and asked, ''Just how much *do* you care about her?''

Mac sighed in resignation. He had spent the afternoon denying to Alan that he still had feelings for Keely, and years denying the truth to himself. ''More than I should.''

"Go after her if she's what you want.''

Mac laughed bitterly. ''Yeah, right. I'm sure her idea of the perfect man is a paraplegic in a wheelchair. A guy who can't get it up and can't hold his bladder half the time. What kind of life would she have with me?''

"Much better than the one she'd have without you,'' Alan said pointedly.

As soon as Mac left the building, Alan raced to the pay telephone and made a call to his wife. If Mac

wasn't going to do what was in his best interest, Alan
would do it for him.

Vicki answered, and the bloodcurdling scream of a
child echoed in Alan's ear. "What in the blazes is
goin' on?" he asked.

"Murder, mayhem and madness," Vicki said
calmly. "The usual."

"Well, tell them to be quiet. I need you to get some
things together and take them over to Mac's before he
gets home."

"Hey!" she yelled at the kids. "Take it to the backyard. And, Savannah, quit tormenting your brothers.
You know that's my job." Several minutes and threats
later, she turned her attention back to Alan. "Okay,
they're tying up J.P. and preparing him for sacrifice,
so I'm free. What do you need me to do?"

"Don't you have a pan of that potato-casserole stuff
Mac likes so much?"

"I think so. Want me to heat it up for him?"

"No, I want Keely Wilson to heat it up for him.
And not just the casserole."

"Who? What are you talking about?"

"Hold on to your panties, woman. Have I got a
story for you."

CHAPTER FIVE

"THIS IS IT," Mac said. "Don't expect anything fancy."

Keely looked through the windshield of the van at the small lots and plain but charming houses of Mac's subdivision. People were walking or working in their yards, and the kids were playing up and down the quiet street the way they probably did in her older more upscale neighborhood on a Sunday afternoon.

"I like it," she said with honesty.

In the middle of the next block he pointed out where Alan and his family lived. Mac's place was directly across the street in a small house with white vinyl siding and green shutters.

A child's bicycle blocked the entrance to Mac's driveway. Grumbling, he parked on the street. "I've told Savannah a million times to watch where she leaves that thing."

"Savannah?"

"One of Alan's kids."

Keely moved to the lift door in the center of the van's side panel and waited her turn to descend. "How many kids do Alan and Vicki have?"

"Three. Bay Alan's thirteen, Savannah's seven, and John Patrick just turned two."

"John Patrick? They named him after you?"

"Yeah," he said, grinning.

"Something tells me you don't mind that too much."

"No, J.P.'s a great kid. Real sweet. All the kids are when they're separated, but together they're like wild animals. I guarantee you've never seen anything like it."

"Are they that bad?"

His expression of horror made her smile. "Real terrors. Especially Savannah. Even I can't take it when they get wound up, and I'm used to coping with screaming kids."

"Oh? Why are you used to screaming kids?"

"Because I raised four of them."

HIDDEN BEHIND THE CURTAINS of her living-room window, Vicki Sizemore watched what was going on across the street and wondered what Mac and the woman were saying. Vicki was dying to get a good look at her.

"Putting the bicycle in the driveway so he couldn't park in the garage was pure genius," she told Alan.

He had poured himself some tea in the kitchen and was just pushing through the door with the glass held between his legs. "I have my moments."

"I wish she'd hurry up and get out. Oh, wait, here she comes. She's about to step on the lift." When the woman moved from the interior of the darkened van into the sunlight, Vicki sucked in her breath. "How old is she?"

"Twenty-seven. Twenty-eight. Something like that."

Vicki conceded that was old enough. "Maybe I should pop over there and pretend I need to borrow something."

Alan quickly nixed that idea. "He won't like it that I asked you to fix the food. If you show up at the door, he'll kill us both." He rolled up next to her at the window and peeked out.

"But I can't tell what she really looks like," Vicki muttered.

"She's cute," Alan said. "Mac was drooling all over himself. Of course, we all were."

Vicki reached down and playfully backhanded him for including himself. "I'll bet she's stuck up if she gets that kind of attention."

"Nah, didn't seem like it. She made a real effort to talk to all the guys and get to know them. Whenever Mac or anyone needed anything, she was right there offering to help. Although Mac did say she has a problem being around him now that he's a gimp."

"She *what?* Why that hateful little—"

"Now, hold on. Don't get all bent out of shape. I started thinking about it on the drive home and it's a good sign. We had eight or nine guys out there today, plus me and Mac, but Keely didn't have a problem with anyone except him. I watched her laugh and fool around with the wheelers, even the amputees, and she wasn't put off by any of them."

"So?"

"So that tells me she's not turned off by gimps, but

by *Mac* being a gimp. And she wouldn't get turned off by Mac being a gimp unless she cared about him.''

Vicki's eyes narrowed. "You may have a point," she said slowly.

He nodded. "Look at it this way. Did you get upset when Mrs. Arnold down the block fell and broke her hip? No," he answered for her. "You felt bad because she's a nice old lady, but you didn't get upset, right?''

"Right.''

"Yet when Mac got that tiny little cut on his finger making J.P.'s rocking horse, you almost had a stroke. Why?''

"Because I love him and I can't stand to see him hurt.''

"Bingo!''

"So maybe I ought to wait until I meet her to decide whether she needs her eyes clawed out.''

"That's my girl.''

Alan put his tea on the end table and patted his lap. Vicki reluctantly gave up her snooping and sat. She rested her head on his shoulder and sighed deeply. "I'd hate it if he got hurt when he's been through so much already. Do you really think he's in love with her?''

"Sure seems like it.''

"No wonder he's never gotten serious about anyone. He's been pining away for Keely Wilson all these years.''

"Not pining away, but I think when he saw her again he realized he still had feelings for her.''

"I'd give anything to be a fly on the wall in *that* house tonight....''

"Yeah, me, too. Nothing we can do about it, though."

As if he'd suddenly thought of something, his whole body jerked.

"What's the matter?" she asked, alarmed.

"What's that I hear?"

Vicki listened, then shook her head. "I don't hear anything."

"Exactly. No screaming. No crying. No fighting. What's wrong?"

She relaxed and laughed. "Bay Alan went to the movies with the Cooper boy, and Savannah and J.P. are next door helping Miss Agnes bake brownies. They won't be back for an hour or so."

"Wait a minute. You mean we're alone in this house for the first time in months and we're wasting it on Mac's love life? Get nekkid!" She giggled as he frantically whisked her top over her head, then pulled off his own. He jerked down the zipper of her cutoff jeans and thrust his hand inside.

Thirty seconds later Vicki didn't give a damn what was going on across the street. Mac was on his own.

"I DIDN'T KNOW you had children," Keely said. The blood rushed to her face. They made their way through the garage to the side door.

"I was talking about my three younger sisters and my brother. I raised them."

"Oh, brothers and sisters." The relief was instant, but Keely didn't like feeling it.

"I was twenty-two when our parents died, and the court allowed me to have temporary guardianship. After a year, when I proved I was able to take care of them, they awarded me permanent custody. Of course, the kids are grown now and scattered all over the country.''

"You raised them by yourself? But you were so young.''

"I couldn't let them be separated, and no one in the family was willing to take in four kids, three of them teenagers. Jilly, my oldest sister, was seventeen, so she was a big help with Brand. He was ten at the time.''

"Still, it must have been hard.''

"It was, particularly when I was also trying to go to graduate school and work, but I'd do it again in a heartbeat if I had to.''

"I remember Brand. He visited you at the track one time when he was on leave from the Marines and got the entire women's team in trouble for gawking and flirting.''

He chuckled. "I forgot about that. None of you could keep your eyes off him long enough to do any work.''

"He was gorgeous,'' she said in self-defense. "And he was your brother, which made him that much more attractive to us, since we all had terrible crushes on you.'' He looked at her with genuine shock. "Oh, surely you knew! We almost swooned every time you spoke.''

"I find that very difficult to believe.''

"Believe it. I had the worst case of lust for you when I was a senior.''

Rendered speechless, he stared at her with his mouth open.

"All female students lust after their coaches," she said quickly, trying to make light of it.

"I didn't know that."

"Oh, sure. Happens all the time."

The door from the garage opened into a laundry room, and he waited for her to go first. Right inside on the floor, blocking the way, was a large covered basket with a note taped to its handle.

"Someone's left you a present," Keely said, stepping back so he could reach it. He put the basket in his lap and pulled off the note. As he read, he made a noise in his throat she wasn't sure how to interpret. "Problem?"

"No, no problem."

Through a second door was the kitchen. Mac put the basket on the table and began emptying the contents. "Alan and Vicki sent over dinner. Potato casserole, salad, bread."

"That was nice of them to do that for you."

"Ah...it's not meant for only me."

He took out two candles, a bottle of wine and a small bunch of multicolored zinnias that looked like someone had just snipped them from a flower bed.

"The dinner is for two," he said unnecessarily, "if you'd like to join me. We don't have to light the candles or use the flowers if it makes you uncomfortable."

Her inner voice warned that she was moving into extremely dangerous territory. By staying, she could be asking for problems she was ill-prepared to handle.

She had once felt a tenderness for this man that strayed beyond the boundaries of a normal student-coach relationship. She was struggling now with conflicting feelings of attraction and revulsion, feelings she didn't understand and couldn't seem to control. Having an intimate dinner, even without the candlelight, would only complicate things.

"How about it?" he asked. "I can't eat this all by myself."

He had the most expressive eyes. They said he really wanted her to stay for dinner, and not because he needed someone to help him eat all this food. He wanted to be with her. The knowledge played havoc with her insides.

"The flowers are beautiful," she said, nodding. "I guess it would be a shame not to use them."

ACROSS THE DINNER TABLE soft candlelight illuminated Mac's face. He had changed into a pale-blue shirt that brought out the few strands of gray at his temples and emphasized his dark hair and eyes.

Some men grew less handsome as they got older, but age had increased Mac's appeal a thousand percent. The tiny lines around his mouth, the slightly weathered skin, added something immensely attractive.

When she was in undergraduate school and he was her coach, they'd sat like this over lunch in the cafeteria many times and discussed her training. And like those days, Keely was in real danger of losing her heart again.

"...gradually add weight-bearing exercises until you've strengthened the soft tissues..."

Her thoughts wandered from the conditioning program Mac was outlining to the shape of his lips as they formed the words. They really were nice lips. Perfect. Enticing. She wondered if they felt as good as they looked.

"...in the biomechanics lab..."

He turned a page in the black vinyl binder in front of him and the fabric of his shirt whispered across his skin like the seductive melody to a song, making Keely nearly moan in harmony.

Mmm, he had wonderful arms and an exquisite chest. Even his neck was sexy.

"...put you in one of those pink ballet costumes and give you a beehive hairdo and red fingernails..."

She had to get her mind back on work and away from those fine taut biceps and those— *What* had he said? Beehive hairdo? Red fingernails?

He'd stopped talking and was grinning playfully.

"I'm sorry," she said with chagrin, hoping she hadn't communicated her thoughts. "I was, um, thinking about something else. What were you saying about joint stress?"

"Forget joint stress." He put aside her progress binder. "Let's wait and go over this later in the week. We have plenty of time, and I think what you need right now is to relax for a change—forget about running and everything that goes with it."

The irony of his words amused her. She hadn't been thinking about running at all.

"How about some wine?"

"I don't usually drink."

"Half a glass? You're no longer on medication, so a little won't hurt you."

"Yes, I think I will."

He poured them each half a glass and she took a sip.

"More casserole? Salad?"

"No, thank you. Everything was wonderful. Thank Vicki and Alan for me when you see them." She paused. "Are you good friends with them?"

"The best. Alan and I met in rehab, so we went through some rough months together. They moved him in as my roommate a few weeks after he broke his neck."

"How was he injured?"

"He fell asleep at the wheel and hit a tree."

"I noticed his hands and arms don't work exactly right, but that doesn't seem to hinder him."

"No, not much slows Alan down. He has a lethal sense of humor, and you never know what he's going to say or do, but he's the best friend you could ever hope for and a great neighbor. I convinced him and Vicki to move here from Valdosta when a job opened up at the college, and I've never regretted it."

"He's on the faculty? He doesn't seem like the college-professor type."

"Oh, don't let that good ol' boy redneck routine fool you. Alan's smart as a whip. He's really *Dr.* Sizemore and is a highly regarded researcher in microbiology."

"Is Vicki disabled?"

"No, she's able-bodied."

Able-bodied. Keely made a mental note of the correct terminology. She wanted to remember it.

"What does she do?"

"Makes gowns for the sorority and fraternity formals, bridesmaids' dresses, majorette costumes, things like that. She must be pretty good at it. She complains of having more business than she can handle. I think she's even made a couple of wedding dresses."

"Must be nice to be so talented."

She started to get up to clear the table, but he stopped her. "Sit here with me a little while longer and let's catch up. We really haven't had a chance to talk today about how your house is working out. Is it as comfortable as it looks?"

"Oh, it's terrific. I love it." She pushed her plate aside, then folded her arms and rested them on the table. "How long have you had this house, Mac?"

"About two years. I have all the space I need and the changes I showed you make things easier for me."

She could see how they would. He had given her a tour before the meal and she'd been intrigued by the way he'd redesigned the house to make it more practical for someone in a wheelchair.

"It's comfortable," Mac said. "I could use more room when Brand and the girls come at the same time, but that doesn't happen too often so it's not really a problem."

"Where are your sisters and brother living?"

"Brand's in Wisconsin. He's a computer specialist with a company that designs product packaging. Jilly's an artist and lives in Santa Fe, and Megan and Christine are both in California. Chris works for a travel company and Megan teaches high-school English and French. The girls are all married and have kids, which means I don't get to see them as much as I'd like."

And that saddened him. She could tell by the tone of his voice. "I'm sorry you're so far apart. You must miss them."

"I do. I never thought we'd be this spread out and it's not what I'd planned for us, but they have their own families and careers, and that's the way it should be. I can't expect them to rearrange their lives for me."

But he had rearranged his life for them; Keely was certain of it. When his parents had died and he'd brought his sisters and brother to live with him, it must have caused an immense change in his life. Twenty-two, responsible for himself and four children…

How many men would have done what he had? None she could think of. The few men she knew or had dated tended to be focused on their careers like her, caught up in their own lives and oblivious to everything else. Mac wasn't the least bit self-centered. He went out of his way to help his students, to help his family, and he didn't seem to expect anything in return. He valued their happiness, but surely he had dreams of his own that weren't tied to other people.

"Did you always want to be a coach?" she asked. "You've spent most your adult life making sure other people achieve their dreams. I'm curious about what you want for yourself."

"I'm happy being a coach."

"I know you are, but did you ever want to be something else?"

"As a young man, sure. I was a runner like you, and I dreamed of being a world-class athlete, but I quickly set my sights on being a good coach, instead. I've never regretted it.''

"But why did you change your mind and go into coaching? If you wanted to run, you should have done it.''

"I had responsibilities that made it impossible for me to even think about something like that.''

"Raising your brothers and sisters interfered with your plans, didn't it?''

"Yes, but I'm not complaining, because having those kids around was the best thing that ever happened to me. I got my chance to be a father.''

His only chance?

He rolled back from the table and pushed to the coffeemaker on the counter. "Do you want some decaf?''

"No, but you go ahead.'' She watched him fill the pot at the sink and get the can of coffee from the refrigerator. She wondered whether it was proper etiquette to ask him if he needed help, but after a minute, she saw that he didn't. He measured coffee into the filter and poured in enough water for two cups, then pushed back over to the table to wait while it brewed.

"When I was young, I was a lot like you,'' he said, continuing his story. "I had my life mapped out, I wasn't responsible for anyone but myself, and I couldn't imagine anything stopping me from going after what I wanted. Then my folks were killed and the kids came to live with me. Suddenly I was responsible for five people. I had to face the reality that my life had changed and that my goals would have to change, too.''

"But don't you have *some* regret about not fulfilling your dream?"

"Honestly? Yes, but I can't waste my life grieving over lost dreams any more than I can waste my life grieving over being in this chair. I meant it when I said I'm happy doing what I'm doing. I'm a good coach. At least, I think I am."

"You're a great coach. And apparently you're also great at other things," she added, remembering what Dean had told her that afternoon about Mac's ability to wipe out the competition when he raced. "I heard about your nickname."

He had just taken a sip of wine and still had the glass to his lips when he suddenly choked and lurched forward, spraying wine everywhere. He dissolved into a coughing fit and grabbed his napkin to put over his face.

"Mac? Are you okay?"

He nodded rapidly but was still unable to talk.

"Do you want some water?"

He shook his head.

He didn't seem to be in any danger, so Keely left him alone to catch his breath. After a minute he recovered enough to talk, but when he did, his words didn't make sense. They held a tone of desperation that confused her even more.

"Who told you about my nickname?"

"Dean. He says you're really good."

Mac's expression said he was horrified to hear it.

"He had no business telling you something like that! I swear things have changed. After I got hurt I was really messed up about being in this chair, and I thought I had to go out and prove my manhood. You understand that, don't you?''

Her forehead wrinkled in confusion. Why was he so upset about being nicknamed the Terminator by other racers?

''Mac, I don't get it. Why does this bother you so much? They gave you that nickname because of how good you are. You should be proud they recognize your talent.''

He gave her an incredulous look. ''Proud of being called the Mouth by women who are only interested in me for oral sex?''

His words were such a shock that at first she didn't react. And then understanding hit her. The Mouth? Oral sex? She was barely able to contain her laughter and her body shook with the effort. Against her will, her gaze slid to his mouth. So, she wasn't the only one who thought it luscious.

''Why, Mac McCandless, I didn't know you could be so naughty. I was talking about wheelchair racing, not oral sex.''

''Oh, hell!''

She grinned. ''Something tells me I just figured out what Rehab 102 is.''

CHAPTER SIX

MAC COULDN'T SLEEP that night for thinking about the stupid thing he'd done. The next day at work, he was irritable and distracted, causing Miriam to remark more than once that he must be coming down with something. A cold, she decided, and fussed at him for not taking better care of himself.

The word raced out in record time, even for the athletic department. Almost immediately, containers of chicken soup and homemade remedies to promote healing began showing up on his desk: garlic pills, licorice candy, a lemon-and-whiskey concoction to swab his throat. Purple-onion cough syrup he wouldn't have taken even if he *did* have a cold.

"What did you do, hire a skywriter?" he asked Miriam. "I'm being overrun by female witch doctors trying to cure me with voodoo remedies."

"I just mentioned to a couple of the women that you were sick."

"I'm not sick," he repeated for the hundredth time.

He had to leave before the women in the building drove him nuts. He grabbed his cell phone from the desk, stuck it in the chair sling and headed down the hill to the track, where the men's team had started drills.

As he pushed up, Scott Madison, a junior and one of the best sprinters Courtland had seen in decades, shot out of the starting blocks a fraction of a second before the pistol, setting off a chorus of curses from the coaching staff and a bellowing reprimand from the head coach, Doug Crocker.

"You've got bricks for brains, Madison. You pull that stunt one more time and you'll never run for my team again, and I mean scholarship or no scholarship. You got that, hotshot?"

"Yes, sir, Coach."

Madison had no more false starts, but later, while the runners were doing drills, the young man again earned Crocker's wrath with his sloppy form. "Madison, get over here!" Crocker threw down his clipboard and chewed out not only Scott but the other runners in the line. Mac watched from the apron of the track with Dean.

"Man," Dean said, shaking his head, "Scott's still got serious problems. Crocker's likely to kill him before the day's over."

Or at the very least demoralize him, Mac thought.

He shifted in his chair to relieve the pressure on his backside, wishing he could do something to relieve the uneasiness in his chest about this whole situation. Technically he should stay out of it. As athletic director, he was no longer just a coach responsible for the women's track team, but an administrator in charge of a multimillion-dollar operation and twelve sports.

He was supposed to let his staff handle the majority of the coaching duties while he ran the department and supervised rehabilitation. If Scott had problems, it was

Crocker's job as coach of the men's team to correct them.

Mac found it hard, though, to do nothing while a young man with Scott's potential slid deeper into trouble.

He let out a shrill whistle and gave Crocker a hand signal. Crocker glared to let him know he didn't appreciate the interference.

"If looks could kill…" Dean said with a chuckle. "He's never going to get over you getting the A.D.'s job, instead of him."

"Yeah, well, he can look at me any way he wants as long as he does his job."

The staff and teaching assistants believed Crocker's hostility resulted from Mac's promotion two years ago, but Mac had felt the beginnings of it long before that, from his first day back at work after his injury. Everyone had been uncomfortable with him in the beginning, even Miriam. Eventually, to his relief, they'd started treating him just like before. All except Doug Crocker. His wariness had never gone away. His anger over the promotion had simply changed it into something more destructive.

Crocker obeyed Mac's hand signal but with clear resentment, scowling as he sentenced Scott to leave the group and run laps. Experienced runners like Scott considered laps an indignity, but Mac had found them to be a much more effective punishment than Crocker's verbal abuse.

"Here comes something much better to look at," Dean said, and Mac turned his head toward the gate.

Using her cane, Keely slowly made her way in their direction. She waved and Dean waved back.

Mac didn't know what to say to her. All day his mind had replayed last night's dinner with Keely, confirming what an idiot he was. The Terminator. He hadn't known the other wheelers called him that. She'd laughed at his mistake until she'd cried.

"Dean, get a racer out of the shed and a pair of gloves for me, will you?"

"Sure," he said, jogging off.

Keely reached Mac. "I burned down our neighbor's workshop when I was eleven," she said.

"What?"

"Mr. Johnson left his cigarettes out there, and I sneaked in and tried to smoke one, but I dropped ashes into some sawdust and the floor caught on fire. To this day, that poor man believes he started it by leaving one of his cigarette butts smoldering."

Mac didn't say anything else, wondering if there was a point to her strange story and if it was forthcoming.

"That's one of the worst things I've ever done. I've always been afraid people would think badly of me if they knew, so I've never told a soul, not even my dad, and he was closer to me than anyone."

Ah, he was beginning to understand.

"We're even now. I know your deepest darkest secret and you know mine. So you don't have a reason to be embarrassed about what happened last night. You don't have to apologize again or feel uncomfortable around me. Actually, I think trading personal secrets like this might make us blood brothers or something. What do you think?''

His gaze covertly skimmed her figure-hugging shirt and shorts. He couldn't imagine her as his brother, but the ''or something'' part sounded intriguing.

''Why don't you sit down and get off that leg, and we'll talk about it?''

''No, I didn't come to stay. I just wanted to drop by for a second and see if you were okay. You ended the evening so abruptly I was a little worried.''

''I was an idiot, not only because of what I said, but how I acted after. I'm sorry.''

''Oh, no,'' she warned instantly. ''No apologizing. Friends need to be able to say stupid things in front of each other and not worry about it. Right?''

He tried not to smile, but he couldn't help himself. ''Right.''

''Good. With that settled, I wonder if I can talk you into coming over one night this week.''

''Did you want to finish reviewing your schedule?''

''No, I had the pool filled this morning and by the end of the week, the water should be warm. I wondered…is it possible for you to swim?'' She turned a little red and added quickly, ''If you can't swim, that's okay. We can just lie by the pool being worthless.''

''I can swim, but I choose not to. I'm not exactly graceful getting in and out of a pool.''

''Oh.''

''But I'm great at lying around being worthless.''

''Then please come. I'd really like you to be the first guest in my house. We can have a late supper on the patio. I make a low-fat vegetarian lasagna that I guarantee you can't tell from the real thing. It smells so good it'll make your mouth water.''

She was trying to tempt him. As if he needed tempting. His mouth was already watering, thinking about that body of hers covered only by a wet bathing suit. Would it be a one-piece suit? Blue like her eyes? Modest or daring? The real thing would probably be nowhere near as exciting as the one he'd just created in his mind.

''Sounds great. How about Thursday night? I should finish here about six.''

''That's perfect.''

After she left, Mac put on gloves and transferred to the racer Dean brought him. He waited until Scott came around the track, then pushed out to join him in his laps.

They did five laps, neither one speaking, settling into an easy pace that Mac purposely dictated. On the sixth lap the kid couldn't stand it any longer.

''Why are you taking my laps with me, Coach?''

''Your laps? These are my laps.''

Scott glanced down at him with a confused expression on his young face. At twenty, he was technically a man, but today he seemed about fifteen, a scared and desperate fifteen.

''What did *you* do wrong, Coach?'' he asked.

''Allowed myself to forget the most important part of my job.''

''What?''

''That I'm supposed to be your friend, as well as your coach. Now, how about telling me what's bothering you. I can't help if I don't know what's wrong.''

THE SUIT WAS RED, one-piece and fit Keely like she'd been melted and poured into it. Mac watched her swim, his serene look a deceptive cover for the battle between honor and desire raging within him. Honor wanted Keely to stay concealed in the water. Desire kept thinking up excuses to entice her out of it.

He checked his watch and smiled to himself. Finally he didn't need to fabricate an excuse to end her swim. "Hey," he called out. "Time's up. You've been in there over an hour, and that's long enough for today."

She swam to the side. "Fifteen more minutes?"

"No, I don't want you to overdo it your first time in. Now hit the deck. And be careful coming up those steps. Hold on to the rail."

"Oh, Mac, I've hardly gotten wet."

"Don't 'Oh, Mac' me. And don't try to wheedle me into letting you stay in there, because it won't work. Come on out."

"Slave driver," she muttered, but she carefully climbed out and limped past him to retrieve her towel, impishly flicking water at his head as she walked by. "Dictator."

The towel retrieved, she limped back to him and began to rub her body briskly. Mac tried not to stare, but his gaze was drawn to every place the towel touched—the slender throat, the long supple arms, the legs that seemed to go on forever.

Casually, so as not to be obvious, he picked up his shirt and placed it strategically across his lap. The erection would fizzle in a moment. It always did.

"You're making progress," he told her. "Your

limp seems less pronounced than it was even a few days ago.''

''You think so?''

''I can tell a difference.''

''So can I, actually. You're taking good care of me.'' She wrapped the towel around her waist and tied it in a knot. ''And now it's time for me to take care of you. I'll get you some ointment and bandages for those hands. I know they have to be hurting.''

''They're okay. They don't need bandaging.''

''I think they do. Let me see them.''

He lifted his palms. Constant training this week had worn holes in his gloves and rubbed his hands raw. This afternoon, when he and the wheelers had run a twenty-mile point-to-point, both hands had bled.

''I'll put something on them when I get home,'' he told her.

''But I have everything here. The longer you wait, the greater the risk of infection.''

''I don't need...'' He stopped, realizing it wasn't such a bad idea. ''Okay. Thanks.''

''Be right back.''

While she was in the house, he transferred from the lounger to his wheelchair and positioned a patio chair nearby.

She returned a few minutes later carrying a duffel bag stuffed with bandages, ointments and wraps. ''Here you go.''

She tried to hand him the bag, but he refused it. ''You'll have to wrap them for me. Sit here.''

Panic spread across her face as she noted how close the patio chair was to him, to his wheelchair.

"Keely, you only have to touch my hands, not my legs. Surely you can do that without feeling sick."

"Did I say I couldn't?"

"No, but you're thinking it might be a problem. The second you thought you had to touch me, you started grabbing your stomach. Look at your hand."

She jerked away the hand that had unconsciously gone to rest against her middle.

"You need to deal with this for your own sake. And mine. Knowing you're afraid of me...it hurts me."

Her face twisted with pain. "Please, don't be hurt. I do feel more comfortable around you than I did. Really."

"Then show me."

The challenge issued, he said nothing more, just waited. Was he doing the right thing? He hoped so. A misstep now could intensify her fear and ruin everything. But he wasn't asking much of her, only to touch his hands. If she couldn't do even that, there was no hope she'd ever get past her revulsion.

Slowly she eased into the chair, careful not to let her knees brush against his, careful not to let her feet touch the foot plates of the wheelchair.

That's my girl. Keep going.

He leaned forward slightly and held out his hands. "A little ointment and some flesh strips and you'll be finished in five minutes. No big deal."

The deepening lines on her forehead marred her perfect face and showed her turmoil. Her hands shook as she removed what she needed from the bag on her lap. Gingerly, fearfully, she placed a dab of ointment on his skin. With soft hesitant circles she rubbed it across one of his palms.

Mac sat quietly and savored the small victory. Her fingers didn't caress or entice, didn't attempt to make him feel good or even try to soothe him. Her fingers touched only what they had to touch. And they touched only because he had given her no choice.

But it was enough.

For now.

CHAPTER SEVEN

June

KEELY UNOFFICIALLY continued to help with the wheelers after classes began in June and put in two hours every day as a teaching assistant to one of the other coaches, helping her with the freshmen runners. She enjoyed the work, but watching the students train was a daily reminder that she was doing little toward her own training.

She walked every day and did deep breathing exercises to improve her lung capacity. But even the next-door neighbor's little poodle, who had started escorting her on her walks, moved faster than she did. She found it depressing to walk with something that had legs only six inches long, could stop and relieve itself on every tree and still beat her back to the house.

Mac kept telling her she had to go easy on herself, but it was tough to hold back when she had such a passionate need to run. Her body was changing, adapting to this new slower way of life, and she was losing ground with every passing week.

She was getting fat, for one thing. Not only had she gained back the nine pounds she'd lost because of the accident, but she'd added two more this month. And for the first time in years, she had a normal period, with bloating, cramps, the craving for chocolate, all those horrible things she had avoided for most of her life.

"Wonderful!" her mother said when Keely mentioned it during one of their Sunday-afternoon phone conversations.

"You're excited I'm having cramps?"

"I'm sorry, darling, but you know how I've always felt about your excessive exercise. Pushing your body like that is unnatural. You'll want a baby some day and at least now you know your body is capable of it. By the way…how's that nice John McCandless doing?"

"Not getting ready to give you a grandchild, if that's what you're hinting."

"I was just asking about the man, Keely, not suggesting you have a baby with him."

"He's paralyzed, remember?"

"Some paralyzed men father children, don't they?"

"No," she said, but then she remembered Alan's two-year-old son. The child had been conceived *after* Alan's accident. Obviously some paralyzed men could father children despite their injuries. "Well, I guess some can, but that doesn't mean Mac's one of them."

"Has he told you he can't have a child? Is he able to have sex?"

"Mother! I haven't exactly quizzed the man about his sex life. Things like that don't come up in the course of normal conversation."

"I'm surprised you aren't curious. He seems nice. He's educated. You should let him know you're interested before someone else snaps him up."

"Whoa! I didn't say I was interested in Mac. I've *never* told you I was interested in Mac like that."

"If you're not, you should be. When's the last time you had a date?"

Keely gritted her teeth. She reminded herself to remain pleasant. Her mother meant well, but she didn't understand that a relationship, with Mac or any other man, wasn't in her plans. Relationships wasted energy. And they never worked for her, so why put herself through the torture? She'd be better off if she *never* fell in love and *never* got married. Her parents' divorce had taught her that lesson.

"Mother, I need to go," she said, yawning loudly. "I've got a test and I need to study."

"You're still not sleeping at night, are you?"

"A few hours, but I usually catch a nap at lunchtime. Don't worry about me."

"I wish you'd go see someone about why you're afraid to sleep."

"I don't need to see anyone. I'm fine. I have my nights and days mixed up is all. Look, I hate to cut this short, but I really do need to study. I'll call you later."

"When?"

"Before the end of the week."

"I'll be expecting it. I want you to call at least once a week from now on. I'd phone you, but I get your answering machine and you don't always return my call."

"I'm sorry. I've been busy trying to get back into the routine of school and I forget. I'll call at least once a week from now on."

"Promise?"

"Yes, I promise."

VICKI SIZEMORE wasn't known for her patience. After waiting three weeks for Mac to introduce her to Keely, she decided she wasn't waiting any longer.

When he answered his phone, Vicki didn't bother to identify herself or go into a lengthy explanation of why she was calling. He knew.

"Keely. My house. Wednesday night after the game."

The Wildcats, the wheelchair basketball team Mac and Alan played on, had an exhibition game to raise money for the rehabilitation hospital. Some of the men, their wives and girlfriends, were coming to the Sizemores' home afterward.

"Tell Keely I've followed her career and want to meet her if you don't want it to look like a date."

"When have you ever seen her race?"

"Never. But I won't say anything if you won't."

"I keep telling you, we're not involved. We're just good friends."

Vicki snorted. "You're spending nearly twenty-four hours a day with the woman, and you can't tell me that's all business. Call and invite her or I will."

"All right, I'll ask her. But I'm not promising she'll come."

"She'd better come. If you can't convince her, I'll take matters into my own hands."

She listened to him sigh loudly and grumble an obscenity she'd never heard him use before. "You're interfering in my life, Vic. You realize that, don't you?''

"Don't thank me, sweetie. You'll make me blush.''

"Mm-mm-mmmm. I love these games. All those half-naked men sweating and grunting. Makes me hot!''

Vicki's latest outrageous comment made Keely bite her lip to avoid laughing nervously. The woman was one of a kind. She talked dirty. She was loud and blunt. If she didn't like someone, she didn't pretend she did. Frequently she'd commented on the way someone looked or talked, although her own Southern drawl was atrocious, and her hair was a bright and fiery red that drew stares.

Keely had liked her immediately.

Certainly part of her appeal was the affection she obviously felt for Mac, but beyond that, Vicki Sizemore had something that made you want to look past her crudeness.

"Y'all won't mind me delaying the barbecue an hour while I jump Alan's bones, will you, girls?'' she asked, and this time Keely couldn't help herself. She chuckled.

"We don't mind waitin' if you don't mind us watchin','' the woman on the other side of her said, and everyone giggled. Keely thought the woman's name was Sandy. She'd been introduced to so many people today she was having a hard time keeping everyone straight.

From the moment she had arrived, however, she'd realized the women were all friends. They shared a camaraderie that sprang from their similar situations—loving men with spinal injuries.

Vicki motioned for everyone to lean closer. "I heard a great joke the other day. Wanna hear it?"

Of course they all did.

"Why are men like parking spaces?"

"Why?" the women echoed.

"Because the good ones are taken and the rest are handicapped."

Everyone howled with laughter except Keely.

Vicki promptly poked her in the ribs. "Oh, lighten up, sweetie. If you're gonna hang around with crips, you've gotta keep a sense of humor and not be sucking up your drawers every five minutes over something somebody said."

Keely was pretty positive she had never once sucked up her drawers, but she got the gist of what Vicki was saying. Not that it made any sense. Fifteen minutes ago they'd all been indignant because Sandy said a waiter at a local restaurant was rude to her husband because of his disability. Now they were laughing at an insensitive joke.

When the others walked over to get soft drinks, Vicki tried to explain the difference.

"Look, it's like laughing *at* somebody versus laughing *with* somebody. We joke around and that's okay because we don't mean any harm. And we're all like family, so nobody's gonna get their feelings hurt. But that waiter was deliberately mean and we don't tolerate that. Understand?"

"I guess," Keely said, but she didn't, not entirely.

She was an outsider, and yet Vicki had gotten on to her when she *hadn't* laughed at the joke.

Keely took advantage of the other women's absence to ask Vicki to match the wives and girlfriends to the players.

"Okay, you know Sandy's married to Dave. He's the one with the mustache. Pam is married to Kevin, the guy with the glasses and kinky hair. Beth Ann, the teeny one with the short-short haircut, is dating Stanley. Felicia and Curtis, and Patsy and Byron are the black couples. Curtis is easy to remember. He has that silver patch in his hair. Now Lisa…"

"I know Lisa. She's going with Chris, the young guy Mac just added to the wheelers, so I've talked with her at practice."

"That just leaves Mike and Bailey," Vicki said, pointing out the two remaining men. "They're both single and didn't bring anybody."

"Which is which?"

Vicki laughed and shook her head. "You're so funny."

"Why? What did I say?"

"Bailey's gorgeous, he's available, he's hit on you twice today, and you didn't even bother to learn his name. I guess that means you've got it bad for somebody else, huh?"

She grinned, making Keely roll her eyes. No matter how many times Keely insisted she wasn't dating Mac, Vicki wouldn't believe it. "You're determined to throw me and Mac together, aren't you?"

"You're already together, sweetie. You just won't admit it. And if it makes any difference to you, I approve, although Alan will make me eat crow over it because I didn't believe for an instant that I'd like you, and he said I would.''

''You didn't think you'd like me? Why?''

''Because Alan told me about you being put off because Mac's a gimp, and I figured you were one of those uppity you-know-what women who think they're too perfect for a man in a wheelchair.''

Keely winced.

''But I've watched you with him today,'' Vicki said, ''and what I see is a woman with real problems and no idea what to do about them. You're attracted to him, but you don't want to be. And you're a little afraid of him, which bothers you more than the attraction because *that* problem he's aware of. He's still clueless about the attraction. So, my new friend, I've decided not to pull your hair out but to help you, instead.''

''Vicki, you're reading this all wrong. Mac and I have known each other for a long time, sure, but I've never thought of him as more than a good friend.''

Vicki just grinned.

''Honestly,'' Keely said. ''But I'll concede you're right about my being afraid. And it makes no sense.''

''That problem will disappear when you work through the other one.''

''I'm not sure I understand.''

''You will.''

The gymnasium crowd gave a loud, collective gasp, and Keely quickly turned her attention to the court. The Wildcats were losing by two points to the Rebels. Two players had tumbled to the floor.

By the time Keely muttered, "Oh, no, Mac," he was back in his wheelchair and rolling down the court again at breakneck speed.

Vicki patted her reassuringly on the leg. "Relax. He's fine. They fall all the time."

"They don't hurt themselves?"

"Nah, it hurts us more than it hurts them."

Keely had tried to act unaffected, but every time someone slammed into Mac or Mac slammed into someone else, she felt it. "I guess I didn't expect this game to be quite so physical," she admitted.

"Did you think because they're in wheelchairs they'd be less competitive?"

"I guess I did."

"They're men, honey, muscle and testosterone. And they're just itching to ram each other. Putting wheels on them just makes them rowdier. They can race faster and hit each other easier. You think *this* is bad, you should watch a game of quad rugby. 'Murder ball' the guys used to call it, and that's a good name for it."

"Couldn't be any worse than this."

Vicki laughed. "Hon, I'm talking about a full-contact sport with wheelchairs slamming into each other at high speed. Alan and Mac really get off on it."

"How can you watch Alan when he does this kind of stuff and not worry?"

"I didn't say I didn't worry. That man's been worrying me to death since I was five years old, and I don't suppose when I'm an old woman it'll be any different. But I've learned not to be obvious about it."

"You knew Alan as a child?"

"Oh, yeah, love at first sight in kindergarten for me, but he was stubborn, so I had to do some persuading."

"What did that involve?"

"I wrestled him to the ground, pinned his arms behind his back and forced him to say he'd be my boyfriend."

Keely smiled, imagining what that must have looked like.

"Even then, he resisted," Vicki added. "He's still got the scar on his shoulder where I bit him."

"How old were you when you got married?"

"Eighteen."

All these years married to the same man. Loving him unconditionally. Raising children together. Vicki had done things the right way, and Keely admired her for it.

She supposed it was unfair to compare her mother's situation to Vicki's, but she couldn't help it. Liz Wilson had bailed out on her husband and her marriage. Vicki had stayed with Alan even through a crippling injury.

"Aw, ref, you're outta your mind!" Vicki yelled loudly. Keely smiled.

No, Vicki Sizemore was definitely not like Liz Wilson—or anyone else Keely had ever met.

CHAPTER EIGHT

THE MEN WERE BATTERED, bruised and lost the game, but it didn't appear to Keely that their spirits had been dampened any. One had a busted lip, another a scratch across his face where someone's fingernail had raked him during a scuffle over the basketball.

Mac had gotten an elbow in the eye in the last quarter, and it was still a bit red. Keely tried to put an ice pack on it when they got to Vicki and Alan's, but Mac insisted the only cold thing he wanted was a beer.

"Here you go," Vicki told him, getting a beer out of the refrigerator and tossing it to him. "Keely, I have juice, tea, bottled water or beer. Which would you like?"

"Water would be great. Thanks."

Alan called out from the backyard for Mac to come and help him cook the ribs and to bring them all another beer. Vicki put some ice, beer and soft drinks in a small cooler and set it on Mac's lap. "That should hold everyone for a few minutes."

"Thanks. Hey, where's the portable phone? I want to call and see how track practice went."

"On the patio."

"You're calling Coach Crocker?" Keely asked, surprised.

"Hardly."

Mac had never mentioned his problems with Crocker, but Keely had seen how hostile the coach was to Mac, and everyone in the athletic department knew the two didn't get along. Dean had filled her in on some of the details. Crocker had expected the athletic director's job when Mike Collier transferred to Georgia Tech, but the job had gone to Mac, instead.

According to Dean, a resentful Crocker had convinced himself it was because the university wanted someone disabled in an administrator's position so they could boast of being an equal-opportunity employer. He called Mac the "token cripple" behind his back, although Keely suspected Mac knew.

"Dean covers practice and he'll fill me in on how things went," Mac explained. "Normally I don't worry about it, but I have a student who's in danger of losing his scholarship and I want to see how he did today."

"Bad grades?" Keely asked.

"Bad judgment. But he'll get over it with some help."

Mac headed out to the backyard to join the others. Keely stayed behind at Vicki's request to help slice tomatoes.

"He's a special guy, isn't he?" Vicki asked.

"Yes, he is. I don't think I've ever met anyone quite like him."

"I just love him to death. He's too nice sometimes, but I guess there are worse flaws in a man." Vicki put her at the table with a plate, a knife and the washed tomatoes, then walked back to the counter where she'd been mixing potato salad. "By the way, when you have questions about stuff, I'm available anytime. All you have to do is ask."

"Stuff?"

"With Mac. Crip stuff." She shot Keely a grin over her shoulder and added, "And sex stuff. You know—how he does it."

Keely almost sliced her finger with the knife. "Mac's sex life is none of my business. I told you earlier that he and I aren't involved romantically. And we're definitely *not* planning to have sex."

"Uh-huh. Well, I want you to know that the day you decide to, you can come to me with questions. Even though the traditional stuff is sometimes out of the question with a para or a quad, sex can be terrific as long as you understand what they can and can't do. I don't want you to get scared off because you don't know what to expect. How much they can do depends on the location of the injury and how bad it was."

"Vicki—"

"Now Alan can still get it up, even though he has problems higher up on his trunk than Mac. But Mac's injury is in a different place and was more concentrated, so—"

"Oh, please, I *don't* want to know this."

They were interrupted by the shrill scream of a child from the adjacent living room, where the Sizemores' oldest son, Bay, was baby-sitting the others. Vicki didn't bother to walk to the doorway. "Savannah, whatever you're doing to J.P., stop it this instant."

"Yes, ma'am," came the reply. The screaming ceased almost immediately.

"How did you know she was the one bothering him?" Keely asked, chuckling.

"Experience. This morning I found him with lipstick on and Savannah trying to put him in a dress. Honestly, I don't know where that child gets her streak of mischief."

Keely thought it was pretty obvious. All three were physical miniatures of their parents: redheaded and freckled. J.P. had soft baby curls in shades of copper like his father. Savannah and Bay had their mother's flaming hair. They also had their parents' personalities, in addition to their looks.

"What were we talking about?" Vicki asked.

Keely quickly brought up a subject less threatening than the one they'd been discussing prior to J.P's scream. "I was about to ask you about Mac and Doug Crocker. Weren't they friends once? They seemed friendly when I was an undergraduate student."

"Not close friends, but friends," Vicki agreed, "and Mac's been really hurt by Doug's attitude. He's made multiple attempts to mend the relationship, but Doug doesn't respond. So Mac's quit trying. Now they just tolerate each other."

"I can't imagine anyone believing Mac didn't deserve that job. He's so good with his students."

"Doug's six years older and he has more tenure than Mac or any of the other coaches, so he thinks he should have gotten it. Plus, he was working with the men's team, which he thought was a more prestigious job than working with the women."

"But he has such a grating personality and the

A.D.'s job involves ninety percent public relations. Doug would have alienated everybody the first week.''

"That's exactly what Alan says. He can't stand the guy, either, although his friendship with Mac probably has a lot to do with that.''

"Will Mac and Doug work it out, do you think?''

"I doubt it. Some people just have hate in their hearts and nothing can change that. Like that woman Mac got shot helping. She never bothered to thank him, even testified he shouldn't have interfered. Can you believe it?''

"I can't imagine anyone doing that!''

"The jerk was trying to bash her skull in with the butt of a gun. If Mac hadn't jumped in, he probably would have killed her.''

"Mac told me he didn't know the guy had a gun.''

"Oh, he knew all right.''

"Then he lied to me. I wonder why.''

Vicki wiped her hands on a dish towel and sat down across from her at the table. "Don't be upset. Despite how well-adjusted he seems, he still has trouble dealing with what happened to him. He tends to downplay everything.''

"What he did was pretty courageous.''

"I think so, but he doesn't. People made a big deal over what a hero he was, but when he was lying in that hospital, dead from the waist down and facing life in a wheelchair, he didn't feel much like a hero. He still doesn't. And I'm not convinced he's completely accepted his condition.''

Keely nodded slowly. She could certainly identify with that.

"You know," Vicki continued, "the sad part is that Mac got hurt for such a stupid reason. I get furious when I think about how that woman supported her boyfriend. I just want to find her and tell her what I think of her. But then I tell myself she probably got what she deserved by staying with a man who beats on her."

"What happened to the man?"

"He got a three-year suspended sentence for assault and had to pay a fine for carrying an unlicensed pistol."

"He didn't go to jail?"

"Not a day."

"That's so unfair!"

"Ironic, isn't it? The only one who's paying for what happened that night is Mac, and I guess you could say he got a life sentence."

"YOU TURNED PRETTY QUIET all of a sudden tonight," Mac said as they made their way down the walkway to Keely's patio door. "Didn't you enjoy the barbecue?"

"Yes, very much."

Mac waited until they were in the kitchen to ask, "What was it about my friends you didn't like?"

She looked at him oddly. "I liked your friends. As a matter of fact, I liked them very much."

"Then what's the matter?"

"Nothing's the matter." She went to the refrigerator and opened it. "How about some fresh juice? You don't have to go yet, do you? It's still early and I'm dying to open the housewarming present you brought me.''

The package sat on the kitchen table where he'd deposited it when he'd picked her up for the ball game.

''The present can wait. Something *is* bothering you and I want to know what.''

Mac was determined to get to the bottom of this. She'd seemed fine after the game and even animated and unafraid when she'd met the other guys on the team. He'd believed she was having a good time. Then suddenly she'd gotten quiet.

''Did someone say something to hurt your feelings?''

''No, no one said anything. Your friends were very nice and I enjoyed myself.'' She got a tray from the cabinet and put the pitcher and two glasses on it. ''Let's drink the juice on the patio where it's cooler. You'll like this mixture. I added a secret ingredient that gives you a boost. I've been experimenting with creating my own energy drinks, and I've come up with one I think is pretty unique.'' She started to walk to the door, but he rolled in front of her.

''If Bailey said something out of line, tell me and I'll kill the guy. I noticed he cornered you a couple of times.''

''Bailey?'' She seemed confused, then she chuckled. ''Oh, Bailey. He flirted a little, but I wasn't offended.''

Mac took the tray from her hands and set it on the counter. ''Then who did offend you?''

''No one offended me.'' Seeing he wasn't going to give up, she shrugged, deciding to explain. ''When we were alone in the house, Vicki told me more about the day you got shot. She said you knew the man had a gun.''

A knot formed in Mac's throat. ''And now you're hurt because I lied to you about that.''

''No, not hurt. Well, a little, I guess. Why didn't you tell me the whole story?''

''I didn't think you'd care.''

The minute he'd spoken, he realized he'd said it badly.

''Now *that* hurts me,'' she said.

''I didn't mean it like that. I meant, when you asked about my injury we'd just seen each other for the first time in several years. The last thing I wanted to do was bore you with the details of my stupidity.''

''Stupidity? Mac! Trying to disarm that man was incredibly brave.''

''No, what I did was incredibly stupid. Don't blow it out of proportion.''

Agitated, he ran his hand through his hair. Man, he hated this, hated the look people got in their eyes when they heard what he'd done. He wasn't brave. He'd reacted without thinking that day. One minute he'd been walking to his car and the next minute he'd found himself in a desperate struggle to get the gun.

He couldn't remember the time in between, couldn't remember any conscious decision to intervene on the woman's behalf. Suddenly he was on the ground with the man and they were both rolling like a kicked soda bottle, the wrong end of cold steel pressing into his stomach.

''I'm sorry I barked,'' he told her.

"Don't apologize. What happened to you is very personal, and there's no reason you should feel obligated to tell the story to just anyone."

"You're not just anyone, Keely."

"No, I'm your friend. And that's why I've felt so strange about this. I felt you needed to know what Vicki told me tonight, but I hated to bring it up. And while we're clearing the air, I think I ought to tell you that I asked Vicki about your relationship with Doug Crocker. I wasn't being nosy, but there's so much speculation among the staff it's impossible to know what to believe."

"Crocker has major issues with me."

"Because you were promoted over him? Or because of your disability?"

"Both, probably. I don't know for sure. I've never been able to get anything concrete out of him."

And Mac regretted that more than he could say, not only because it kept them from resolving their hostilities, but because of the gossip they generated.

"Can we not talk about this?" he asked. "I try to leave problems at work and not let them intrude on what little free time I have."

"Okay, enough depressing talk for tonight." Keely wagged her finger at the package on the table. "Besides, I can't stand it any longer. Are you ever going to let me open that gift? You're cruel to bring it here and then tell me I can't open it."

"I'm trying to teach you patience."

"Fat chance of that and we both know it." She picked up the drinks tray and set it on his lap. "Let me change clothes and I'll be out in a second. Then you can show me what you brought.''

Mac took the juice out to the patio, then went back for the flat rectangular package he'd picked up earlier in the day.

Keely walked out a few minutes later, wearing an oversize T-shirt that went to her knees and hung precariously off one shoulder to reveal an expanse of creamy skin.

She liked to be comfortable. That was one of the first things he had discovered about her, and she hadn't changed in the past ten years. She wasn't an exhibitionist, but she wore as little as she could get away with and still be decent.

She wouldn't wear a dress if she could wear pants. She didn't wear pants if she could wear shorts. And he suspected she probably removed the shorts and everything else when she was alone.

Judging by the nipples that strained against the T-shirt, underwear wasn't high on her list of priorities at the moment, either. She'd obviously shed her bra. But surely she had something on under that thing. Shorts. Something.

''I hope you like it,'' he said, handing her the package. ''I had a hard time deciding what to give you.''

''You didn't have to give me anything.'' Her eyes glowed with childish glee. ''But I'm glad you did. I love getting presents.''

She flipped on the outside lights, then put the gift on the patio table and tore into the paper, as eager as a six-year-old on her birthday. She gasped with delight when she saw the large framed photograph of her and her father embracing. "Oh, Mac, this is wonderful!"

He'd thought long and hard about an appropriate gift, deciding it should be something personal but not too personal. Cleaning out a file drawer a few weeks earlier, he'd run across an old media guide for the women's track team. This photograph from Keely's freshman year had been used on the cover. The university archives still had the negative, so he'd borrowed it and had a local photo store make an enlarged print.

Keely touched her fingers to the glass, as if she could touch her father's face beneath. "I remember this. It was taken after my first conference title. My dad ran out on the track to hug me when I crossed the finish line. This is most thoughtful thing anyone's ever done for me."

"So you like it?"

"I love it. Thank you!"

She leaned down, and for a moment he thought she might hug him, or better still, kiss him on the mouth. But all he got was a quick peck on the cheek.

Pulling back, she smiled at him softly, but then her sweet expression turned to—God help him—longing. He had never expected this and it stunned him, weakened his resolve.

He'd had a hard enough time resisting her when she thought of him only as her coach and friend. But to see passion in her eyes, to know that a part of her didn't fear him but desired him as a woman desires a man, stripped him of all reason.

He reached for her. "Keely…"

Abruptly, she straightened and backed away. She picked up the photograph. "I should put this inside before the dew ruins it." She fled through the patio door before Mac could stop her.

He expelled a breath in frustration, understanding suddenly what had eluded him before. She wasn't afraid of him. She was afraid of *wanting* him. A relationship was a threat to her running plans.

His chin dropped to his chest. If his adversary had been another man, he'd know how to fight for Keely's heart, but it wasn't a flesh-and-blood person. She was in love already—with being the best runner in the world.

"How do I compete with your dream, Keely?" he wondered out loud. Sadly, he realized that was a fight he could never win.

CHAPTER NINE

August
Pensacola, Florida

KEELY PRETENDED that night on the patio had never happened. To Mac's disappointment she also seemed determined to remind him as often as possible over the next few months that regaining her career was the only thing of importance in her life.

Maybe it was. Maybe he should do himself a favor and accept that. Whatever desire she'd felt for him had been an aberration, gratitude for her housewarming gift disguised as desire.

She intended to run again, and she'd made it perfectly clear that no doctor, no therapist and certainly no paraplegic coach wearing his heart on his sleeve was going to interfere with her plans. Yes, indeed. She had her life all mapped out, and the name Mac McCandless wasn't anywhere on the map that he could see.

He watched her now, giving an interview to a Pensacola television reporter outside the city's sports complex. He knew what she was saying without actually hearing the words—knew because the words were rehearsed, along with the assured smile that always accompanied them.

Yes, I'm back in training.

No, I'm as strong as ever and completely recovered from the accident.

The Olympics in Sydney? Of course I'm going to compete. She even believed what she was telling the guy. She used the same convincing lines on Mac at every opportunity.

True, she was doing well, better than he had anticipated. The leg and hip had healed, and she'd graduated from walking to light running. Her limp had even disappeared. But her weakened lung would never allow her to do more than run for pleasure.

He shook his head and pushed off through the crowd of race spectators and wheelers before Keely could see him and wave him over. No way was he going to be put on the spot.

After her accident he'd managed to dodge questions about her chances of a comeback by feigning a lack of firsthand knowledge about her condition. He couldn't do that now. The reporters knew she'd been back at Courtland with him through the summer. They knew he was in charge of her training. Sooner or later someone could turn a camera on him and ask, ''Will Keely Wilson run professionally again?'' He'd have to lie or tell the truth. And he wasn't sure which was worse.

Two of his students were about to race on the adjacent track, so he quickly made his way over to them. The Courtland team had arrived in Pensacola late that morning after a six-hour drive that was supposed to be four—the oldest van in their three-vehicle caravan had blown a tire. Keely had surprised him by driving down to Florida on her own to watch the events.

"Hey, your guys look great," a buddy called out to him as he passed the wheelers from the Hartford rehab hospital.

"Thanks, Steve."

"You racing in Detroit next month?"

"Not this time." He pushed aside the regret that accompanied his response. Maybe next year, when his life was a little less hectic, he'd concentrate a bit more on his own racing.

On the track the race was about to begin, so he quickly gave last-minute instructions to his students while Dean reloaded the camera. After that, Mac got the team together near the fence. "You guys had a great morning. This heat's a killer, so watch yourselves during the lunch break. Let's meet back at this spot at about one-forty."

They wheeled off in different directions, some to meet girlfriends, others to find a shady spot and eat snacks provided by the race officials. Mac was contemplating finding a shady spot himself, hoping to catch up on the sleep he'd missed because of their middle-of-the-night departure from Georgia. As he headed toward the concession area for something to drink, a slim man approached. He asked Mac if he was the Courtland coach. Mac said he was.

The man started to say something, stopped and then sneezed. He sneezed several more times before he could talk again.

"Sorry," he said, wiping his nose with a handkerchief he'd pulled from his pocket. "Allergies. Drive me insane all year. This ocean air will probably kill me."

Mac felt sorry for the guy. He sounded as if someone had stuffed socks in his sinus cavity.

The man stuck out his hand. "Beatty Redmond of Coxwell Industries down in Miami. I've been hearing wonderful things about your team. Watching them today, I'd say the praise was well deserved. Very impressive."

"Thanks."

"I was wondering if you might have a few minutes to talk to me. Our company president is interested in sponsoring a team and sent me here with specific instructions to, to... Oh, excuse me a moment."

He started another sneezing spell.

"To what?" Mac prodded.

"To..." (sneeze) "find..." (sneeze) "the best team" (sneeze). Redmond blew his nose so loudly that people around them turned to look and laugh. "I think your team might be it. Do you have a few minutes?"

"Mr. Redmond," Mac said, hardly able to keep the excitement from his voice, "you can have as much of my time as you need."

"YOU'RE KIDDING. Thirty thousand dollars?" Keely pushed aside the bottle of mineral water she'd taken from his motel room's minibar and leaned across the table toward him, as if she hadn't heard correctly. "And he's giving you more this fall?"

"Fifty for the next fiscal year. He's also going to provide uniforms."

"That's wonderful!"

"The company has a licensing agreement for some new kind of breathable material that not only wicks moisture but uses your own body to regulate temperature. Insul-something or other. Redmond thinks within two years everyone will be wearing it, even nonathletes."

Dean slapped Mac on the shoulder in congratulations and flopped down on the bed. "Does this mean we can finally buy a team van and burn that wreck you got from the baseball team?"

Mac grinned, hardly able to suppress his glee at what they might finally be able to do. Buy equipment. Manage travel expenses. The offer wasn't eight hours old and he'd already started to calculate the possibilities.

"*Maybe* we can buy a van. But let's not make any plans or tell the team until we actually have the money. I still have to clear the sponsorship with the university."

"Do you foresee any problem with that?" Keely asked him.

"No, it should be pretty much a formality."

"I think we ought to celebrate tonight," Dean said. "Food? Beer? Dancing? The over-twenty-one crowd will hit the Aquarium. Want to join them?"

"You want to go look at fish?" Keely asked.

"No, I want to go *eat* fish. This place has the best seafood you ever ate, a huge dance floor, and it's gimp-friendly." He looked at Mac. "You in?"

Mac nodded. "You know it. But I'm buying."

"No argument from me," Dean told him. "Keely, you in?"

She hesitated, and Mac wondered how she was going to get out of Dean's invitation. Keely got up at five every morning to work out and rarely stayed up past ten. He was pretty sure she didn't date, although she had plenty of opportunities; he knew she did very little that wasn't directly related to her training. Chances were, she hadn't been to a nightclub in years, if ever.

"I don't eat anything fried or drink beer," she reminded them. "The dancing is pretty iffy, too."

"Dean's grandmother has more fun than you do," Mac said, giving Dean a wink.

"Yeah, Mac," Dean said, "let's dump her and find some younger women. This one's too old."

Keely's hands flew to her hips in mock indignation. "I am *not* too old."

"You just act old, then," Mac said. Getting her out for a good time might show her that running and relationships could coexist. "You need a night out, Keely. Do you even know *how* to dance?"

"Of course I do! I just haven't done it in a long time."

"How long?"

"Uh, years."

"Unreal!" Dean said. He pulled her to her feet and toward the door. "Mac's right. Go change clothes. You're in serious need of a good time and we're the guys to provide it."

THE AQUARIUM had once been what its name indicated, a seaside tourist attraction with fish, dolphins and a whale show. The outdoor facilities were no longer open, but one tank remained with an underwater viewing window. The current owners had converted an enormous rectangular room in the main building to a combination restaurant and nightclub.

The place was popular not only with the wheelers in town for the race but with the military from the nearby naval air station. Sailors in uniform, and women apparently hoping to catch one, crammed the place. Men and women in and out of wheelchairs moved across the center dance floor, creating a sea of flesh and metal that seemed to undulate in rhythm to the rock and country songs the band played.

Nets, shells and boating memorabilia hung from the ceiling and three of the walls. The fourth wall was the focal point of the room, the lighted tank stocked with strange and colorful creatures that swam right up to the glass and looked at you as you looked at them.

The place fascinated Keely, and yet it had its drawbacks. The music was too loud. The air carried the fishy scent of the ocean, which was fine if you were standing on the beach or eating fish, but not so fine if you were trying to eat salad. Even worse, she felt a disturbing alien emotion each time someone pulled Mac away from the table to dance.

The women—and there had been an endless parade of them—seemed most interested in the slow songs, when they could sit sideways in Mac's lap and nestle against his chest. The woman nestling against him now had her arms around his neck and was telling him something funny that had him braying like a jackass.

"I didn't realize people in wheelchairs could dance," Keely told Dean, mentally berating herself for caring that Mac's right hand had shifted from the wheel on that side to the woman's jean-clad thigh.

"Not a whole lot crips can't do when it comes right down to it," Dean said.

"So I see." Obviously Mac could move the chair with one hand while groping women with the other. Well, it wasn't exactly groping, but it bothered her to watch, anyway.

Was he trying to torture her in exchange for that night on the patio? Or was she simply getting very good at *self* torture?

Someone touched her shoulder, and she turned to find Steve Sasser, one of the Hartford wheelers Mac had introduced her to. "Would you like to dance?"

"Oh, no, thank you. I haven't danced in so long I don't remember how."

He patted his lap. "All you have to do is sit. I'll do all the work."

She contemplated saying no again, but then relented. He was nice. A good-looking man. She couldn't think of a single reason she shouldn't dance with him.

After Steve came Jimmy, Ben, Wade, Erik and two dozen more men, both disabled and able-bodied. "This is getting ridiculous," she told Dean. "I'm exhausted just walking back and forth from the dance floor."

"Yeah, but having fun for a change, right?"

Yes, she admitted, she was having fun, though feeling a little guilty about it. Growing up, her dad had often hammered into her the consequences of breaking training.

"Act like ordinary people and you'll be ordinary," he was fond of saying.

He'd been right, of course. During high school, while her friends worked on their summer tans, Keely worked on endurance and strength. She'd skipped the parties, the dates, the hours on the telephone talking about boys. Instead, she'd concentrated on making the Olympic team. She'd won her first silver medal at seventeen.

Adhering to her father's rules all those years had paid off. The lessons she'd learned had followed her into adulthood, and she was loath to deviate from them too often. When you were bad, you paid for it with poor performances and you lost the respect of the people counting on you. It wasn't worth it.

Not that she was a complete social misfit. The very nature of her business dictated that she attend dinners and put in appearances at various functions. She dated occasionally. She'd even had a physical relationship that lasted a whole six months. It had turned out badly, of course, and the failure had been entirely her fault, but that was the way things worked. With so much time and passion expended on her career, she had none left over for a man.

"My turn to dance with you," Dean said, standing. He held out his hand. Keely allowed him to lead her through the crowd.

"I don't know if I'm ready for this," she shouted as the slow song segued into a faster one.

"Just be careful and don't throw that hip out. Mac would kill me."

Maybe it was the music. Maybe it was Dean's youthful exuberance rubbing off on her. Whatever it was, Keely allowed herself to flow with it, letting her natural rhythm guide her body and release her from her inhibitions. Dancing, she rediscovered, was like running, controlled by an inner mind that moved you without true conscious thought.

The next song was slow. Dean insisted they dance to it, too, but his attention—like her own—was more on Mac and his current partner. The girl was young and petite, with dark hair that fell past her waist. "She's very pretty," Keely commented.

"Beautiful."

Dean's gaze kept going back to the couple.

"Do you know her?" Keely asked. "She looks familiar."

"Ginny Sasser. Steve Sasser's daughter. I met her here last year and I've bumped into her a few times since then at races. You probably saw her at the track this morning."

Ah, that was it. Keely didn't remember the face, but that long hair was hard to forget. "Is she single?"

"Yeah. And smart. She's in her second year of law school."

Keely grinned at him. "You sure seem to know a lot about her."

"I've had a bad case of the hots for her ever since I met her last year."

"If you're attracted to her, why haven't you done anything about it? I haven't seen you dance with her once."

"You should talk."

"Meaning?"

"You know exactly what I mean. You and Mac. You've spent all night trying to stay away from each other, yet you can't keep your eyes off him and I'd bet money he could name every man you've danced with."

Was he watching her? She hated being thrilled at the thought of it.

She wasn't going to allow herself to be drawn into a conversation about Mac, so she ignored Dean's comment and told him again to go ask Ginny to dance.

"I haven't worked up my courage yet," he said.

"Do it now, Dean. You can't simply stand back and worship her from a distance."

"She might turn me down and then I'd be crushed." He grinned. "The rejection might scar me for life."

"Oh, sure, like anything would ever scar you for life. Go on—do it," Keely said again.

"She might be tired of dancing."

"Then ask her if she wants to go look at the fish with you."

"Well…maybe. I'll think about it."

As they looked at Ginny, she smiled at them. Or more precisely, at Dean.

"See?" Keely said. "She's sending you signals. She wants you to come over."

"Think so?"

"I'm positive. She obviously likes you, too."

Keely took the lead and danced them closer to Mac and Ginny.

Dean danced her back the other way. "What are you doing?"

"Helping you out." She danced them forward.

"I don't need help." He danced them back.

"Quit being difficult and let's get over there."

She nearly had to jerk him this time, but he followed her lead. They ended up dancing right next to Mac as the song ended and Ginny got up from his lap. Perfect timing.

"Hi," Keely said.

"Hi," Mac replied.

Keely turned her attention to the girl. "I'm Keely and this is Dean. We're friends of Mac's."

"I'm sorry," Mac said, and took up the introductions. "I think you already know Dean. Ginny Sasser, meet Keely Wilson. Ginny is Steve's oldest daughter."

"Oh? Steve's daughter." Keely pretended ignorance. "I'm glad to meet you. Are you here with your dad?"

"Uh-huh, just my dad." She cut her gaze to Dean. "I mean, I'm not here with a date or anything."

Dean seized his opportunity. "If you're not otherwise engaged, would you care to walk over and look at the fish?"

Ginny quickly nodded assent. "I'd love to see the fish with you." She turned to Mac. "Thanks for dancing with me, Coach McCandless."

"Thank you, Ginny."

"Nice to meet you, Keely."

"You, too, Ginny."

Dean took Ginny's hand. "See you guys later." He winked at Keely over his shoulder and mouthed, "Don't wait up," as he led Ginny off to the aquarium wall.

"'If you're not otherwise engaged'?" Mac mimicked Dean. "What was that all about? Who talks like that?"

Keely chuckled. "I believe young love does something to the syntax."

Mac's forehead wrinkled. "You're kidding. You mean those two…"

"Uh-huh. The heat between them nearly singed my eyebrows. I had to force him to come over here, he was so nervous about talking to her."

"Man, I must be getting old if can't recognize sexual attraction anymore."

Probably because he was too busy radiating sexual attraction himself.

The soft slow intro of the next song filled the air, and men and women around them began to move into each other's arms. Putting Dean together with Ginny left Keely alone with Mac and both of them partnerless.

Mac gazed up at her expectantly. "Looks like my dance partner deserted me."

"Looks like it."

"And it was partly your fault because you forced Dean to talk to her."

"I…I guess it was." She knew what was coming next, but was uncertain how to handle it.

"You'll have to take her place, you know."

She didn't move an eyelash. Inside, though, her vital organs were turning to jelly.

Dancing with him…the intimacy of it…buttocks to groin. One breast pressing against his chest. With the other men she hadn't given it a thought, but this was Mac. Mac, who made her feel liquid. Mac, who with a simple smile could make her breath catch in her lungs and her heart flutter like a thousand hummingbirds in flight.

She wasn't sure she could dance with him. Yet she couldn't walk away without being cruel. Deep down she suspected the tiny part of her that longed for intimacy with Mac had even purposely put her in this terrible situation.

Physical fear of him still stood as a wall between them, a lower wall than when she'd first learned of his injury, but a wall nonetheless. Over the past months, he'd helped her learn to touch him without cringing, but dancing with him was a big jump from putting ointment on his scraped hands or rubbing sunscreen across his shoulders. His hands and shoulders weren't paralyzed. His legs were.

She worried how his legs would feel under her. How did they look?

She'd never seen him when he wasn't wearing long pants. Even on the hottest days this summer, he'd worn sweats or a long-legged body suit. For work he preferred khakis or jeans, although the rest of the staff dressed in shorts. Tonight his legs were covered again, in a dark-gray pair of cotton twills.

He held out a hand at her hesitation. "Remember

how much fun we had dancing the night of your graduation?''

"I remember. You had some pretty fancy moves, as I recall.''

"I still do,'' he said, grinning. When she didn't move, he sobered. "Come on, Sport Model. This is Mac. Your best buddy. You don't have any reason to be afraid of this. I promise.''

Sport Model. He'd given her the nickname in college, teasing that she was built for speed like a fancy racing car.

As if disconnected from her body, she saw her hand inch forward and into his, without having made the decision to move it.

"That's it,'' he coaxed, gently urging her down toward his lap. "Trust me and everything will be fine. You know I'd never ask you to do anything that would hurt you.''

Her pulse pounded in her ears. The first contact with his lap sent a sizzle of fear through her body, but the fear quickly turned to a delicious curl of pleasure that stretched like a contented cat in the pit of her stomach and below.

His legs felt fine. The curves of her backside settled in against them without any problem, and her lower legs found a comfortable place to nestle between his.

Her arms and hands were a different story. She didn't know where to put them. Her right arm was the one closest to his body, and she moved it this way and that, trying to find an appropriate place for it, until he took the decision from her and hooked it on his shoulder.

He pulled her forward a bit and placed her other hand against his chest. She knew his soft cotton shirt hid muscle and delicious masculine angles, and her fingers ached to touch the naked flesh in reality, as they had done so often lately in her dreams.

She had danced with Steve Sasser the very same way only thirty minutes ago and the position had felt merely functional, a way to keep her off the wheels of the chair and balanced in his lap. With Mac, it was more of an embrace.

"This okay?" he asked. "If it's not, all you have to do is say so."

"It's fine." Sexual arousal had taken root at the heart of her and was making her feel a little bold.

As they began to move to the lazy rhythm of the song, she remained aware of the people around them, but her focus reduced itself to one man, to the musky smell of his cologne and the warmth of his breath against her cheek.

His face was just a whisper away and she studied it, the contours of his jaw, the crinkly lines at his eyes, the ever-so-slight dip in the center of his chin. They were flesh-and-blood magnets drawing her with an invisible charge.

And that mouth. A torture device for women if she'd ever seen one. Perfect teeth. That tiny, heart-shaped bow at the top of his upper lip.

She was thankful she wasn't alone with him. Had they been alone, she might have pushed foolishness to recklessness and touched her lips to his, just to see if they really felt as good as she imagined.

"This isn't so bad, is it?" he asked, giving her a

reassuring smile. She liked the way his eyes seemed to smile right along with his mouth.

"No, it isn't so bad." She didn't think it was wise to tell him that, in fact, it felt very very good.

Their gazes held for a moment, for too long a moment. In the dark depths of his eyes she saw her wildest dreams and her worst nightmares. He desired her. He wanted to make love to her.

Quickly she looked away, afraid her own eyes might reveal the truth: she wanted the same thing. And it wasn't that other Mac she wanted, the Mac from ten years ago who had run so gracefully and been so physically perfect. It was *this* Mac. The older Mac. The Mac who couldn't run and wasn't perfect. The Mac who'd been to hell and survived it.

She wanted the Mac in the wheelchair.

WHEN HE TOOK HER back to the motel that night, awkwardness made her tongue-tied. She stood at her door, shuffling from foot to foot, not knowing what to say or how to act, hoping she could say good-night without throwing herself on top of him.

He was attractive, charming, witty and oozed sexuality from every pore of his skin, a dangerous combination of traits in any man, but downright deadly in this one.

Her brain cells screamed for her to get away, and as quickly as possible. Every time he touched her arm tonight, or smiled at her, or whispered something amusing in her ear, it put another chink in the wall she had erected against him. The wall was beginning to crumble.

Now she needed time to repair the damage. Time alone. Sleep, if possible. Maybe even a few notes jotted in her journal to soothe her. She had to force her concentration away from him and back to her goal. She couldn't allow herself to become distracted.

She thanked him for a good time and scurried into the room as fast as she could without being rude. As on countless other nights, she found she was afraid to sleep or even turn off the lights, so she got out her journal and read back through past entries.

May 7: Mac says I'm making great progress, but he treats me as if I might break. He's always around. He's always looking out for me. It's annoying at times. Other times I find I like it way too much. Have to work on that.

June 28: Mac let me increase my exercises slightly today. He's such a sweetheart. I need to thank him somehow. Dinner out as my treat? A gift? The leather shop at the mall has a briefcase in the window that's perfect. It's the same incredible brown as his eyes.

August 17: Today Mac...

Mac this. Mac that. It read more like a teenager's diary than the journal of a grown woman. She was supposed to be recording her training progress, not talking about Mac McCandless.

In disgust she tossed the journal back into her bag. This was ludicrous! She couldn't give in to this... this...admiration.

Admiration? Who was she trying to fool? Call it by

its real name—lust. Wet, aching, nipple-hardening, I-want-to-rub-myself-all-over-you kind of lust.

As Dean might phrase it, she had a bad case of the hots for Mac. And she had to find a way to control herself—before she ruined everything.

CHAPTER TEN

September

"Please, Mac, let me ride you. I'll try not to squeal this time."

"Aw, Linda, not today. I've got tons of work to do."

He had appointments all morning, a board-of-trustees meeting that afternoon and a stack of telephone messages on this desk left over from yesterday.

"Yes, today. Please, please, let me. Just an itty-bitty ride?"

The secretary gave him a pleading look, dissolving Mac's better judgment. He'd always had trouble resisting a woman when she wanted something. All she had to do was poke out a lip or act hurt, and he melted quicker than butter on a hot ear of corn.

"Pleeeeeeeeease," she whined again.

"Since when am I an amusement ride?"

"Since you got these fun wheels. Oh, come on. It won't take five minutes."

He sighed, knowing he was defeated. Okay, he'd take her for a ride. It wasn't seven yet and few people were at work. No one important would see them. As long as the other women he worked with didn't find out, it was okay. If they did, they'd want a ride, too, and he didn't have time to entertain them this morning.

"Climb on," he told her. "But we've got to be quick. And you have to promise—no squealing. You know I hate squealing."

"I promise."

She plopped down in his lap. He shifted her sideways so her hips wouldn't touch the wheels. Pushing off was difficult, but in seconds he had overcome the slow start and the added weight of his passenger. Quickly they picked up momentum. By the time they hit the ramp at the end of the hall, they were flying.

"Eeeeeeeeeeee," she squealed despite her promise, just like they'd both known she would.

They barreled up the ramp and onto the concourse, scattering people in their wake, picking up speed again as they left the carpet and hit the concrete floor. As they whizzed through a group of students, someone yelled, "Go for it, Coach." Another opened a door.

Mac raced through the upper level to the outside without slowing. The college had placed ramps across one end of both sets of steps and he hit the first one with a loud *whomp*. The chair nearly jumped the second one, becoming airborne and slamming onto the pavement with a jolt that bounced Linda several inches off his lap. The planters loomed ahead.

"Hold on," he warned, but there was no real danger. He had maneuvered this course so many times he could do it in his sleep. The trick was maintaining the right speed so he didn't have to brake, cutting to the right of the first tree to avoid the uneven pavement and making sure he didn't hit anyone.

"Coming through!"

The student athletes on their way into Coach Layton's early-morning conditioning class scrambled onto the planters and out of the way, cheering Mac on as he expertly snaked through the trees and toward the street. As always, he waited until the last possible second to brake. And as always, Linda screamed loudly as they slid to a stop inches from the curb.

This time he looked up to find he had also stopped inches from Keely.

"Keely! Hey."

She opened and closed her mouth several times. Finally she whispered, "Excuse me, I have to go," and slipped around them.

"Oops," Linda said with a chortle. "Mac, do yourself a favor and let your friend know I'm an old married woman who dearly loves her husband."

"Huh?"

She rolled her eyes, then knocked on his head as if it were made of wood. "Think about it, you big dunce and maybe you can figure out why she's upset." She hopped up. "Thanks for the ride. See ya."

"See ya, Linda."

Mac pivoted the chair so he could better watch Keely's progress up the long walk. She charged ahead at full steam, almost at a run, forcing people to jump out of her way. Clearly something *had* upset her.

When the answer hit him, he wanted to knock himself on his own head for his stupidity.

"SLOW IT DOWN a bit," Dean said from behind, sounding like he was beginning to tire. "We still have over 1200 steps to go."

Instead of slowing down, Keely began climbing faster. The sound of her soles hitting the concrete steps was like a drumbeat, urging her to run faster, to make it up and down the steep rows of the coliseum without stopping to rest.

"If you can't keep up, Averhardt, don't blame it on me," she said, ignoring the growing pain in her side.

"Don't start this again, Keely. You know you're pushing too hard. For some reason you've been antsy ever since we started today."

Running the lower circle of the 1,956 steps of the coliseum with Dean was a twice-weekly ritual Keely enjoyed, but his constant admonishments to slow down and not overdo were getting on her nerves. Today of all days she needed to push herself. She needed to feel strong and alive, to feel she had overcome her injuries.

September twenty-seventh. A year ago today, she'd been hit by that car and nearly died. This day marked a whole year away from competition. Other elite women runners were celebrating victories and breaking her records right and left. She, meanwhile, was stuck here in classes that bored her to tears and being nagged by Mac and Dean every time she lifted a leg to exercise.

Seeing Mac this morning with that woman on his lap hadn't helped her feelings, either.

She needed to work a little harder, run more miles, exercise another couple of hours a day. By spring maybe she could race again.

"I'm not slowing down," she told Dean, taking two

steps at a time. She called over her shoulder, "And I'm doing all twenty-four rows without stopping."

"You're *not* doing all twenty-four. That's crazy."

"Oh, yes I am."

The pain deepened, making Keely struggle to bring in more oxygen. Faced with the unexpected barrier, she did what she always did; she denied the pain and pushed herself harder.

"Please slow down," Dean urged again. "You've been doing so great these past few months. You don't want to do anything to wreck your progress."

"Ooh, you're such a nag."

"Fine. Don't listen. You're on your own, then. I can't handle this pace."

Dean pulled back, letting her go ahead without him.

She reached the place where the steps met the top-most aisle, raced over to the next row and began the descent. Down she ran to the floor, then up again to the top, moving as fast as she could. Down. Up. Down. Up.

The pain in her side worsened, but pain was good. Pain meant she was alive.

Focus, she told herself. *Work harder.*

An image of Mac riding that woman on his lap flashed in her head to intrude on her concentration.

Focus!

She pressed ahead. Down. Up. Down. Up.

A couple of steps into her descent on the next row, someone hit her in the ribs with a brick—at least, that was what it felt like. An intense fire consumed her side and made her cry out, propelling her forward. One second she was on her feet and the next she was sprawled facedown, bumping down the steps on her belly and feeling every hard edge.

"Keely! Are you all right?" Dean's voice seemed miles away.

Finally she thumped to a stop. She rolled onto her back and lay there with her eyes closed, trying to catch her breath.

Not again, she prayed. *Please, not again.*

Dean was next to her now, giving his best imitation of a man having a panic attack. "Did the hip go out? Did you break anything? Is it your lung?"

She struggled to turn around and sit up. She put her head between her knees, frantically drawing in oxygen through her mouth. One of the athletes doing steps on an adjacent row called out to ask if she was okay and did they need help.

"Tell her—" she paused to take a couple of deep breaths "—I'm fine."

"Are you sure? I can have one of the trainers here in two minutes."

She shook her head.

Ten minutes passed before the fire in her side died out and she could breathe and talk normally.

"You cut yourself," Dean said, wiping blood off her arm and below her eye with his shirt. "And I think you're going to have a shiner."

The throbbing in her cheek told her he was right. She must have hit the edge of one of the steps with her face when she fell.

"What happened?" Dean asked.

"I fell over my own feet." She glanced sideways to see if Dean believed the lie. He didn't.

"You were gasping for breath and your face was purple," he pointed out. "For a second there I thought your lung was about to collapse again. You scared me to death."

"You're making a big deal out of this when all I did was trip and fall down a few steps."

"Keely, I don't buy that excuse. You cried out and grabbed your side before you fell."

"Dean, please."

The last thing she needed was him running to Mac with some wild story. Admittedly the lung was still bothering her, but even the respiratory therapist she'd worked with after the surgery said that was to be expected for a while. She'd had a lobe removed; she'd lost tissue. She hadn't yet built back to full capacity. The lung would be okay. She only needed a few more months to recover.

"You know Mac's going to ask me what happened," Dean said. "I'm not going to lie to him."

"I'm not asking you to. I *told* you what happened. I tripped. That's all there was to it."

Regardless of whether or not he believed her, Dean had the good sense not to bring it up again. He walked her downstairs to the locker rooms and left her with a reminder to take care of her eye as soon as possible.

She doctored her cuts and stretched out on a bench with an ice pack on her face. Soreness in her arms and legs set in immediately, a combination of falling and not cooling down properly. As soon as she was able to drag herself upstairs, she went to Mac's office, hoping to talk to him before Dean and do a little damage control.

Mac wasn't in. The monthly board-of-trustees meeting, Miriam said. He'd be gone most of the day and would even miss wheeler practice.

"I can leave him a note," Miriam offered, not looking up. "He probably won't see it until morning."

"No, don't bother. I'll catch him later."

For Keely "later" meant that night. Dinner at seven. Three or four nights a week they had dinner at his house or hers while she studied and he graded papers. Sunday afternoons, if he wasn't gone with the football team, he grilled fish or chicken on her patio. A couple of times they'd taken day excursions out of town: the zoo, the art museum, the Egyptian exhibit up in Nashville.

Somehow they had settled into the routine of an old married couple, and it was, for the most part, comfortable, like slipping your foot into a soft old shoe. The fit was good.

Lately, though, it had become less comfortable for her and she suspected for him, too. The attraction between them hung in the air all the time; it colored every decision, every action. She found herself carefully choosing her words. She avoided sitting too close to him, not sure she could keep her hands to herself. The effort that went into being friends, being *only* friends, was wearing her out.

"What happened to your face?" Miriam asked, just now looking up.

"I took a little tumble down the steps."

"You're going to have a black eye."

"Do me a favor and don't mention it to Coach McCandless, okay? I'd rather tell him about it myself."

"Sure, hon, but be prepared. He's going to have a fit when he sees it."

CHAPTER ELEVEN

KEELY WENT to wheeler practice that afternoon, but she skipped lab, opting to go home early and take a hot bath to ease her aching muscles.

After that, she made her weekly call to her mother, since she'd missed doing it the previous Sunday. Holding the receiver between her ear and shoulder, she stood at the bathroom mirror and dabbed makeup on her face. The skin of her cheek and around her eye was an artist's palette of purple in varying shades. The makeup didn't hide the bruises.

At six she drove from her house to Mac's and used the spare key he'd given her, letting herself in through the front door. While the squash and broccoli cooked, she fixed her homemade chocolate pudding and stuck it in the refrigerator to firm, a consolation for Mac who wasn't crazy about vegetables and enjoyed a calorie-laden treat. The pudding wasn't really chocolate and didn't have a gram of fat or sugar in it, but he didn't know that.

She tore lettuce for salad as she skimmed a chapter of the advanced chemistry text she'd picked up at the campus bookstore a couple of days earlier. Finally something interesting!

She made a mental note to talk to her adviser about

auditing a class. Her nutrition class was okay, had already given her an idea for an electrolyte drink she was itching to put together, but the rest of the classes...bor-ing. She deserved an A for simply staying awake in Principles of Recreational Management. If she could get access to one of the chemistry labs to have a little fun, she might actually survive this quarter.

At six-thirty she heard Mac's van pull into the garage.

Upbeat. Calm. That was the way she had to play this. She was pretty sure Dean hadn't yet had a chance to tell Mac about her fall, and that would work in her favor. Quickly she rehearsed what she was going to say.

He pushed through the door, calling out a tired greeting. "When's supper?" he added. "I'm starved."

"Ten minutes," she said, not turning around. She continued to stand at the counter, tearing up the lettuce, although she'd already broken the leaves into minuscule pieces.

"Can I help?"

"No, it's nearly finished. Just relax. How was your meeting?"

"Long and uneventful." She heard him toss his keys on the table and put down his briefcase. The fragrance of roses filled the air. "How was your day?"

No, he definitely hadn't talked to Dean yet.

"Well," she said, clearing her throat, "there *is* something I need to—"

Before she could get the rest of the sentence out,

the telephone rang. Her shoulders slumped. Now she'd have to work up her courage all over again.

He pulled out his cell phone. "Hello. Hey. Yeah, I just walked in the door. What's up?"

He paused to listen to something the caller said. When he spoke again the hard inflection in his voice put Keely's senses on full alert. "No, Dean, I haven't talked to her. Maybe you better tell me what happened before she fell."

Her body stiffened.

Listening over the next few minutes to the one-sided conversation was like waiting in front of a firing squad while the executioners loaded their guns. Dean, no doubt, was recounting every gory detail of this morning's mishap. Mac said little in response, but that in itself was an ominous sign.

"…No, Dean, you did the right thing. No, I'm sure she won't hold it against you." He hung up the phone and Keely braced herself. "I believe you have something to tell me."

"I fell down a couple of steps. Surely I'm not the first person to do that."

"Keely, turn around."

He swore loudly when he saw her face. He made her sit at the table so he could study the damage. A bouquet of red roses lay on his nearby briefcase, and she inhaled their heady fragrance as he assessed her injuries.

His hands trembled as he lightly pressed his fingers against her cheek. "I don't think you chipped the bone, but have Doc Ramsey take a look at it in the morning to see if it needs an X ray. You'll probably have a tiny scar from that cut, but you'll hardly see it.''

"One more won't make any difference.''

He examined a cut on her forearm and a second one on her hand and dismissed them as minor. "That all of them?''

"Yes.''

"Any hip or knee pain?''

"No, just muscle soreness. I soaked in the bathtub and it helped, but my legs are still really sore.''

"I can take care of that.''

He moved his chair at an angle. Before she could protest, he picked up both her legs and placed them across his lap. He still had on the suit he'd worn to his board meeting, and he looked like a million dollars.

"I'll mess up your suit.''

"Forget my suit.''

He began to run his hands over her calves, feeling the muscles through her thin leggings, stroking to lengthen and relax them.

Oh, my! All protest died on her lips.

"Tell me what happened before you fell,'' he said, working his way up her right calf.

"Dean already told you what happened.''

"I want *you* to tell me.''

"I was going too fast. Dean warned me to slow down, but I was feeling edgy this morning and wanted to see how far I could get. You know me. Miss Impatience. But it's no big deal, because I'm fine.''

Lord, he had great hands. She could die right now and be content. Forget checking the broccoli. Forget supper completely. She just wanted to sit here in this chair and let him put his hands all over her.

"Did you have trouble breathing before you fell?"

"Hmm?" Concentrating on his words was hard when he was doing such erotic things to her. "I guess I was a little winded. That's natural, though, isn't it?"

"Did you have pain?"

"No, just trouble catching my breath. You aren't going to cut back on my training schedule, are you?"

He didn't indicate one way or the other, telling her he'd wait until Doc Ramsey had a chance to check her over before he made a decision.

"Are you angry with me?"

"Furious."

He didn't seem furious. He seemed concerned but calm. He hadn't even given her a lecture for disobeying his orders.

He nodded at the bouquet of roses and baby's breath. "I stopped and got those for you on the way home. They aren't much, but I thought they might help cheer you up."

"They're gorgeous. Thank you. But...you didn't know about my fall until a few minutes ago."

"No, but when I looked at the calendar this morning and realized what day it was, it occurred to me that you might be feeling a little down. Today's the anniversary of your accident, isn't it?" She nodded. "Depressed?"

"A little. I've lost the whole last year of my life. Falling down those steps today didn't help." *Or seeing that woman's arms around your neck.*

His hands slid upward to her thigh, making her breath catch in her lungs.

"Four thousand years ago the ancient Chinese used massage to treat not only physical symptoms but emotional ones," he told her. "They believed that touch was necessary for the well-being of the soul and that a good massage could do wonders for you when you had a bad day."

That made sense to her. At this very moment she felt better than she had all day, possibly in her entire life. Heat infused her. Little ripples of pleasure radiated through her body.

"Close your eyes. Relax."

If she got any more relaxed, she might fall from the chair, but she closed her eyes, anyway, and let him work on her aching spots. One of his hands was kneading her upper thigh, his fingers only inches away from sending her to heaven, while the other had slipped behind her knee to gently massage. She had to bite her lip to keep from moaning out loud.

As he worked, he told her about the importance of massage to the Greeks, how warriors in Egyptian, Persian and Japanese cultures received massages both before and after battles and bathed in public pools scented with fragrant oils to relax.

The tension of strained muscles gave way to tension of another kind that made her body quiver. Her blood raced through her veins. Desire pooled between her legs.

"You're boiling over," he said.

Her eyes flew open. "What?"

"You're boiling over." He pointed to the stove. "The food."

The water in the pot sizzled as it hit the burner. The vegetables. Oh! He was talking about the vegetables!

His face was a mask of pure innocence, but she thought she saw a twinkle of amusement in his eyes.

Blushing, she jumped up and quickly removed the pot from the burner. "I, um, supper should be ready in a few minutes," she told him, struggling to regain her equilibrium. She had a sneaking suspicion he knew how aroused he had gotten her. Even worse, she suspected he'd done it on purpose.

AFTER SUPPER, Mac changed into jeans and a T-shirt, then joined Keely in the living room. She was curled up on the couch with her shoes off, using the remote to click through the TV channels.

"No homework tonight?" he asked.

"Finished." She stifled a yawn. "I only had one chapter to read."

"Maybe you should turn in early. You've had a rough day."

"Are you kicking me out?"

"No, of course not."

"Then, can I stay here with you for a while? If I go home, I'll only sit around that empty house and get depressed again."

"Stay as long as you want. How about we find a movie to watch?"

"Okay, but I get to pick. Your taste in movies is as bad as your taste in music. If I never have to watch *Rio Lobo* again, it'll be too soon."

He chuckled. They had a friendly, ongoing squabble over what radio station to listen to when they rode in the van. He liked country. She liked the weird New

Age stuff the campus station played. Their respective tastes in movies were incompatible, as well. They always disagreed on what to watch. But they'd learned to compromise.

"You choose tonight," he told her. "Scoot over, and I'll sit with you."

He transferred to the couch, pushing his chair to the side, out of the way. Keely scanned the channels and stopped on one that showed a fake-looking squid attacking a submarine.

She smiled at his expression of disbelief. "Just kidding," she said, changing to another channel. "Here we go. *The Quiet Man*. John Wayne for you. Ireland for me. And it looks like it just started."

"Good choice."

They settled in to watch, but it wasn't long before Keely's chin dropped and she nodded off to sleep. She swayed, fell against him, then jerked awake. "Sorry." The second time she fell, she didn't move.

"Keely."

No answer.

Careful not to wake her, he lifted his arm and let her slide the rest of the way down. She snuggled in with a sigh, her face in the crook of his neck and her arm loosely around his middle.

Mac closed his eyes to capture the moment, knowing it might be the only intimate one he'd ever have with her. Years from now, he wanted to be able to instantly recall every detail: the way she felt in his arms, the soft sound of her breathing, even the clean fragrance of her hair. She must have dusted herself with powder or sprayed on perfume because she smelled like flowers. He inhaled deeply and pressed the alluring scent into his memory.

The movie ended and another one began. When a loud commercial came on, he looked for the remote to turn down the volume, but it was on Keely's other side, out of his reach. She mumbled something and stirred. Then she lifted her head and looked at him with eyes that didn't want to stay open. It took her a moment to realize where she was. *And* that she was plastered to his side.

She didn't draw away in horror, as he expected. Instead, she dropped her gaze to his mouth. An invitation, he told himself, so he lowered his mouth to hers.

Nice. Her lips were sweeter than he'd imagined. Even nicer was the fact that she began to kiss him back. Her hand slid up to his neck. A little gurgle of pleasure escaped her throat.

Heat poured into him. His equilibrium shifted. If blood could boil, it was boiling in him now.

Touching her, being touched by her, caused the dam inside Mac to break. The feelings he'd kept carefully hidden rushed out, filling him with an urgent need to hold her close to his heart. He gave in to that need because he had no choice.

By the end of the kiss, they were both gasping for breath. She stared at him in wide-eyed confusion. Her face carried a bright red flush and her lips the dampness of passion.

"We shouldn't have done that," she said, still clinging to him.

"Why not? Felt damn good to me."

"You're my coach."

"I'm also a man, Keely."

"Believe me, I'm aware of that."

She moved from his arms. She stood and found her shoes. Her backpack was on the floor, and she stuffed her books inside it.

"You're not leaving?"

"It's late. I'm tired." She picked up her keys. "Bye."

"Wait!" He took a fortifying breath. "Stay here tonight."

"In your bed?"

"Yes. With me. In my bed."

Her brief hesitation gave him hope. But then she shook her head. "I can't."

"You can't? Or you don't want to?"

"I don't want to."

Fair enough. At least she was honest. But it didn't take away the sting of her rejection.

"Okay. But if you're determined to leave, I'll follow you home."

"I'd rather you didn't. I'll see you tomorrow."

By the time he got into his chair, she was already out the door and in her car. He watched in frustration as she cranked it and drove off.

There was a pattern here. He got close. It spooked her. She retreated.

But what could he do about it?

Be patient, he supposed. Let her come to him when she was ready. *If* she was ever ready. One thing was certain, he wouldn't be foolish enough to ask her a second time to share his bed. The next move was hers.

CHAPTER TWELVE

THE FRONT LAWN of the Sizemore house looked like a toy department after an explosion—bikes, bats, balls, tanks, toy soldiers, brightly colored plastic cars you could sit in and peddle, enough action figures to fill a railroad car, some with missing legs or arms, a few with missing heads.

Keely picked her way through the graveyard of overturned bicycles and rang the doorbell. A herd of trumpeting elephants answered it.

"Ma-ma, company!" Savannah yelled as she ran past without a backward glance. Six or so little girls, all chattering at the same time, and several older boys followed her.

"We're goin' to Jack's," Bay yelled, bringing up the rear of the pack. He and the boys jerked up bicycles and prepared to ride off.

Vicki appeared at the door with J.P. on her hip. "You be back by noon, Savannah," she called after her daughter. "And Bay Alan, don't you make a pest of yourself with Mrs. Wyatt." She smiled at Keely, a genuine smile that told her she was glad to see her. "What a nice surprise. What brings you out so early on a Saturday morning?"

"I need to talk to you if you can spare a minute."

"Sure, come on in. Don't you just love this autumn weather?" She led the way to the kitchen. Black fabric covered the table. A crisp white apron and cap lay on a nearby chair.

"I love the cooler temperatures but I'm not ready for it to drop below freezing," Keely said. "Who's the pilgrim costume for? Savannah?"

"Yeah. I'm trying to get a jump on her costume for the Thanksgiving play, since this is my busiest time of year." Putting J.P. on the floor with a cookie, she joined Keely at the table. "I'm glad to have someone to visit with this morning. Alan's tailgating with Mac and some other guys before the football game."

"I know, and that's why I hope you don't mind me dropping in. I need to ask you something and I don't want either one of them to know I'm here."

"Mm, sounds wonderfully sinister. I like it already. What secret are we keeping from them?"

"No secret really." Nervousness made her fumble with the cuffs of her sweater. "I feel awkward talking to you about this."

"We've gotten to be friends these past months, haven't we?"

"I wouldn't be here if I didn't think so."

"I promise whatever we talk about will stay between us. Now, what is it you want to ask me?"

She took a deep breath and let it out. "I have some questions concerning Mac."

"Uh-huh." Vicki didn't look surprised.

"He and I have become…much closer lately. I guess you've noticed."

"Hard to miss. You spend so much time together

Alan has started referring to you as the Siamese twins.''

''I've tried not to be attracted to him, but I am. I've tried not to act on the attraction, but I do, anyway. It's like I'm no longer in control of my brain or my body. I find myself brushing imaginary pieces of lint off his shirt so I can touch his chest, or asking him to look at something in a textbook so I can put my head next to his just to smell him. To smell him! Isn't that the most awful thing you've ever heard?''

''Absolutely horrible.'' Vicki looked as if she was trying not to laugh.

''And suddenly I'm jealous of every woman he's nice to. A few weeks ago I bumped into him while he had one of the secretaries on his lap. You know how they're always bugging him to give them a ride. I literally saw green. Here was this woman sitting on him, with her arms around his neck, and I wanted to scratch her eyes out.''

''Did you?''

''No, of course not! I walked away. But I came *this* close to telling her to get her bony behind off him if she knew what was good for her because she was sitting in *my* seat!''

Vicki broke up then, laughing loudly.

''This isn't funny!''

''Oh, sweetie, I'm sorry, but listen to yourself. You're a normal woman with normal desires and he's a very attractive man. What you're feeling is natural. Why are you fighting it?''

Keely wasn't sure she knew. For months she'd been telling herself that a relationship with Mac wasn't possible because he could distract her from her training. But she couldn't be any more distracted than she was already. Her mind wandered. Her timing was off. Whenever he watched her workout, she couldn't concentrate on what she was doing and ended up dropping weights or stumbling.

Yesterday, while he was bent over her ankle taping it, she got so turned on by how sexy the back of his neck was that she leaned forward to get a better look at it and fell off the table, nearly knocking them both to the floor. She'd decided right then and there that she had to do something. She had only two choices—either get away from Mac or get closer to him.

"You're not still afraid of his physical condition, are you?" Vicki asked. "That's not what this is about?"

"No, not afraid of his condition exactly. I'm afraid more of doing something stupid, hurting him, humiliating him, expecting something from him that he's physically unable to do."

"You're afraid of your *ignorance.*"

"Yes. That's it. Also…I've only had sex with one man before, so my expertise is sorely lacking. I'm not sure I even know how to go about this."

Keely let out a breath, relieved to finally put a name to her fears and to talk to someone who would understand.

"Vicki, you told me once that if I had any questions, all I had to do was ask. Well, I'm asking. Mac's wary of me, so if anything's going to happen between us, I'll have to be the one to initiate it. Only…I don't know how."

"You need the Vicki Sizemore crash course in seduction."

"Exactly. But how on earth do I seduce a man in a wheelchair?"

Vicki's eyes sparkled with mischief. "His birthday's in a few days. Let's put together a surprise he'll never forget."

THE SOUND OF KEELY singing and the soft fragrance of perfume met Mac when he opened the door. He stopped in the kitchen for a moment and savored both, realizing how much he'd missed having a female around since his sisters had grown up and moved away.

He sighed at his own foolishness. Miss stockings hanging over the shower rod? Miss makeup cluttering his bathroom vanity?

Yes, he had to admit he did. Women added disharmony to a man's life, but there was something comforting about that disharmony. He couldn't explain it, but the chaos created by women was somehow necessary for a man's survival, and he had lived too many of the last few years alone and without it.

Keely walked out of the bedroom and around the corner, jumping in fright when she saw him. "You aren't supposed to be here yet!" She took a nervous glance behind her. "I wasn't expecting you for another fifteen minutes."

"I finished early." In truth he'd left a mountain of paperwork on his desk. Knowing she'd be here waiting for him to celebrate his birthday had shot holes in his concentration.

He put his keys on the table, along with the box filled with birthday presents given to him by the staff, then made a more leisurely examination of Keely's outfit. The blue strapless dress sparkled and showed a generous amount of both breast and leg, two of his favorite parts of her anatomy.

"You look nice."

She smoothed her hand across an imaginary wrinkle. The dress didn't have enough material to wrinkle, but Mac couldn't say he minded.

"I thought we'd dress up for dinner tonight since it's your birthday. You don't mind, do you?"

Not if it meant getting to stare at her in that dress, he didn't. "No, I don't mind." His gaze roamed over her again with appreciation, then stopped at her feet. "But I think we'd better find you some shoes."

She laughed and wiggled her bare toes. "I brought some heels. I just don't want to put them on until I absolutely have to." She walked over and kissed him lightly on the forehead. "Happy birthday."

"Thanks."

"Do you feel older?"

"Older and *old*," he admitted.

"You're not old. I was just thinking a little while ago that you're even more handsome now than when I first met you ten years ago." She brushed her fingertips through the hair at his temples. "This little bit of gray is incredibly attractive. And these little lines by your eyes—" she slowly slid her finger along one "—somehow make you even sexier."

"Wrinkles are sexy?"

"On you they are." His heart bubbled into his

throat as she caressed his jaw, then slid her hand across his chest in a gentle intimate motion that set his skin on fire. "You certainly don't have the body of an old man. Of course, I haven't seen all of it yet."

Yet? "Keely..." He reached out to touch her, but she grinned and scooted back. What was she up to?

"Your brother called earlier," she said, making sure she stayed just inches past his reach. "Did he catch you at work?"

Mac nodded. "I talked to him."

"You also have a package from California. I assume it's from one of your sisters. And Vicki brought over a cake and some gifts from the kids."

"I'll open everything when we get back. Where did you make reservations?"

"Mm...I can't tell you. That's part of tonight's surprise."

"Am I allowed to eat real food, or are you going to make me have bean sprouts and all that other stuff you eat?"

She smiled. "Tonight you get steak. Now hurry up and have your shower. I want this to be a very special night for you and I'm anxious to start."

He pushed into the bedroom, found underwear and socks, then got his best suit out of the closet. He threw everything on the bed. Shrugging out of his shirt, he tossed it in the hamper, then took off his belt, shoes and socks. He rubbed his hand across his stubbled jaw. Maybe he'd shave first.

The bathroom door was closed. He slid it open, pushed forward and stopped in surprise. What...?

Glowing candles filled the room. "Keely!" he called, going inside.

She walked up behind him. "I'm here."

He turned his chair so he could see her. "What's this?"

"Your appetizer." She leaned toward the vanity and pressed the button on a small CD player that hadn't been there that morning. Soft music spilled out. "I thought it might be fun for us both if I gave you a bath."

He swallowed hard. His body tensed. Was she serious?

"You'd enjoy that, wouldn't you?" she asked. "The two of us naked in the tub?"

Numbly, he nodded.

"I thought you might."

She reached back and unzipped her dress, purposely moving it down an inch at a time while she swayed to the rhythm of the low seductive music. His gaze was glued to the riveting sight as bare breasts, a bare midriff and then a bare stomach danced into view. Finally the dress pooled around her feet, revealing her perfect—and perfectly naked—body.

Her breasts were breathtakingly beautiful, as if they had been carved to exact proportions, and were tipped with nipples that were rosy and erect. Her hips flared gently from a tiny waist before melding into those impossibly long legs. The hair between her legs was blond, like that on her head.

She had the sleek body of an athlete. Her muscles added delicate curves that were exquisitely feminine and lovely.

Mac sat there staring, stunned, wanting to touch her but afraid of making a move that would alter their relationship forever. Once they crossed the boundary from friends to lovers, there was no going back for either of them.

She stepped out of the dress. "I've been reluctant to have a relationship with you because I thought we might both get hurt by it. But something very strong is going on between us, and I think that trying to suppress it is hurting us more. I don't know if what I'm doing is right or wrong. I don't have much experience with romance or sex, and I'm probably making a fool of myself. But if I am, I don't care. I'm tired of fighting my attraction to you. I want to be with you more than I've wanted anything in a very long time. If you want to be with me."

She rubbed a hand across her breasts, down to her feminine mound, then back up to her breasts, while Mac watched, mesmerized. The shadows created by the candles danced on her skin. Her own shadow danced in tandem on the wall behind her.

The slow sensual motion of her hand was meant to seduce him. He didn't need any prompting, but did she realize what she was letting herself in for?

"You understand I can't... Physically, I can't..."

"I know, and it doesn't matter. You don't have to hold me or touch me or even say a word to me if you don't want to. Ever since I saw the seat that goes across your tub, I've been having the naughtiest thoughts about you sitting there while I slowly wash you. You have an incredible body and I want to touch every part of it."

"Some parts aren't the least bit incredible. They don't work like they're supposed to."

She reached for his T-shirt and he lifted his arms automatically so she could pull it off. "That honestly doesn't matter to me. If you can't do anything more than take a bath with me, it'll be enough."

Oh, he could do a little more than that. And he intended to show her.

She helped him out of the rest of his clothes. For a moment, when she peeled off his underwear, he felt self-conscious. He wondered if she would ignore the lower half of him as women tended to do, perhaps even be unwilling to look at him. She'd once been so afraid of his body.

"You're beautifully made," she said, and he suddenly felt that way for the first time in a long while.

He transferred to the seat across the tub. She stood behind him washing his hair, an act he discovered could be wildly sexual, although his head was all she touched. He closed his eyes and let her work her magic, feeling all traces of tension ease out of him as she scratched his scalp lightly with her nails. She was making love to him with just her touch and her words, and it was as arousing an experience as he'd ever had.

"I know you're very sensitive in places," she said in a throaty voice. "When I get through with your head, I'm going to find every one of those places and see just how sensitive they are. I might touch them with my fingers or my lips...or run my tongue over them."

He groaned and begged, "Touch them now."

"Be patient. We have all night."

"Do we?"

"Yes. If you don't feel like going out, I can cook. Steaks and vegetables are marinating in the refrigerator. We can lie around here being sinful, feeding each other...and doing whatever else comes to mind."

"I don't have to dress up?"

"You don't have to dress at all. In fact, I'd greatly appreciate it if you didn't so I can enjoy looking at you."

"Lady, I didn't know you could be so wicked."

"Me, neither, actually. I like it."

Finally, when he didn't think he could stand it any longer, she rinsed his hair with the hand shower and soaped his shoulders and back, tormenting him with the gentleness of her strokes. She teased his sides and his neck slowly and deliberately; she ran her tongue along the back of his ears and nipped them playfully with her teeth.

He sat without moving and let her have her way until she soaped her breasts and began to rub them across his back. "Do you like that?" she asked with a low purr in his ear. The last of his control deserted him.

"You're killing me."

She chuckled with glee. "That's the idea. You've been killing me for weeks, Mac McCandless, and now it's payback time."

"Come around to the front where I can touch you, too."

"Not yet. I'm in charge here. Just enjoy."

"Obey your coach and get over here."

"You're not my coach tonight. You're my lover. And I want to give you pleasure."

Her *lover*. He liked the sound of that. "Please, come around before I lose my sanity. I can't stand much more of this."

"All right, but I'm not through playing and, remember, I'm still in charge."

She rinsed them both, stepped over the seat and moved in front of him. This was fantasy come to life. Her lips were dewy. Her skin was flushed from passion. But it was the wantonness in her eyes as she looked down at him that did him in.

"I'd give my soul," he said, "to be able to move inside you."

She skimmed her fingertips across the muscles of his chest. "Vicki assured me that people with spinal injuries who can't have traditional sex can at least have a satisfying experience if they stop worrying about what they *can't* do and concentrate on what they *can*. She says they have to be inventive."

"You told her you were planning this?"

"I had to. I needed advice. When you and Alan were at the Auburn game, I went over to the house."

"Were you worried about having to touch me?"

"Yes," she admitted. She kissed his forehead. "I won't lie to you. Anticipating what something might be like and actually doing it—well, they're two different things. Even though I wanted this, I was still a little afraid of it."

"And now?"

"And now, I can't imagine how I went so long

without touching you. And I want to know what it feels like for you to touch me back.''

He didn't need a second invitation. Her breasts were at just the right level to take into his mouth, and he did so with the right and then the left, licking and sucking the hardened nipples while his hands touched her hips, her back, her buttocks—all the places that had been forbidden to him before.

He pulled her down to straddle his lap. Following his instructions, she lifted her legs over the seat and wrapped them around his hips.

He touched her gently at first, wanting to drive her to the edge without going over it too quickly. He held her gaze and watched the emotions play across her face, watched desire turn her eyes to molten blue, as he slid the pad of his thumb back and forth between the folds and across the sensitive nub hidden there.

''Is this a prerequisite for your class in Rehab 102?'' she asked thickly.

''Are you interested in my class?''

''Can I be teacher's pet?''

''You already are.''

He quickened the motion of his thumb and slipped his fingers in and out of her, using her own moisture as lubrication. She gasped in pleasure, threw back her head and closed her eyes, tightening her legs around him.

Tomorrow he would have bruises where her fingers clutched his shoulders, but it was worth it to see that wild look on her face.

Her body began to slide back and forth toward release, moving against his hand, forcing him to increase the pressure. He slipped his other arm around her waist and aided her in her rocking.

Faster. Harder. She was soaring now and he was soaring with her, fueled by the incredible sexual energy she was creating. Her deep moans infused his blood with fire.

She cried his name, and the explosion in her body washed through him like a giant wave, carrying him along. Keely was on the crest of the wave and he was somewhere in the churning water below, but it was still a pleasurable trip—and unexpected. He had heard paras and quads talk about feeling "something" during sex that was like a climax, but he had never experienced it firsthand.

He almost cried from sheer joy.

Keely had collapsed on his shoulder, unaware of the wonderful gift she had just given him. He stroked her back, realizing suddenly what had made the difference between tonight and the times before.

This time, he loved the woman in his arms.

She moaned as if in pain. "No fair," she said. "I was supposed to make love to *you*."

Mac hugged her close. "You did, sweetheart. You did."

KEELY STRETCHED against Mac's side and let out a long sigh of contentment. Lying in bed with him was sheer bliss. She could do this every night for the rest of her life and never get tired of it.

Their lovemaking had exceeded all her expectations. Intimate and special, it had been the most wonderful experience she'd ever had. Finding out he'd also gotten pleasure from it had made her weep.

"Want more?" he asked now.

"Mmm, yes, more," she said suggestively, putting aside her plate of half-eaten birthday cake.

He chuckled. "I meant *food*. My, my, but you've turned into a lusty young thing."

"You make me lusty." She ran her hand over his middle. He really was beautiful, despite his injuries. His legs were a little thin from atrophy, but other than that he was taut, well shaped. The dark hair across his chest was just thick enough to be sexy without obscuring his lovely muscular form.

The tattoo on his hip had been a surprise, very out of character for Mac. Once he'd explained Alan's role, though, it made perfect sense.

The circular scars on his stomach and lower back had also given her a moment's pause when she'd undressed him, but only because they were so small, so inconsequential-looking, and she had prepared herself for something horrible. How puzzling that a bullet could cause such little damage on the outside yet be so devastating.

He picked up another piece of birthday cake from his plate and took a huge bite. The man's diet was a disaster, full of fat and cholesterol. His kitchen cabinets were a junk-food addict's paradise. The only time he ate vegetables or fruit was when she prepared them.

"I don't see how you can eat the way you do and still look so good."

His mouth was stuffed with chocolate and cream filling. "Itz-er-zize," he managed to get out.

"Exercise?"

"Uh-huh. Itz-er-zize."

"You need to eat something other than cake and Doritos." They never had gotten around to cooking dinner, so Mac had made a raid on the kitchen for snacks. "Why didn't you bring back some of the raw carrots and cauliflower I cut up? They're full of vitamins."

"Ugh! Vim-ma-mins."

He was hopeless. "Keep eating like that and you'll be too fat to fit into your new gear."

He swallowed the rest of the cake and licked icing off his thumb. "You shouldn't have bought all that stuff for me, Keely. You spent too much money."

"You'll need it now that you'll be racing more. You're forty, and you can't use your students as an excuse any longer. You can race seriously." He didn't say anything. "Right?" she pressed.

"Maybe."

She sighed at his indecision. "I don't understand your attitude. You're so good. With some discipline in your life and diet, and some intensive training, you could be one of the best wheelchair racers in the country. In the world."

"I'm not sure I want to make that kind of commitment. I don't have the time unless I take it from something else I love. My students need me. My wheelers need me."

And Keely Wilson needed him, too. The time he spent coaching her he could use for his own training. But she was too selfish to give him up. Without him, she didn't believe she'd race again.

"Maybe we could train together," she suggested. "That would help with your time problem, wouldn't it? You're always saying we make a great team."

"That might shortchange you, and I'm not going to risk that."

"No, it wouldn't. Ooh, you're so self-sacrificing it makes me furious. You're so busy taking care of other people that you don't take care of yourself. For a change, do something because it helps *you*."

"You sound like Alan."

"Well, Alan's right." She lifted her head so she could see him better. "You told me once that you couldn't pursue your own dream of being an athlete because of family commitments. Maybe God is giving you a second chance."

"You mean He crippled me just so I could race wheelchairs?" he said with a smile, but she didn't think it was very funny.

"No, of course not. But you're always telling me people have to accept their physical *disabilities* and rise above them. Isn't that the same thing as accepting your physical *abilities* and using them? Seems pretty hypocritical to me that you urge to your students to go out and try their best, regardless of their physical condition, but you won't do it yourself."

His smile faded.

"Will you at least think about it?" she asked when he didn't say anything.

"Yes, but not tonight. The only thing I want to think about tonight is you and me." He set his plate on the bedside table and pulled her up to lie on top of him. She put her hands on his chest and leaned her chin there.

"Did you *really* feel something when we made love?" she asked. "You're not just saying that to make me happy?"

"I really did feel something, but I want you to understand it probably won't happen every time. It might never happen again, and if it doesn't, I don't want you disappointed or thinking I didn't enjoy it."

"I understand. But the more we make love, the more opportunities you'll have to feel something, right?"

Her logic made him chuckle. "I guess that's one way of looking at it."

Wiggling her eyebrows, she asked, "Ready to try again?"

He rolled, taking her with him, pinning her to the mattress beneath him. "Lusty *and* demanding. What am I going to do with you?"

She slid her arms around his neck and pulled him down for a long hard kiss. He tasted of chocolate. "Mmm, does that give you any ideas?"

"A few. Sit up here in front of me and I'll show you one."

She followed his directions. "Are you about to do what I think you're about to do?"

He put her legs over his shoulders and buried his dark head between them. The feel of his mouth on the most intimate part of her brought an embarrassingly loud moan to her lips. Her breath nearly stopped.

Rehab 102. Her first class.

"Can I get a degree in this?" she wondered out loud, and his body shook with amusement.

THEY CLUNG TO EACH OTHER in the dark, Keely sleeping soundly, Mac only half-awake. He needed to get up and prepare properly for the night, but she felt too good. Her head was on his shoulder, and her body was half on top of his, seeking his warmth in the cold room. He pulled the covers over her back and kissed her on top of her head.

He'd waited so long to hold her like this. He would wait one more minute before getting up. Just one more. Maybe two.

He drifted into sleep, feeling confident about himself and their relationship. Things were going to be okay. She cared about him and he cared about her. The problems he'd imagined hadn't materialized.

He slept soundly, waking only when the first rays of dawn streamed through the window. He glanced at the clock, relieved to see it was before five and he hadn't overslept. Still, there was something wrong. He wasn't sure yet what it was.

Keely stirred just as the horrible truth struck him. Humiliation washed over him and sent heat to his face and chest.

She awoke and made a sound of disgust. "What in the world? What is this?"

She crawled to her knees, turned on the lamp and pulled back the covers. The sheet, the blanket, even the shirt she had on were soaked.

"Oh, please!" he prayed out loud. Not now. Not with this woman. But it was already too late for prayers, too late to do anything but wait for the awful reality to destroy the dream. The stupid cripple had done the one thing he feared above everything else. The stupid cripple had wet the bed.

CHAPTER THIRTEEN

HE COULD RECALL every humiliating experience in his life. In fifth grade he'd touched Lucy Henderson's breast—an accident, of course, because actually trying to touch a breast hadn't occurred to him until a couple of years later.

Lucy hadn't had much of a breast to touch, even by fifth-grade standards, but she had screamed, anyway, and called him a pervert in the middle of art class, accusing him of trying to "feel her up." The humiliation had stayed with him a long time past the punishment—a three-day suspension from school and an I'm-disappointed-in-you lecture from his dad.

He'd thought nothing could ever embarrass him like that again, but he'd been wrong. This was worse.

At the rehabilitation hospital, he'd been hoisted in and out of the pool for therapy with a harness-and-pulley mechanism that treated him like a packing crate and made him feel just about as human. He'd been bathed and dressed as if he were a child, until he'd learned to do it himself. He'd suffered the horror of having a nurse stick a sixteen-inch tube into his bladder several times a day just so he could take a leak.

Those months after the shooting had been the worst of his life, and probably nothing could surpass the pain he felt when he thought about them. But this came close. This came damn close.

"Hosing the bed" while with a partner was one of his greatest fears. In rehab he and the other single men with spinal-cord injuries had talked and worried about it a lot. And now he'd gone and done it, ruining any chance he had of making Keely forget his physical problems and think of him as normal.

But who had he been trying to kid? He wasn't normal, hadn't been for a long time. Why was he trying to pretend he was?

That's right, McCandless. Start feeling sorry for yourself. Start wallowing in self-pity again and make everything that much worse.

This wasn't the first time he'd waited too long to use a catheter and had wet himself, but it *was* the first time he had wet someone else in the process. He hated that the "someone else" was Keely, the one woman he'd hoped would never see him as less than a man.

"I'm sorry," he said stiffly. He swore to himself, knowing that no matter how often he apologized, it would never erase what had happened. Might as well just accept that things between them would never be the same.

"Mac, there's no reason for you to be upset," she said, her luminous blue eyes reflecting compassion rather than the disgust he'd expected. She tried to smooth back his hair, but he turned his head, not wanting to be touched right now. How could she bear him when he couldn't bear himself?

"I don't want to talk about it," he said.

"All right. We'll just forget it."

Fat chance of that.

They had both showered and changed into dry clothes, Keely borrowing one of his shirts so she wouldn't have to put on her dress, and Mac slipping into a pair of sweatpants. He was struggling to change the sheets and the waterproof pad on the mattress, but he was so angry with himself he couldn't get them right. He jerked a corner down only to have the opposite corner pop up.

She walked to the other side of the bed. "Let me help you."

"I can do it myself," he snapped. "I'm crippled, but I'm not helpless."

She let go of the sheet and straightened, throwing up her hands. Now he saw disgust in her eyes, but it wasn't because he had wet the bed; it was because of the way he was handling it. "Did I say you were helpless?" she asked.

He was being an ass and it wasn't like him, but he couldn't seem to help himself. Why didn't she just go home? He didn't want her here. He wanted to sulk in private, go a little crazy for once, maybe even throw something, but he couldn't do that with her looking at him, trying to touch him every two seconds. He didn't want her witnessing just how far into self-pity he was about to sink.

Several minutes later, after an almost comical battle with the fitted sheet, he got the bed made. He pushed into the kitchen and on to the laundry room, where he threw the sheets into the washing machine. Back in the kitchen, he filled the coffeemaker. A jolt of something was what he needed, and since even he couldn't stomach a beer this early in the morning, he figured caffeine and the sugar high from some powdered doughnuts would have to do.

She followed him and leaned against the counter silently watching, the wet hair and too-big shirt making her more desirable than any woman had a right to be before six in the morning. This time he knew for sure that she wore nothing under the shirt, because he'd seen her put it on.

And it was hell knowing.

Memories of the night before flooded back to torture him—that erotic striptease she had done to coax him into the bath, her exquisite body aroused, her legs wrapped around his waist as she screamed her release. He had been with a lot of women, before and after his injury, and enjoyed every experience, but none had given him as much pleasure as this woman had last night. None had gone beyond the physical aspect of sex to touch the man underneath.

He loved her. Heaven help him, he'd tried not to fall for her again, but he'd tumbled like a stone the second she'd come back to town. The relationship had no chance of working, though. This morning's fiasco was proof of that.

"Go home," he said sharply. "Getting involved with me was a mistake. I'd rather go back to being just your coach."

She shoved herself away from the counter and stood in front of him. "A mistake?"

"A big one."

"I understand you're embarrassed, but why do you want to throw away our whole relationship because of one unpleasant incident? That doesn't make a bit of sense.''

''I'm not talking only about what happened this morning. All kinds of things make this impossible, things you don't even know about. I don't want to go through this every day as you find out the bad side of being with a paraplegic.'' He turned the chair around and pushed forcefully toward the bedroom, intending to get dressed. ''We'll both be better off if you'll go home and forget last night.''

''So it was a big lie when you acted like you cared about me?''

He stopped abruptly and turned the chair enough so he could see her. ''I didn't lie.''

''You must have, or you wouldn't be trying to hurt me like this.''

Her statement was like a fist to the gut. ''I don't want to hurt you and I do care about you.'' *I love you,* he wanted to say, but it would only make things harder. ''You deserve more out of a relationship than a paraplegic can give you.''

Her forehead crinkled in thought. She chewed the inside of her cheek. ''Well, let's see. I know you can give me a satisfying sexual relationship, so you must mean you can't give me something else I need. What? Friendship?''

''You know what I'm talking about.''

''Understanding? Compassion?''

''That's not what I'm talking about and you know it.''

''How about…time together? A shoulder to cry on? A confidant? Can you give me those things or does that take someone who can walk?'' He didn't answer because she was exaggerating, saying something ridiculous to make a point. ''I need someone to tell me when I'm being bratty. Can you do that or is it too much for a paraplegic to handle?''

''Yes, I can. You're being bratty right now.''

That made her smile a little.

''I'm talking about my physical problems and how they can affect a relationship. They can kill romance in about thirty seconds flat. I don't want you repulsed by me again.''

''Ah, now I understand where this sudden desire to flee is coming from.''

She sat in his lap against his objection, but this time he let her smooth his hair from his brow. The touch of her fingers raised goose bumps on his flesh.

''Mac, I have limited experience with romance, so I don't know what the standard is, but last night was the most romantic night of my life. And I don't mean because of the sex, although that was fantastic. Just lying in your arms and having you stroke my back as I fell asleep made me feel safe. Do you know, last night was the first time in over a year that I've slept through the entire night?''

''A year? Why?''

''Since my accident I've had this irrational fear of the dark and dying in my sleep. I've only been able to sleep a few hours at night. That's why I take so many naps and get cranky in the afternoon. I think maybe it's because the accident made me realize how fragile I really am and how little control we truly have over what happens to us.''

"You should have told me. I could have helped you find someone to talk to."

"You're right. I should have told you and not let it continue so long. And I guess I have talk to someone about it eventually. But I'm telling you now to show you how important last night was to me. I felt so cared for and so contented being with you that I dropped off to sleep without the slightest hesitation."

"And then I ruined everything this morning."

"No, you didn't. I'm sorry about what happened because it's upset you so much, but it didn't bother me. It doesn't bother me now. I don't care if you wet the bed every night as long as you let me sleep with you once in a while. More than once in a while." She put her arms around his neck and kissed him lightly on the lips, but he remained unyielding. "Getting to this point took us so long, Mac. Please don't mess things up over something so stupid."

"Keely…"

"You're not getting rid of me, so you might as well quit arguing."

"Baby, it's no good. You and me together—it won't work. I fooled myself last night into believing it could, but now I see that was just wishful thinking."

She blew out a breath in impatience. "Please, don't do this. Please don't throw away what we've found together just because you're embarrassed."

"That's not it at all."

"Oh, no? Well, answer this—what if it had been me?"

"But it wasn't you."

"Well, what if it had been? What if I was the one

who'd wet on you? Would you want me to be embarrassed about it? Would you allow me to be so embarrassed that I ended our relationship?''

"No, but that's not the situation here. And you didn't wet on me, so you have no way of knowing how I feel.''

She looked at him oddly.

"What?'' he asked, wondering what she was thinking.

"You're absolutely right. Maybe you'd feel better if we evened things out.''

"Evened them out?'' She didn't say anything, only sat there contemplating something. Then he realized what. "Oh, hell, you're not thinking...?'' She nodded. "You wouldn't!''

But she would. And she did.

Before he could push her off his lap the crazy sweet wonderful woman wet on him.

THE GREEN PEPPERS were out of season and outrageously expensive, but full of vitamin C. Keely picked over them, found some she liked and put them in the cart. She checked them off the grocery list.

"You're insane,'' Mac said at her elbow.

"I know. A dollar a pepper is highway robbery, but I've got a taste for them.''

"I was talking about that crazy stunt you pulled this morning.''

"Oh. You're never going to let me live that down, are you?''

"I can't get it off my mind.'' He grabbed her hand

and gave it a little squeeze. "Thank you. No one's ever done anything like that for me before."

"The situation was drastic and called for drastic measures."

"You shocked me into submission."

"I couldn't think of anything else to do. Pleading with you wasn't working." She playfully tweaked his chin. "You're awfully hardheaded at times."

Mac had been so overwhelmed by what she'd done he had given up trying to send her home. With a great deal of coaxing she'd been able to convince him that he was overreacting to his little mishap in bed and she could handle any problems his condition caused in their relationship.

He'd tried to scare her off, telling her in graphic detail about the problems paraplegics deal with every day. She'd taken a deep breath and told him the truth—those things frightened the wits out of her and she wasn't sure she'd handle them with any degree of grace. But she *would* handle them.

"My legs are thin and ugly," he'd said.

"I wouldn't care if you didn't have legs," she'd countered.

That had done it. He'd given in, knowing further argument was useless, although he'd made her promise to be open with him about her fears.

They had also agreed to be discreet. Technically there was no conflict of interest. Mac wasn't her supervisor, her teacher or responsible for her grades. Their coaching arrangement was private and had nothing to do with the university. But the gossips would have a grand time if they found out she was involved with him.

And she was very much involved with him. Physically. Emotionally. Whether it was only a killer case of lust or went deeper, she wasn't sure. Trying to label it would probably be useless, maybe even dangerous. She had little experience with romantic love, particularly how it felt when it happened to you, so this might be something else entirely.

She only knew she liked being with Mac more than she had ever liked being with anyone. She trusted him, liked him, desired him. Definitely desired him.

When they'd settled things this morning, they'd made love, and again when he'd come by to pick her up after work for their weekly grocery-shopping trip. She couldn't seem to keep her hands to herself now that she was allowed to touch him. And every time she touched him, even looked at him, she wanted him.

Like right this minute in the middle of the produce section.

"I laughed all day," he said, unaware of the devastating effect he was having on her and the naughty things she was imagining. "Miriam thought I'd lost my mind. I almost busted a gut when she told me that whatever was wrong with me, I needed a daily dose of it."

"Maybe you do."

"Oh, no! You're not getting a second chance."

"Behave and I won't need one. Act up again and next time I'll wet on your *head* instead of in your *lap*."

He laughed but warned, "And I'll get you with my

grabbers.'' He clicked together the two metal hands of the tonglike device he used for getting cans and boxes down from the shelves. He pointed it at her crotch.

Keely slapped it away. ''Stop it before someone sees you.''

She looked both ways in the aisle, relieved that none of the other shoppers had observed his latest bout of mischief. He was full of it tonight, using his grabbers to pinch her on the behind every time she turned her back to him and bent over.

They had decided there was probably no harm in continuing to shop together, since people would just assume she was helping him. She *was* helping him, although he managed just fine by himself if he was careful about how he packed his laptop basket.

In truth, they simply liked shopping together. They ate together most nights, anyway, either at her house or his, so it seemed senseless to make separate shopping trips.

Usually her biggest problem was keeping him from putting junk food in the basket when she wasn't watching. This teasing tonight was considerably more difficult to deal with because while it was embarrassing, it was also fun. She liked his playful side; she liked to see him happy and smiling.

''Behave. Let's find the stuff on this list so we can get out of here. I still need to read over my notes for class tomorrow. Coach Stewart is letting me teach by myself for the first time.''

''Solo? Are you nervous?''

''Terrified. Actually, I could really use help preparing. Want the job?''

"What does it pay?"

"Oh, hugs. Kisses."

"Scratch my back and you've got a deal."

"Done."

"I don't know why you're nervous. You're a good teacher and coach. The couple of times I sat in on the nutrition class you're helping with this quarter I was really impressed. Even I learned something."

"Too bad you don't practice what I teach."

"Yeah, but as you've pointed out to me at least a million times, I'm a hopeless case." She smiled. He had that right. "You're a good teacher and coach, Keely. One of these days you're going to realize it."

Maybe. She still wasn't comfortable in front of a class, and the thought of teaching by herself scared her to death. She liked it okay, but she'd much rather spend her time in the weight room or playing around in the chemistry lab. Her teaching assistant's job and her courses were all right temporarily, but as soon as she was able to run again, she'd put them aside.

And it wouldn't be long now. She'd already decided what she wanted her first race to be—the Los Verdes Marathon in April, which gave her five months to train. Five months to prove to Mac that she was ready. She glanced at him, wondering how he was going to react when she told him.

"Have you given any more thought to what we talked about last night?" she asked. They moved down the aisle and Keely picked through the poor offering of lettuce.

"What specifically was I supposed to think about?"

"Wheelchair racing. We could even go together.

You know, pick some races that have a wheeler division so we can both compete. How does that sound? Wouldn't that be fun?''

"Mmm," he said noncommittally.

"Maybe this spring we could try it."

"Yeah, right, like either one of us would be ready for that." He plucked the list from her hand and started reading as if the conversation bored him. "What else have you got down here?"

She hid her disappointment. Maybe this just wasn't the appropriate time to bring up racing. "Potatoes," she said.

"I'll get them."

He pushed over to get potatoes, or so she thought. He came back with a bag of chips and a container of onion dip in his lap basket. He transferred them to the cart.

"That is *not* potatoes," she said. "Can't you get something else?"

He grinned. "You're right. I forgot the beer." He took off around the corner.

"Hopeless," she muttered. "Utterly hopeless."

One aisle over, she strained to reach for a box of no-fat crackers on one of the upper shelves when a masculine arm reached around from behind and got them for her. She squealed and whirled, coming up hard against the man's chest. He grabbed her elbow to steady her.

"Whoa! Didn't mean to scare you," Doug Crocker said, his own eyes wide with shock. "Sorry."

"Coach...I..." She stepped back, feeling uncomfortable at his closeness, then laughed at his expression, realizing she'd scared him as much as he'd scared her. "I didn't know it was you."

He chuckled. "That's okay. You looked like you were having some trouble, so I thought I'd give you a hand." He passed her the crackers.

"Thank you. They always seem to put the things I want on the top shelves." She glanced quickly past him, wondering where Mac was and whether he knew Crocker was in the store.

"I'm glad I ran into you, Keely. I've been wanting to tell you what a good job you're doing with the freshman runners. Laura Stewart says you've been a great help with the fall conditioning program."

"Oh? Well, that was kind of her. I don't know how much help I've been, but I've enjoyed it."

"You have a real knack for coaching."

"I appreciate your saying that."

She smiled politely, wondering what he wanted. He was being too friendly. Crocker didn't give compliments, and he hadn't said more than ten words to her in the months she'd been at Courtland.

"You and McCandless seem to be spending a lot of time together lately. I guess that's part of the arrangement he has worked out with you. Or is it personal?"

Ah, now she understood. He was fishing for information about Mac. Well, he wasn't going to get it.

"Coach McCandless is a very generous man. I've been lucky he's willing to help with my training."

"I bet that's not too much of a hardship for him, although I guess it might be for you."

"I'm sorry, I don't know what you mean. Why

would working with Coach McCandless be a hard-ship?''

''Him being a cripple, I meant.''

Her blood pressure soared. ''Coach McCandless may be in a wheelchair, but he's less *crippled* than anyone I've ever met. He's a fine coach and a fine man. If you spent more time talking *to* him than *about* him, you might realize that.''

He smiled, but it wasn't sincere. ''Ah, now I've offended you, and here I was getting ready to ask you to have dinner with me. I thought you might like to know what it feels like to spend time with a real man for a change, instead of half a one.''

Before she could tell him what she thought of his invitation, Mac pushed up from behind him. He had obviously heard every word. His complexion was ruddy; his eyes were hard and cold as ice.

''The lady prefers cripples to asses, Doug. And for the record, Keely's with me tonight, tomorrow night, every night. Got it?''

Crocker looked between them, his hard gaze mirroring Mac's. ''So it's like that, is it?''

''Yeah, it's like that.''

Keely groaned inwardly. So much for being discreet. Now the whole world would know they were sleeping together.

She saw that Crocker had clenched his hands, but now he opened and closed them rapidly, as if he wanted to jam one into Mac's face.

''Go ahead,'' Mac said, sensing the same thing Keely had. ''You've been itching to do it for a long time. Take your best shot.''

Crocker didn't move. Finally, giving Mac a cold smile, he dipped his head. Without apologizing to either one of them for his rudeness, he turned and stalked away.

"Sonova…" Mac muttered.

"He's definitely that."

"I meant me."

"You? Are you crazy?"

"Yeah, me, because I lost my temper with him and I hate giving him the satisfaction of knowing he has the power to do that. But when I heard him hitting on you, I couldn't help myself. I saw red."

"I don't know why you don't get rid of him and end your misery. He's given you more than enough cause. He's disrespectful to you in front of the staff, and he says awful things about you behind your back. He even tries to undermine your orders. No one would blame you for firing him."

"Yeah, I know, but he used to be a good coach and he could be again, if he'd just put his feelings for me aside. Besides, I owe him."

"Owe him how?" He looked away, as if he'd said too much, but she made him face her again. "Owe him how?"

"Never mind. I was just running off at the mouth."

"Oh, no. You're the one who brought it up, and now I want to know what you're talking about. How could you possibly think you owe Doug Crocker *anything* after all the things he's done?"

"Because…sometimes…" He frowned. "Sometimes I think he may just be right and that one of the reasons I got the A.D.'s job, instead of him, was so I could be the university's token cripple."

CHAPTER FOURTEEN

THE BACK DOOR opened that evening and Keely raced by like a whirlwind, the force of her entrance and the cold wind that followed her scattering the tests Mac was supposed to be grading for his Sport Management class. He quickly slapped a hand down on them before they flew off her kitchen table.

Glancing at Keely to make sure she wouldn't see the racing magazine he'd been reading, he put it in his briefcase. He wasn't sure why he'd bought it, or circled the upcoming races with wheeler divisions. Even if he decided to enter one, he'd have a hard time getting ready physically.

Crazy. Ridiculous. He didn't know why he'd allowed Keely to put the idea in his head. He was forty, after all, too old to be thinking about racing professionally.

"Did you have a good workout?" he asked, suddenly noticing Keely's silence.

"No."

"Problems?"

"No."

"Want me to fix you something to drink?"

"I don't care."

He heaved a heavy sigh, wondering how long she

was going to stay upset over the stupid comment he'd made in the grocery store. Her mood was even worse than it had been before she'd left to ride her bicycle.

"I can't believe you're still worked up about this," he told her, putting the papers in order.

"And I can't believe you would even *think* you didn't deserve the job as athletic director."

She was wrestling with her jacket and grumbled under her breath when she got the fabric caught in the zipper. Unable to get the zipper up or down, she pulled the jacket over her head, then stepped out of her tights.

Mac watched with fascination as she retracted her arms into the sleeves of her T-shirt like a turtle, did some kind of contortionist maneuver with her bra and pulled it out one of the armholes. She tossed the flimsy piece of cotton on top of the tights on the floor. Getting a bottle of water out of the refrigerator, she sank with a groan into the chair next to him, wearing nothing but her T-shirt and panties.

"I couldn't keep my mind on my workout because of what you told me," she said, pushing sweat-soaked hair out of her eyes. "I got upset every time I thought about it, and I'm especially upset with you for throwing something like that at me and then refusing to talk about it. How can you expect me to just forget it?"

"Because it was a stupid thing to say, and it's not worth discussing. I wish you'd just drop the subject before we end up fighting."

"You wouldn't have said it if you didn't believe it."

"You're going to nag me about this all night, aren't you?"

"Yes, I am. You know how irritating I can be when I set my mind to it, so you might as well just give in and talk to me."

He chuckled despite his frustration. Even her railing could be endearing.

"Listen," he began. "Sometimes I let the prejudices of people get to me. I feel a little insecure because of being in this chair and I think dumb things. I'm entitled to be human and have an occasional lapse in good judgment, aren't I?"

She started to argue, then her hard look faded. "Of course you are. You're so easygoing and you never complain, and I guess I forget what a rough time you've had dealing with your injury. Oh, I'm such an idiot for bugging you about this! Especially considering how I acted when I found out about your paralysis. I'm the last person in the world with the right to give you a lecture."

"It's okay. Forget it." The misery on her face made him add, "And I don't honestly believe I got the job because I have a disability, so you can quit worrying."

"You don't? Really? You promise?"

"I promise."

"But Crocker planted a seed of doubt and made you worry just a little, didn't he?"

Mac answered carefully, not wanting to upset her again, but not wanting to lie to her, either.

"I guess that's true, but I also know I'm good at what I do. If my disability did play a role in the search committee's decision, even unconsciously, I've proved I'm as capable as any able-bodied person. They got the best person for the job. I wouldn't have taken it if I didn't believe that.''

"Mac, I'm absolutely positive you were the best person and you should be, too. You're a great coach and a great athletic director. You're good with the athletes. You never show favoritism for one sport over another. You set a wonderful example for the staff.''

"And next week I apply for sainthood.''

"I'm serious.''

"I know you are, and I like that you think I'm such a paragon of virtue even if I'm not.''

"You *are* a paragon of virtue. You're kind and compassionate. Handsome. Sexy. Incredibly sexy. I had a terrible time keeping my hands off you when we were in the store. I almost attacked you in produce and again in frozen foods.''

He reveled in her description of him, even if it wasn't accurate. "We aren't in the store now," he said with a lazy grin.

She grinned back. "No, we're aren't, but I'm hot and sweaty and I probably stink, so I doubt you want me too close until I've cleaned up.''

He leaned toward her and sniffed. "Yeah, Wilson, you stink. Go take a shower.''

"Come in there with me and I'll make it up to you for getting mad." Her voice had turned low and throaty.

"If I'm playing with you, when am I supposed to get these test papers graded?''

"I'll help you after supper, and you can help me study for my teaching assignment tomorrow. Come on. Thirty minutes in the tub isn't going to put either one of us behind and it'll relax us." Her eyes darkened with the suggestion of passion. "You've had a hard day. Let me scrub your back and take care of you."

He let his gaze slide to her breasts, remembering how she'd rubbed them against his back last night and driven him to the brink of madness. With a mental groan he forced himself to look up. If he wasn't careful, he was going to develop an obsession with those breasts. He already had one with her legs and that curvy little backside.

"I like it when you want to take care of me," he said, "but you're forgetting one very important obstacle to this plan of yours. I can't get in and out of your bathtub."

"Mmm, yes, you can."

"And why is that?"

Her teeth toyed with her bottom lip, as they often did when she didn't want to tell him something.

"What have you done?"

"Bought a transfer seat for the bathtub so you can take a shower here whenever you want."

"Agh!" He threw down his pen. "You promised you wouldn't make any more changes to the house."

"The seat's portable and inexpensive. It lifts right off and you can even take it with you when you go out of town with the teams."

"You shouldn't have spent any more money on me."

"I didn't spend much, and when I cooked up my little seduction scheme, I got to thinking that if it worked, you'd occasionally want to spend the night here and take a shower. And if it failed and you *didn't* want me, I'd just give you the seat as a gift.''

''You really believed there was a chance I wouldn't want you?''

She looked at him with sincere confusion. ''Well, yes. I'm certainly no prize, and you could have any woman you want. They throw themselves at you all the time, baking you brownies and sweet-talking you into riding them on your lap.''

''That's only because I'm in this chair. A disability brings out the mothering instincts in a woman.''

''No, it's you, not your disability. You're a magnet for anything female between the ages of eight and eighty. I've seen the way those young coeds drool over you. And I'm seriously considering strangling that red-head in the Sports Information office if I see her stick those big boobs of hers in your face one more time on the pretense of fixing your collar.''

Amused, he tried not to laugh.

''Please don't be mad at me for buying the transfer seat,'' she pleaded. ''I want you to feel as comfortable here as you do at your house, and it was such a tiny expense.'' She lifted a leg and put it in his lap, rubbing back and forth across his midriff with her toes. ''Besides, it's as much for me as it is for you. It gives me more opportunities to get you out of your clothes.''

Mad? How could he be mad when she looked at him with those enormous eyes and told him she wanted him naked?

Caressing her leg from ankle to thigh, he followed the soft curve of her calf and ran his finger along the scars that marred the otherwise perfect flesh. The bones were healed and the rod attached to them should be removed, but he knew she wouldn't agree to surgery right now. He wouldn't even bring it up.

"I'm not mad, Keely, but I wish you'd check with me before you do things like this. Is the seat all you bought?" She nodded. "Do you promise?"

"Yes. Well, except for the bathtub faucet gadget and some extra grab bars." She grimaced at his look of exasperation. "And a few other very minor things. But that's it."

Her thoughtfulness overwhelmed him. She had a wide streak of generosity in her, too, although she tried to conceal it. He'd seen it over and over again in her treatment of the students, particularly the wheelers. They had come to rely on her not only for instruction, but for a sympathetic ear about their romances and personal problems.

"I'm suddenly reminded of what I like most about you," he said. "You always keep me slightly off balance. Just when I think I've figured you out or I'm sure I know what you're going to do, you surprise me."

She smiled. Her dimples peeped out to lure him. "Come play in the bathtub and I'll give you more reasons to be crazy about me."

Without a word he took her arm and pulled her into his lap. In two seconds he had her shirt over her head and her body angled to the side. He rubbed his big hand across her small perfect breasts, teasing the peaks, making them harden.

"Is this a yes?" she asked, laughing.

He slipped his hand lower.

"Mmm. Definitely." Her laughing turned to a cat-like purr. "John Patrick McCandless, I *do* love the way you say yes."

THE QUICK BATH melted into a leisurely one, taking far longer than the thirty minutes they had planned. The transfer seat fit fine on the tub in the bathroom off the hall, but Mac suggested they see if he could get in the larger tub in her private bathroom, instead. The tub was like a five-foot-square shallow swimming pool, and its tiled side proved high enough and wide enough for him to slip down onto it and into the water without help.

Once in, he didn't want to get out, especially with Keely naked and fussing over him. Only one tiny thing spoiled the fantasy-come-to-life.

"This stinkin' stuff wasn't part of the deal," he grumbled as she worked lavender-scented soap into a frothy lather and rubbed it across his back. When she was through with his back, she poured shampoo in her hand and massaged it into his hair. He got a whiff of herbs and groaned. "Ah, Keely."

"Now, Mac, don't be a baby. Did I whine when I had to use your shampoo and soap this morning?"

"No, but my shampoo doesn't make me smell like I've been dragged through a flower garden."

"No, but your shampoo makes me smell like I've been drenched in men's cologne. This is so much nicer. Quit squirming or I'm going to get it in your eyes. Hold your head back."

He obeyed and let her rinse his hair. "Remind me

to wake up early enough in the morning to go home and wash off this smell before I go to work. I'll get laughed out of the locker room if anyone gets a whiff of me.''

"I thought you liked my smell.''

"On *you* I love it.''

"Complaints, complaints.''

She slipped to the front and sat between his legs, facing him so she could soap the rest of him. He took her legs and hooked them over his, then grabbed her bottom and pulled her onto his lap.

"You've got a great rear end, Wilson. I get turned on just thinking about the way it undulates when you run.''

"Undulates? My rear end does *not* undulate. And you're supposed to be watching my running form, not my behind.''

"Baby, I'm no fool,'' he said, making her giggle.

Several minutes passed and she still kept washing, lingering on his shoulders, giving extra attention to his chest. The playful movement of her fingers across his flesh had him fighting for control.

He eased his hand up and tweaked one nipple, but she slapped it away. "Uh-uh-uh,'' she scolded, playing coy. "Not your turn yet. When I get tired of touching you, you can touch me.'' Running both hands slowly over the muscles of his arms, she added huskily, "But the way you're built, that might never happen.''

With an impatient growl, he pulled her forward until their bodies touched intimately. She laughed, but it turned to a moan when his mouth covered hers and he kissed her deeply. She put her arms around his neck and kissed him back, coyness replaced by eagerness.

With his hands locking her in place, he rubbed her against his slight arousal, although he had no sensation there and the pleasure of it was all in his mind. For her, thank God, the pleasure was real. She moaned again, a sound that was halfway a sigh, and ground herself against him, letting him know she wanted more.

Pain mingled with his desire. The act of penetration was only a memory to him now, but it was powerful enough to make him ache for what he could never have again. He loved her with his heart. He wanted also to love her with his body.

Perhaps she sensed his pain; perhaps he'd unknowingly hesitated, for she whispered exactly what he needed to hear—*"I never knew being with someone could be this perfect."*

The flame within him flared to a roaring fire.

Sweet heaven, it *was* perfect, better than anything he'd experienced prior to his paralysis. He had no reason to grieve for what he'd lost. *This* was what lovemaking was meant to be, not just a sensory experience, but a melding of the physical being with the emotional. Body touched body, but spirit also touched spirit. Two fused to become one.

"Fly for us both," he told her, moving her faster and harder against him. When her climax ripped through her like an explosion, she cried his name, and he was certain he had never heard sweeter music.

MAC TRAVELED to Augusta with the football team for
a Thanksgiving Day bowl game, and wasn't expected
home until late Sunday night. Keely backed out of
going to Atlanta to spend the holiday weekend with
her mother. She thought she'd enjoy staying in Courtland and having some time to herself. But by Friday
night she was irritable and bored. Lonely, she realized.
Without Mac around, nothing seemed to interest her.

Saturday she ran with Dean and was further off her
time than the previous week, which concerned her.
Then she had lunch with him and two of the other
female teaching assistants, which ended in disaster
when a fan made a nuisance of himself and she finally
had to ask the manager to make him leave the café.

"I felt bad about it," she told Vicki that night, when
she went over to the Sizemores' for coffee and dessert.
"But he just wouldn't take no for an answer."

Vicki hung Keely's jacket in the hall closet, and
they walked to the den, where Alan played Chutes and
Ladders with Savannah and J.P. on the floor. Bay was
stretched out in front of the TV.

"You handled it the right way," Vicki said. "If it
had been me, I'd have probably decked the guy."

"Decked who?" Alan asked.

"Some jerk who wanted Keely to sign her auto-
graph on his body."

That tickled Alan, who wanted to hear the details
and couldn't stop laughing when she got to the part
where the guy lifted his shirt, hefted his beer gut onto
the table and handed her a pen.

Keely found herself laughing along with him, no
longer feeling down. "I'm glad you two talked me

into coming over here tonight. I needed to be around friends after the day I've had.''

"We wish you'd come over more," Vicki said. "You don't have to wait until you're with Mac."

Mac. Keely continued to smile, but her insides constricted at the mention of his name. She wondered what he was doing. Her watch said eight-fifteen, and the game had been over for about four hours. This morning when he called, he'd said he would probably go out with friends tonight. The team had won, according to the radio. They'd want to celebrate.

"Daddy, J.P.'s eatin' the game again," Savannah complained.

Alan quickly pulled the toddler forward and took away the cardboard cutout Savannah had been using to move around the board. As a result the usually good-natured J.P. began to cry. When Alan tickled him, he immediately stopped, but the child was obviously sleepy and getting fussy.

"Time for this one to wind down and go to bed," Alan said.

Vicki walked over and picked him up. "I'll take him. He needs a bath first. Come on, Keely. You can help."

"Uh, okay, but I warn you the only thing I've ever bathed is a dog."

Alan snickered. "Kids aren't that different. Clean their ears, neck and tail good, and don't let them shake water all over the floor."

"I can handle that."

"Good," Vicki said, leading the way to the bathroom. "You can put him to bed, too. Know any lull-abies?"

"Not a one."

"Improvise."

MAC CAUGHT a commercial flight home Saturday night, rather than waiting to ride back on one of the team buses Sunday, but the flight nearly did him in. He hated to fly commercially, hated having to be carried into the plane like spoiled royalty, hated especially having to check his wheelchair and worry that it might get broken.

The airline hadn't broken it, but when he landed in Columbus, Georgia, he discovered they'd temporarily misplaced it. Agony was a mild word for what he experienced until the baggage handler brought it out. To add to his irritation, he had to pay for an expensive shuttle trip from Columbus to Courtland because he'd left his van parked at the athletic department.

Now, finally home, he felt a bone-deep weariness. And anticipation. He took out the sack of presents for the kids and tossed his suitcase in the house. Keely's car was parked in Alan's driveway, so he headed across the street, wondering how he was going to explain his arrival a day early.

But Alan didn't seem surprised when Mac appeared at the door. He seemed downright amused. "Well, well, well. Look who's back. What's wrong, Mac? Did you miss me and have to rush home?"

"Yeah, I couldn't stand being away from you another minute. Broke my heart."

Savannah had to hug him, and Bay, currently going

through a fascination with airplanes, wanted to hear about his flight. Mac took an aviator's cap out of his sack and handed it to him.

"Oh, wow! Thanks, Uncle Mac."

"Me. Me," Savannah begged, jumping up and down. He buckled a Mickey Mouse watch on her wrist and showed her the button that made Mickey announce the time.

"Don't drive your mom and dad crazy pressing that," he warned her. "Only every once in a while, okay?"

"'Kay," she promised, immediately pressing it. She pressed it twice more before she sat down.

Vicki walked in and kissed him on the cheek. "Hey, I thought you weren't coming home until tomorrow. What gives?"

"I had things to do. You know." He glanced down the hall. Where was Keely? He felt as if he hadn't seen her for a month. If he had to wait one more minute, he was going to explode. "J.P. still up? I brought him a little something."

"Keely's putting him to sleep. Tell us about your trip."

Mac groaned inwardly. "We won. Nothing special."

"Are you hungry? I have an apple pie in the oven, or I can fix you a turkey sandwich."

"Later, Vic," Alan told her. "Can't you tell the man has other business?"

"Huh?"

"Sweet thing."

"Oh!" She chuckled. "Sorry. Go on back. I know she'll be as eager to see you as you are to see her."

He pushed down the hall to where the two younger children shared a room, hearing soft singing. The door was partly open and he could see Keely lying on the bed next to J.P., lightly patting his back as he fought sleep, singing him a very slow version of "A Hard Day's Night." Mac smiled. Only Keely would use a Beatles song as a lullaby.

As he watched her, watched the pleasure on her face at the simple act of putting a child to bed, happiness turned to regret. With him, she could have no children to sing to at night. With him she would have to be content to love someone else's children. The thought of it filled him with a pain that was almost physical.

Of all the things he had lost because of the shooting, losing his ability to father children bothered him the most. Fatherhood might theoretically be possible, but the odds against conception were high. He didn't know anyone among his paraplegic and quadriplegic friends who had tried artificial insemination and been successful.

He slowly opened the door. Seeing him brought surprise to Keely's face and then a look of joy that was a tonic to his weary body. She checked J.P. and finding his eyes closed, eased from the bed. Two seconds later she was in Mac's lap, kissing him wildly, making the difficulties he'd endured to get home seem unimportant.

"Let's get out of here." He was nearly breathless from wanting to be alone with her.

"I'll race you to the door."

"WELL?" ALAN ASKED from across the room, urging Vicki to hurry up and have a look out the window. He'd bet her twenty dollars Mac and Keely wouldn't make it across the street to Mac's house before they kissed.

"Shut up and let me... Oh, my goodness!" Vicki walked over to her purse, got some money and handed it to him. Included with the twenty was an extra ten.

Alan grinned. She must have seen a lot more than a kiss. "Well, way to go, Mac!"

CHAPTER FIFTEEN

DECEMBER ROARED IN, bringing colder-than-normal
temperatures to Georgia. Mac and Keely spent most
nights at his house on a quilt in front of the fireplace,
the open fire a luxury that safety prevented him from
having while alone.

The quilt had belonged to his mother and was a
crazy jumble of patterns, textures and colors. The
scraps came mostly from clothes she'd sewn him and
his siblings growing up. Some were special, like the
piece leftover from Megan's baptismal gown. Others
were more ordinary but still held a memory of some
sort. A patch in one corner represented Mac's favorite
pair of shorts at the age of five, the ones with the little
cowboys on them. The ''S'' from Brand's Superman
pajamas was there, as was a patch from Christine's
favorite sundress, with the big daisies.

Keely called it his ''memory quilt'' and insisted he
drag it out every night to cover the hardwood floor.
Comfort wasn't the reason. She'd become fascinated
by the quilt, by the stories behind each scrap of fabric,
and begged to hear a new story whenever he was willing to indulge her.

With her curled against his side, her hand under his

shirt stroking his chest, Mac didn't mind indulging her often.

"And what's this one?" she asked one night, pointing to a triangle with tiny flowers in the design.

Mac chuckled, remembering a happy time and place. "You'll love this story. That was Jilly's party dress when she was about thirteen. I think she was in the eighth grade, or maybe the ninth. She and her best friend, Lisa, weren't old enough to date, but the party was at a neighbor's house, so my mom and Lisa's mom got together and agreed it would be okay if these two boys in their class escorted them. Jilly talked nonstop about the party for weeks and couldn't wait for that night to get there. Only, things went a little haywire, thanks to Brand."

"What did he do?"

"About ten minutes before the kids came by to walk Jilly to the party, Brand handcuffed her to a kitchen chair."

"Oh, no," Keely said with a snort of laughter.

"Brand had gotten a magic kit for his seventh birthday and was the only one who knew how to open the handcuffs. But he wouldn't, and no matter how much we coaxed, he just stood there with his arms crossed, shaking his head, saying a magician never reveals his secrets. Dad was so furious he threatened him with every kind of punishment he could think of, but it still didn't do any good. Dad was yelling, Mom was pleading, and Jilly was bawling her head off. In the middle of this chaos Lisa arrives with these two boys in tow who couldn't wait to run down the block and tell all the other kids what was going on. So five minutes later we had a kitchen full of laughing kids.''

"Did Brand finally turn her loose?"

"No, my dad had to cut off the handcuffs with a hacksaw. Brand couldn't watch TV or sit down for a month.''

"I'll bet he never pulled a stunt like that again.''

"You don't know Brand. He was a terror back then, especially when it came to his sisters. To tell you the truth, he still plays pranks on them every chance he gets.''

When she stopped chuckling, Keely let out a wistful sigh against his shoulder. "You're so lucky. I always wanted sisters to pull pranks on. When I was little, one Christmas I somehow got it in my head that Santa was responsible for bringing sisters. Christmas morning I woke up expecting to find at least one under the tree and was shattered when I didn't. My mother had to sit me down and explain where babies really come from. And, of course, I was disgusted by that.''

"Did your parents ever consider having other children?"

"I don't really know. In the few years after I was born, I think they might have tried, but my mother never got pregnant again to my knowledge. I'm not sure if something was wrong or they simply stopped trying. They fought so much I doubt there were too many opportunities to conceive a child.''

"Sometimes even the nicest people aren't nice together.''

"I guess so, but my dad was such a great guy I can't imagine anyone having trouble getting along with him. He took me to the track almost every weekend when I was growing up so I could practice, and I never heard him complain about all the hours of free time he gave up for me. He was never very good at sports himself, but he saw something in me and he encouraged it. He supported me a hundred percent.''

''Your father would be proud of you if he could see you today. All the titles you hold. All the medals you've won.''

''All but the gold. That one has always eluded me for some reason. In 1996 I thought I finally had it in the bag because I'd trained hard and the Olympics were in my hometown. But that morning it rained and turned cool. I hadn't expected that and it threw me. I got a slow start and was never able to gain any momentum.''

''But you still got a silver.''

''Yes, but the gold is what's important. I wanted it. I still want it.'' She sat up and turned cross-legged to face him. ''When I was little, my dad made me a medal out of a piece of wood. He painted it gold and threaded it with red, white and blue ribbon. He put it around my neck and said, 'One day, kitten, you'll win the marathon and this will be a real Olympic gold medal.' I still have a piece of the ribbon and I wear it for good luck when I race. It's all faded and falling apart, but I keep it because it represents my dream. *Our* dream. Mine and my dad's.''

An uneasiness grew in Mac's chest. Until now, he hadn't realized how closely her running was tied to her feelings for her father.

''I *have* to win that gold. I have to. I've dreamed

all my life of taking that victory lap around the Olympic stadium and holding the American flag high while thousands of people cheer. I want that for myself and I want it for my dad. You remember how supportive he was of me when I was running for Courtland. Every weekend we had a meet, if it was within driving distance, he'd be there to watch.''

"I remember.''

"I could always count on him to be in the stands rooting for me, encouraging me to do my best.''

"But he wasn't alone.'' She cocked her head in confusion. "Your mom was always with him,'' Mac reminded her. "I don't remember a time your dad came that your mom wasn't right there, cheering you along.''

Keely looked away, but before she did, he saw a flash of pain in her eyes. "I suppose she was,'' she said softly. "I really don't remember.''

KEELY'S UP-AND-DOWN relationship with her mother moved toward a crisis the following week, and Mac found himself in the middle of it. Liz called to say she was driving over Friday night and bringing her male friend, Everett Lathom. The unexpected visit sent Keely into a panic.

"You have to come and help me entertain them,'' she said. She sat on the corner of his desk sticking pencils in his electric sharpener, grinding them one after another into useless nubs. "Good grief! I call her every week without fail, and I've already promised I'd spend a few days with her between Christmas and New Year's. What more does she want from me? I can't *believe* she's going to pop in like this without an invitation.''

''Maybe she got tired of waiting for an invitation. Or maybe she's afraid you'll back out at the last minute like you did at Thanksgiving.''

She gave him a hard look. ''Whose side are you on?''

''Are there sides?''

''Yes, of course there are.'' Then she realized how ridiculous that sounded. ''I don't really mean it.''

''I know you don't. Look, I think you should do this alone. You haven't seen your mother in months. And it also couldn't hurt you to get to know this Everett fellow better, since she seems serious about him.''

''I won't survive without you there.''

Survive. A strange word to use for getting through a visit with your mother.

In the end he agreed to come, not because he believed Keely really needed him, but because he figured Liz Wilson might.

When he got to Keely's house shortly before seven Friday night, she was at the stove stirring the red beans she was planning to serve over rice. Judging by her expression, he would have sworn she was going to a funeral, rather than having dinner with her mother and her mother's friend.

''You know it's pretty stupid for you not to be comfortable around your own mother,'' he told her.

''You don't understand. My mother and I can't spend five minutes together without fighting. And I can't imagine why she insisted on bringing that man with her.''

''What's so wrong with this guy that you can't stand to be in the same room with him?''

Two hours later Mac knew exactly what was wrong with the guy—nothing. Except that he wasn't Keely's father. And in Keely's book, that was an unforgivable sin.

Everett Lathom was friendly, interesting and clearly crazy about Liz. Mac also had to give the guy credit for effort. He was bending over backward to be nice to Keely, to draw her into the conversation, but she was as sullen as Mac had ever seen her.

Liz and Everett were pretending they didn't notice, but the air was so thick with tension, it would take a chainsaw to cut it. Mac was pretty sure he'd count this among the longest nights of his life.

''This is such a lovely meal,'' Liz said, and Mac wondered how she could do it with a straight face.

''And such a beautiful house,'' Everett added.

Keely mumbled an almost unintelligible thank-you, then pointed out—for the third time—the photograph of her father hanging on the wall to the left of the fireplace.

''Mac gave it to me,'' she said.

Her mother's smile was laced with indulgence. ''Yes, dear, you told us, and it's a wonderful gift. Such a good likeness of you.''

''And Daddy.''

''Yes, and Daddy.''

Liz and Everett exchanged glances. Mac could almost hear Liz's silent plea for Everett to continue being patient with Keely—and not to be offended by her latest reference to her father.

They had decided to eat in the living room at a small table set up near the fireplace for the occasion. Liz reached over and patted Mac on the arm, acting as if nothing was wrong. "John, I'm so glad Keely invited you to join us. I was thrilled when she told me tonight you two are seeing each other."

Mac smiled, but Keely made a noise of impatience. "He likes to be called *Mac,* Mother. Nobody calls him John."

"Actually, quite a few people still call me John," he said. Keely gave him a hurt look for not supporting her, but he ignored it. "They're mostly people I grew up with. I didn't become Mac until my dad died. He'd been called that all his life."

"Where did you grow up?" Liz asked.

"Benevolence, a little town about fifty miles from here."

"I have a cousin who married a man from Benevolence and lived there for several years," Everett said. He turned to Liz. "Honey—" Keely jerked at the endearment "—you remember Reba and Charles Abernathy, don't you? We ran into them at the symphony last year when they were in Atlanta visiting."

Liz put her hand over his, a loving gesture that didn't escape Mac's attention, or Keely's. "Yes, I remember the Abernathys. Nice people."

"Charles Abernathy," Mac repeated. He called up a memory from more than twenty years ago. "I played high-school football with a Charles Abernathy. He was a big guy with thick black hair. He was a senior when I was a freshman and went on to play for Georgia.''

''That's him,'' Everett said, chuckling, ''although he lost that thick hair a long time ago.''

A lengthy discussion ensued among the three of them about the Abernathy family, then about their own families. Mac told them about his siblings and pulled pictures from his wallet to show off their children. Everett responded with pictures of his two grown daughters and their children.

Mac was impressed by Everett and Liz. They didn't seem that much older than him, probably in their early fifties, and they had an easiness about them he liked. The open affection they showed each other reminded him of how things had been between his own parents.

''Mac, Liz tells me you and Keely are working with some wheelchair racers at the college. How's that coming?'' Everett asked.

''Really good. Keely's been a great help. She's turning into a first-class coach.'' He glanced at her, hoping for a comment, but he didn't get one. ''I was really proud of how well she did last quarter, and she's doing even better this quarter. I know it hasn't been easy for her—going back to school, being a teaching assistant and training at the same time, but she's really put everything into it.''

Still no response. Keely sat stoically, picking at some stewed apples.

''Are you still enjoying school, sweetheart?'' her mother prodded.

''It's all right.''

''Just all right? What's your favorite class?''

She shrugged. "I don't have one."

"She does great in my Rehab 102 class," Mac said, hoping to make her giggle or at least shock her out of her stupor, but all she did was pinch him under the table.

"Oh?" Liz remarked, looking at Keely. "What do you do in that class?"

"It involves a lot of oral presentations," she answered without a change in expression.

This time Mac pinched Keely under the table.

"And what about your other classes?" Liz asked her. "What kinds of things are you learning?"

"I don't know. Nothing really exciting."

"I would think you'd be more enthusiastic about school, considering how well you're doing. And if John—Mac—thinks you'd make an excellent coach, perhaps you should consider that."

"School and coaching are just temporary diversions, Mother, until I can run again. I'm only doing them because Mac made them a stipulation of my training. I don't *enjoy* them, for heaven's sake."

Temporary? She didn't enjoy them? Mac couldn't conceal his surprise or hurt at her revelation. Just what else, he wondered suddenly, did she consider a temporary diversion? Him?

He muttered a low expletive that let Keely know she'd pushed him too far tonight with her childish behavior and spiteful tongue. "Should I strangle you now or wait until the company leaves?" he whispered through gritted teeth.

Keely ignored him, but he was certain he saw a smile touch the corner of her mother's mouth.

Everett cleared his throat and made a desperate attempt to salvage a situation that was rapidly going downhill. "Well, er, I'd like to see one of these wheelchair races sometime. I didn't know there was such a thing. Do you use special chairs?"

Mac took a deep breath and regained his composure. "I have photos with me from some of the practices and races," he told Everett stiffly, choosing to postpone the confrontation with Keely until they were alone. He pulled the photo pack out of the sling under his seat. "I brought them along because I thought you and Liz might like to see what Keely is helping me do."

When they'd finished eating, Keely cleared the dishes and Mac arranged the photographs on the table, where Liz and Everett could both look.

Liz picked up one of the photos and looked at it more closely. "Why, that's Ross Hewitt. I didn't know he'd been down from Chicago."

Liz pointed out a dark-haired man talking to one of the wheelers at the race in Pensacola. "No," Mac said, "that man's name is Redmond. He represents a company that partially funds our program. He's really been a lifesaver. I've been able to replace our old chairs and create a decent expense fund for the athletes, something we've never had before."

"I'd swear..." She leaned over to Keely and showed her the photograph. "Doesn't that look just like Ross?"

Keely glanced at it and released a dismissive snort. "No. It favors him a little, but Ross has a much bigger build. And the hair is different."

"Oh, Keely! How can you say that? This is Ross Hewitt. I'd stake my life on it."

"Who's Ross Hewitt?" Everett asked.

Keely stood so abruptly she almost overturned the chair. "A little cheese and fruit would be nice, since I don't have dessert," she said, plastering a smile on her face. "Let's put the photographs away so they don't get messed up."

She reached for them, but Mac grabbed her hand and entwined his fingers with hers. "In a minute," he told her, suspicious of her behavior. "We're not finished." She tried to pull away, but he wrapped his other arm around her hip and held her close.

"Ross is Keely's agent and business manager," Liz said, clearly oblivious to the drama being played out across the table. "He manages her investments. A nice man, but he has terrible allergies and this awful voice because of them. He coughs and sneezes constantly."

The uneasiness that had haunted Mac the moment Liz began this conversation now hit him full force. No, he'd told himself, it couldn't have been Hewitt he talked with at the track that day in Pensacola. Redmond must coincidentally resemble him.

But the voice…the allergies…

Liz was going on about Ross Hewitt, how helpful he'd been to Keely right after her accident, but Mac only half listened. He looked up at Keely, praying he would see innocence on her face, but all he saw was a guilty stain creeping up her throat, and eyes that confirmed what she'd obviously hoped he would never find out. Through Ross Hewitt—the fictitious "Beatty Redmond"—*Keely* was covertly sponsoring Mac's wheelers.

CHAPTER SIXTEEN

KEELY SLAMMED the lid on the pot she was drying, bent down and tossed it with more force than necessary into the cabinet. The other pots crammed inside tumbled to the floor in a chorus of clanging metal.

It was bad enough that she'd suffered through two hours of watching old what's-his-name paw her mother, and right beneath the photograph of her father, too. It was bad enough that Mac—the one person she'd thought she could count on to support her, no matter what—was furious at her for having Ross pose as the fictional Beatty Redmond, but her mother had shattered what nerves Keely had left by announcing over the fruit and cheese that she was planning a spring wedding. She was actually going to marry that old geezer!

"You acted like a spoiled three-year-old!" Mac yelled from behind her, continuing the verbal attack he had started the second they were alone. "I can't believe you pitched that fit. I've never been so ashamed of anyone in my life!"

She plopped down on the floor and started picking up the pots, stacking them in the cabinet so they'd stay this time. Her hands shook with anger, and the tears that had threatened for days began to come now, even though she tried to hold them back.

The news hadn't been unexpected, just more devastating than she had imagined. All week, since her mother's call, she had worried that an engagement announcement might be the reason for the visit. All night she'd been waiting for the bomb to fall. And it finally had, widening the emotional fissure between her and her mother.

"I didn't pitch a fit," she told Mac in defense of herself, although she knew he was right. She'd pitched a humdinger of one. But it just hurt so much to see her mother and old what's-his-name happy.

"Like hell you didn't pitch a fit! You were abusive and deliberately rude to both of them. You made your mother cry when you said you wouldn't be at the wedding, and for that alone you ought to be ashamed of yourself. You'll be lucky if she ever speaks to you again after what you've done."

The lines in his face and the narrowed eyes showed just how angry he was. So did his voice.

"How can you be so selfish? Don't you think your mother has a right to happiness and to marry the man she loves without you acting like she's committing a crime?"

"I didn't tell them not to get married. I only said I thought they hadn't known each other long enough. I'm not going to pretend I like it when I don't. But they're adults. They can do whatever they want."

"And thank God for that. At least they're smart enough not to let your childish behavior keep them from going ahead with their plans."

She slammed the cabinet shut and stood, planting her fists on her hips. "You know, I'm getting really tired of you calling me names and treating me like you do. You tell me I'm selfish, yet you get furious when I try to do something unselfish for your wheelers. You accuse me of being childish, but you treat me like a child, always having to approve every step in my training, not allowing me to run when you know I'm ready. I'm sick to death of you smothering me. You swore you wouldn't let our sleeping together affect my training, but that's exactly what you're doing."

"Now wait a minute! Don't twist this around to make it sound like I'm to blame here, and don't pretend this has anything to do with us sleeping together. You and Ross Hewitt were wrong setting up that bogus sponsorship and lying to me about it. If you didn't think you were doing something wrong, you wouldn't have had him pass himself off as someone else."

"I've already explained all this. The sponsorship isn't bogus and neither is Coxwell Industries."

"You just happen to own the company."

"Yes, I own it. Ross had been bugging me for a long time to license the InsulCare formula and produce it, so I used the money from my buyout of the Aztec contract. I had a company and you needed a sponsor for the wheelers. What was so wrong with me trying to help?"

"Nothing, except you went behind my back, you lied and manipulated me, and I don't like that one bit. That tells me you don't really care about my feelings."

''That's not true! The only reason I went behind your back is because you wouldn't have taken the money from me otherwise. You're so irritatingly noble at times.''

The veins in his face looked like they were ready to pop. ''You don't know what I would have done, because you took the choice away from me!''

She bit back her scalding reply. Okay, he had a point about the money, but she'd honestly been trying to help. She had assumed his pride wouldn't allow him to accept if she offered it outright, so she'd come up with a way to give it to him. She'd told a few white lies. But they certainly weren't worth getting this upset about.

He took her silence as an admission of guilt.

''Sometimes, Keely, I think you purposely try to be hard to get along with, and when problems don't materialize the way you expect, you invent them. Just like this thing with school. You love school, but you sat here tonight and made us all think you hate it. You love coaching, but you won't admit to yourself or anyone else that it's something you'd like to try professionally.''

''Why on earth would I consider coaching when I'll be running again soon?''

''You know why. You're afraid of the truth.''

''I don't have the slightest idea what you mean.''

She turned to the dishwasher and busied herself, filling it with tonight's dishes. All the activity was an excuse to avoid looking at him. She didn't like the way he could see inside her and recognize what was going on when she didn't always understand her own feelings.

"Keely, don't lie to me and don't lie to yourself anymore. You worked hard and you gave this comeback your best shot, but it wasn't enough. The reality is, even if you want something badly, that doesn't mean you're going to get it."

"You don't know what you're talking about."

"I don't? Can you look at me in this chair and tell me I don't understand what it feels like to want something so badly you'd do anything to get it?"

She didn't answer him, didn't know *how* to answer him.

"Well, can you?"

"You're comparing my situation to yours and they're not the same at all," she said. "We're totally different. Just because you stopped believing in dreams and miracles doesn't mean I have to."

He pushed up close and took her arm, forcing her to turn around. Then he held her tightly by both forearms. "Listen to me. It's exactly the same thing. We've both been permanently injured and we both have to accept that nothing we ever do is going to change that."

"I am *not* permanently injured."

"You can barely breathe when you run."

"That's not true! I could run a race tomorrow if I had to. I've already gotten my entry form for the Los Verdes Marathon in April."

He let go of her abruptly. His jaw worked back and forth in anger. "That just proves what I said a little while ago. You're not honest with me. You go behind my back and do things you know you shouldn't.''

''Would you have supported me if I'd told you I was thinking about entering a race?''

''No, because physically you can't run it.''

''That's not true!'' she said again. ''You're not in my body. You don't know what I can and can't do. From the way you hold me back, sometimes I think you don't *want* me to run again.''

''Do you really believe that?'' He gave her an incredulous look.

''No,'' she said honestly, body sagging. He had done everything he could to help her. She was just angry about tonight's events, and taking it out on him was easy because he was here. ''I know you'd never do anything to hold me back. But I'm starting to get the feeling you never believed I could do this, not even in the beginning when you agreed to help me.''

He didn't respond.

''Well?'' she prompted. ''Did you?''

A sickening knot formed in her throat because she was afraid she already knew the answer. Tears streamed down her face.

''Keely, you're upset. I'm upset. Right now isn't a good time to talk about this. When we're both calmer, we can—''

''It's true, isn't it? I thought at least *you* believed in me, and that's what kept me going all these months. Whenever I got discouraged or afraid I couldn't do it, I'd remind myself that you would never have agreed to help me if you didn't think I had a chance of racing again. So I'd work harder and I'd push a little bit more. But you've been lying all this time, haven't you?''

"Wait a minute. I've never lied to you."

"Then, what *is* the truth? Did you believe for an instant that I *could* race again? And if you've ever cared for me, don't lie to me now."

The anger seemed to leave him in one great expulsion of breath, to be replaced by an overwhelming sadness. "No, I never believed you'd race again," he said with obvious regret. "You're counting on a miracle that's never going to happen."

KEELY CRIED HERSELF into a sick headache and fell into bed. Mac was afraid to leave her alone. He cleaned up the kitchen and put the leftover food away.

Later, when he was sure she had no more tears left to spill, he went to her in the darkness and pressed himself against her back, wrapping his arm around her. She hadn't even bothered to take off her clothes. She lay awake but unresponsive on top of the covers.

He kissed her neck, longing to make love to her, but knowing she needed something different from him right now.

"I wasn't trying to hurt you," he said softly. "I wanted you to have your chance, even if it didn't work out, and I knew from my own experience that it was going to take you time to accept things."

"You should have been honest with me." Her voice was flat, emotionless. "You yelled at me tonight about not being honest, and all these months you've been deceiving me. How honest is that?"

He clenched and unclenched his jaw. "You're right.

I should have told you the truth in the very beginning and not agreed to coach you. I did it to stall for time."

"To waste my time, you mean."

"How was it a waste of your time if it helped you heal? The past months have been great for you. You've gone back to school and now you have the chance to try coaching as a new career."

"I don't need a new career. I already have one—running. I *will* run again. I *will* be the best in the world. I *will* win a gold medal in Sydney. And no one, not you or anyone, is going to tell me not to try. I'd rather go after my dream and fail than be like you—afraid of even trying."

He forced down the anger rising in him again, ignored the sting of her words. He smoothed her hair. "Baby, you can't run."

"Yes, I can!"

With a sigh Mac rolled onto his back, put his arm under his head and stared at the shadows on the ceiling cast by the pale light in the hall. Continuing this conversation was useless. She wasn't going to listen to him, didn't want to listen him. Nothing he said would to convince her.

He could think of only one way to make her see the truth, but it would probably kill them both.

CHAPTER SEVENTEEN

December

THE MORNING WAS COLD and clear, the ground still covered with a thin layer of frost the sun had yet to burn away. On the side of a four-lane road, Keely paced and stretched to keep her muscles warm and tried to rid herself of the uncommon nervousness that clawed in her belly.

Stay focused, she warned herself silently. *Be patient. Conserve your energy.*

She took several deep breaths and visualized the test marathon course ahead of her; it would follow the by-pass for nearly a third of the twenty-six miles, taking her along the newest, and for the most part, uninhabited section of the road. The surface was smooth and the road had a bike lane she could use. The only hill was at mile six, when she would be warm but not tired.

At mile eight, before the first traffic light, she would exit right onto a meandering dirt road for less than a mile, then take a left that would put her on a relatively flat two-lane country road for eleven miles. Miles twenty-one to twenty-six, the hardest part of any marathon, would be another country road with a slight downhill grade.

The course was incredibly easy, with every part of

it working to her advantage. She was certain Mac had intentionally drawn it that way, just as she was certain he had given her every other advantage within his control.

Exams were over, so she didn't have to worry about school. The three-week Christmas break had begun two days ago with a mass exodus of students, which meant the streets in and around Courtland were virtually deserted. She wouldn't have to worry about the bypass being crowded with other runners, or running in heavy traffic, which made her uneasy since her accident.

As the only participant in this "race," she wouldn't be jostled at the start or fighting for position at the finish. It would be just her against the clock.

Even the weather was cooperating, she thought, as she jogged to Dean's truck and took off her jacket and the old sweats she'd put on over her running tights. The cool air would reduce her chances of dehydration from sweating. Since their arrival a light tailwind had come up to push her along the course.

"Drink," Dean said. He handed her a cup of a carbohydrate-replacement solution, and she stopped jogging to sip it. "I know you said you don't usually eat during a race, but Mac made me get bananas, dried fruit and energy bars just in case." He offered her a banana. "Want to eat something before you start?"

Grimacing, she waved it away. "I've carbo-loaded for days. I don't think my stomach can handle anything solid right now. My butterflies might not appreciate it, either."

"Nervous?"

"A little. Mostly excited." She drained her cup and placed it in the trash sack on the floorboard. "I've spent months working toward this day."

"I wish I felt as good about it as you do. You haven't run a full marathon in practice, and that worries me."

"Mac gave me more than four hours to finish," she reminded him. "And I always run better in a race than in practice. I can handle it in that time with no sweat."

"Maybe, but it might not be as easy as you think. You know what happens when you try to push yourself."

"I'll be fine. I haven't had problems in months."

Reaching into her bag, she brought out a baseball cap and her father's ribbon. She rubbed the ribbon for strength before pinning it to her shirt. Everything depended on her performance over the next few hours.

According to Mac's deal, she only had to finish today's trial within an hour of her *worst* recorded time at this distance. She could make it. And when she did, Mac would have to concede that she was able to return to racing.

His sweetheart of a deal, though, had come with a big stipulation: "If you don't make it, Keely, you have to retire. No more comeback attempts. No more putting off the inevitable. You have to accept that your career is over and give me your word that you'll go on to something else."

She had agreed. She had no reason not to. Her training had gone well over the past months, except for a few setbacks she blamed on tension caused by the situation with her mother. Recently she'd done extensive hill work, deep-pool running, and speed work on the track, returning her muscles and cardiovascular system to top form.

She jogged back and forth for a few yards, then did easy stretches, testing her muscles. They felt good.

"If you need to drink between the designated stops," Dean reminded her, "wave and I'll pull around."

"Will do."

"I'll be right behind you if you need anything."

"Just don't follow me if I suddenly plunge into the woods to drop my tights."

"Got it," he said with a chuckle. He closed the door of the truck. "You greased up and ready to go?"

She nodded but looked to her right, hoping to see Mac's van approaching. The gloomy sight of an empty road met her. A horrible thought worked its way from her head down her spine. Maybe he wasn't here yet because he wasn't coming.

Admittedly, things had been strained between them for the past two weeks. Dean had relayed his messages and helped her with her prerace training program. The couple of times she'd tried speaking to Mac directly he'd been maddeningly businesslike, as if she was just another of his students.

Two nights ago on the telephone, they'd had a terrible argument because of Mac's insistence that one of the team doctors be here today in case she had problems. She hadn't talked to or seen Mac since.

He wanted her to quit and she wouldn't. She wanted him to believe in her ability and he couldn't. Their difference of opinion over her career had driven a wedge between them that had wrecked both their professional and personal relationship.

But regardless of their problems, she'd expected him to be here for her start. *Wanted* him to be here.

Taking her gaze from the road, she looked at Dean for reassurance, but he was wearing an uncomfortable expression.

"He isn't coming, is he?" she asked.

"He had things to do—checking the course, picking up Doc Ramsey. They're ahead of us somewhere."

Disappointment brought a lump to her throat. "Did he give you a message for me?"

Dean shifted in place, like a little boy asked by his mother to confess a sin. He knew she and Mac had argued about her unwillingness to retire.

"No, I'm sorry, he didn't."

Keely looked away, trying not to feel upset but failing. Mac wasn't coming. He wasn't even going to bother to wish her luck.

"I can get him on the radio."

She realized Dean was still talking to her. "What?"

"Do you need me to get Mac on the headset?"

"No, it's okay. I don't need him," her mouth said, but her heart said she needed him very much, not only today, but every day. And more than she'd realized until this moment.

"MAC, WE'RE ROLLING. Starting time nine-zero-seven and thirteen seconds."

Dean's voice startled Mac, although he'd been waiting for the signal. He made a note on his clipboard and tossed it onto the dash. The sound made Doc

Ramsey, who'd been half-asleep in the passenger seat of the van, sit up and rub his eyes. Mac raised the microphone arm on the headset so he could respond.

"Okay, don't crowd her, but stay close enough to tell when she starts having problems. If she even stumbles, I want to know about it."

"Will do. Where are you and Doc?"

"Parked at the fire station. We'll move and stay just ahead of you. We can be there in a couple of minutes when you need us."

"Copy." There was a moment of silence on the line. "Hey, Mac…"

"Yeah?"

"This thing between you and Keely is none of my business, but I think you should know she seemed hurt you didn't come see her off."

Mac's heart gave a lurch. He'd debated for two days whether to see her this morning and had spent a sleepless night worrying about it. Ultimately he'd decided it was better to stay away. Better for Keely not to get angry right before she had to run. Better for him because his insides couldn't survive another fight with her.

And the truth was, the thought of talking to her this morning, when he knew she was about to get the biggest disappointment of her life, was more than the coward in him could take.

"Mac, did you hear me?"

Mac glanced at Doc, thankful the older man didn't have a headset on and couldn't hear the conversation. "Yeah, I heard you. Sorry to put you in the middle of things."

"No problem. I just hope, well, you know, y'all can work things out after this is over."

Me, too, Mac thought. *Me too.*

EVERYTHING WENT SMOOTHLY until ninety minutes into the run when Keely began to feel an increasing pressure along the ribs on her bad side. Taking shallower breaths helped, but that robbed her of oxygen and slowed her pace, something she couldn't afford in this middle leg when she needed to record her fastest miles.

A slow start. A fast middle. A moderate end. That was the pacing plan Mac had devised to keep up her energy and bring her in at four hours. With the tailwind, she'd expected to gain some time, but she hadn't. Instead, she was steadily losing time. And she had to make it up.

Ignore the pain. But it was difficult to ignore. It was so smothering.

She tried to concentrate on keeping her form smooth and efficient, to gain time through economy of motion and block out the burning that now consumed her whole side.

Breathe normally, her mind screamed at her. She tried, but every time she inhaled deeply, it felt as if someone was jamming a spear in her ribs.

Suddenly Dean drove around and pulled over, indicating a water stop. Keely almost cried with relief. Mac had ordered her to stop and drink, rather than drinking on the run, and the few seconds of rest at each stop had helped keep her moving. The few she'd get at this stop would mean the difference between staying on her feet and going down.

Dean thrust a cup in her hand when she got to the truck. "You look bad and you're still slowing down. Are you okay?"

She nodded and drank the liquid as fast as she dared. Too slow and she'd lose precious seconds. Too fast and she'd be fighting stomach cramps.

"Answer me orally," Dean ordered. "You know procedure."

According to Mac's rules, she had to orally respond to questions at each water stop. If she didn't, Dean wasn't supposed to let her continue. So far, she'd been able to. This time, she tried but no sound came out.

"That's it," Dean said, reaching in the cab to get the headset. "I'm pulling you in and calling Mac."

Ignoring him, she tossed the cup and headed out, Dean's curses following her.

"Mac!"

"Yeah?"

"I got no oral response at this stop and she's fighting for air. I tried to pull her in, but she got away from me."

"We're on the way."

Stubborn infuriating woman! She was already so far behind time she had little chance of finishing, but that wouldn't stop her from injuring herself trying.

Mac drove like a wild man to intercept Keely. He passed her and Dean, then made a quick U-turn and pulled up next to her so Doc could talk to her out the window of the van. Dean hadn't exaggerated. She was laboring for breath and pushing herself forward on willpower alone. Only by a miracle was she was still going.

She tried to wave them away. Where she got the strength to lift her hand, he didn't know.

Mac watched for oncoming traffic while Doc visually assessed her condition. Doc asked her to touch her pulse monitor and give him a reading. She followed his instructions, and the reading was in line with what Doc expected, easing Mac's concern, but only slightly.

"As long as her vitals and fluid intake stay okay and she can communicate, I think it's safe for her to continue," Doc said. "Let's start checking her at each stop."

"Your call, Doc," Mac told him, not trusting himself to decide. "Her safety is the issue here. Nothing else matters."

"Her oxygen intake is the only thing really concerning me right now," he told Mac, then turned back to Keely and asked, "How's your respiration? Are you feeling any pain in your chest? Any pressure when you inhale?"

She shook her head.

"Just tired and hot?"

She nodded.

"C'mon, talk to me so I'll know you're breathing okay and can go on."

No response.

Mac leaned forward on the steering wheel and yelled, "This is insane! Give it up before you hurt yourself."

Still no response.

"Talk to me," Mac warned her, "or I swear I'll bring you in and physically restrain you."

She turned her head and looked at him, and he could see the determination in her eyes, along with the pain she was fighting. She opened her mouth to speak, but the three words she forced out were the very ones he didn't want to hear. "I...won't...quit."

KEELY TOOK A FEW BREATHS of oxygen from the portable unit Doc passed through the window. That eased her pain, revived her temporarily, so they did it several more times over the next few miles and let her continue to run.

But Mac frequently expressed his unhappiness with the situation and wouldn't let her out of his sight. He was in front of her now in the van, leading the way. Keely focused on his emergency flashers and just kept putting one foot in front of the other, trying not to think about how far behind she'd fallen.

At each water stop she sat in the side door of the van and let them fill her with liquids. Doc checked her vital signs and made sure her temperature didn't get too high. Dean gave her oxygen and rubbed her leg muscles to keep them from cramping while she wasn't moving.

Mac, frustrated by his inability to get down on the floor to help, barked orders at everyone from the driver's seat.

Repeatedly they urged her to quit, but Keely kept going. She kept going when her energy deserted her and the oxygen no longer did any good. She kept going when the pain in her lungs became so intense she felt she was inhaling fire with every breath.

Even when her watch told her she had only four minutes to finish—and seven miles to complete—she kept going.

"SHE'S DOWN! She's down!"

Dean's words ripped through Mac's brain at the same moment he looked in the rearview mirror and saw Keely collapse.

Doc was out the door before Mac could pull off the road and stop.

Doc and Dean hauled her in the side door of the van and put her on the floor. Cursing his useless legs, Mac threw himself from the driver's seat to the floor, dragging himself to her side.

As he reached her, the timer beeped on her watch—the death knell of her career.

"Maaaaac…"

"I'm here, baby."

He held her in his arms and tried to comfort her as the first sob racked her body. She didn't have enough liquid left to produce tears, and her wails were punctuated by great gasps for air. Her face, etched with the pain of what she had endured, also carried the anguish of failure.

"I…couldn't…" She clung to him and tried to cry. "I…couldn't…do it."

"It's okay," he said, pulling off her baseball cap to cradle her head. "Everything's going to be okay."

"I tried…so hard."

"I know you did, baby. You did everything you

could.'' He put the oxygen mask Doc handed him over her nose and mouth. ''Now just breathe for me and don't worry about anything. I promise everything's going to be all right.''

Her temperature had risen to 103, high enough for concern, so they plied her with more liquids, changing to watered-down fruit juice when the sugar in the replacement drink made her throw up. Doc kept a continuous check on her blood pressure.

Her arms were scraped and bloody from elbow to wrist because of her fall, but they weren't a priority at the moment. Helping her shocked system was. With Dean on one side and Doc on the other, they walked her back and forth along the road to keep blood moving to her muscles and stave off post-race collapse syndrome.

After several agonizingly long minutes, they brought her close enough to the van for Mac to talk to them. He had pulled himself into his wheelchair and used the lift to get down onto the road. ''Is she dizzy?'' he asked Doc when they approached. ''Headache?''

''She's okay,'' Doc said. ''Breathing easier and keeping down undiluted juice. She's stabilizing.''

Mac had set up a recovery unit at the athletic department, where she'd spend the next few hours replenishing her body fluids and getting her blood sugar back to normal. His only thought now was to get her there as soon as they had her regulated.

But when he suggested it, Keely balked.

''No...I have...to finish,'' she said as they helped her sit in the open door of the van. Her skin was bright red and her muscles quivered, making her hands shake so badly she could hardly hold the cup Dean had given her. Although her breathing had improved, she still had to breathe through her mouth to get enough oxygen, which made talking difficult.

Her pronouncement that she had to finish the race had the three men looking at one another with concern. Mac knew they were all thinking the same thing—she must be out of her head.

"Sweetheart…" Mac folded his hand around hers and brought the cup to her lips. He helped her drink. "You're dehydrated and confused. The trial is over. There's nothing to finish."

"Not over. Have…to finish." She stopped to catch her breath, then continued in her halting speech, determined, it seemed, to make them understand, to prove she wasn't out of her mind. "Not confused. Have to…keep going. Have to cross…the finish line."

"No! Absolutely not! There's no way in hell I'm letting you go on!"

"Please…listen…please."

"You don't have to finish. We all know you ran the best race you could."

Dean and Doc expressed their agreement.

"Matters to me," Keely said. "Please…this is my…last race. Know I can't go out a winner. But…don't want to go out a quitter."

"No, no way. You aren't physically able to run."

"No, but, Mac…I can still walk."

SHE CROSSED THE FINISH LINE eight hours after she began, walking, instead of running. It was a small victory compared to what she had expected of herself today, but in the eyes of the three men who watched her take her last faltering steps, she might as well have won the gold medal in the Olympics.

"That woman is ninety percent guts," Doc said, sounding a little choked up.

"And the rest is heart," Dean added.

Mac swallowed a lump in his throat the size of a baseball. He'd never felt more love for anyone, never been prouder of anyone, in his life.

They drove her to the recovery unit at the athletic complex. She lay on a table with her feet elevated to ease the flow of blood to her heart and prevent edema in her legs. Doc swabbed antiseptic on her scraped arms and helped her change into dry clothes.

Physically she seemed okay, no worse off for having walked those last seven miles, although with every step Mac had agonized over his decision to let her do it.

"Please, Mac," she'd pleaded with him, "let me go out with some dignity."

He hadn't been able to refuse her.

Her emotional health was what worried Mac now. She couldn't stop crying—quiet private tears, not the sobbing he expected—which tore at his heart every time he tried to talk to her. "Try and sleep a little while," he told her. "That might make you feel better."

She looked at him with big sad eyes that said nothing would ever make her feel better. "What do I do now, Mac? How do I go on without the one thing that made me who I am?"

"You just will." He wished he knew the right words to say, but instead, he felt useless. "You'll dig down and grab hold of some of that incredible strength you have, and you'll find a new direction in your life."

"I can't imagine any other life."

"Can't you? I can. When I met you, you were a gangly seventeen-year-old kid with the best set of legs I'd ever seen on a runner and no idea how to use them. I came away that day sure of two things—You were going to be a champion and you were going to steal my heart. I wasn't wrong about either prediction."

He stroked her hair. He hadn't intended to say any of this now, but the words tumbled out.

"The feelings I have for you started as physical attraction and admiration for your talent, but they've had a lot of time to grow into something stronger. I love you. You're hurting right now and it's going to take a while to put the hurt behind you. But don't think for an instant that your life is over, because it isn't. If you'll have me, I intend to spend the next sixty years making you glad to wake up every morning."

"What are you saying?"

"I'm asking you to be my wife and grow old with me."

"Marriage?"

"Yes. Marry me. I know I can make you happy."

For a long time she didn't respond, and he began to regret the suddenness of his declaration. She had too much to deal with now. When she was feeling better, when he had champagne and a ring, he'd ask the proper way.

"You don't have to say anything right now or even

think about it,'' he told her. ''Close your eyes and rest. We'll talk when you're feeling better.''

With intravenous fluids, she improved steadily over the next hours. At nine-thirty that night Doc checked her a final time and decided she was well enough to go home.

''I think I should stay with you tonight,'' Mac told her in front of the men, propriety having crumbled the minute he'd taken her into his arms in the van. ''You shouldn't be alone.''

She nodded but said nothing.

At her house, Mac fixed dinner while she took a shower. When he went to tell her it was ready, he found her asleep on the bed, her face stained with tears and her father's ribbon clutched in one hand. He covered her with a blanket but left the lamp on the bedside table burning. He looked in on her several times during the night, until he himself fell into an exhausted sleep on the couch sometime around dawn.

He didn't wake until after noon. He pushed to the bedroom and peered inside, but she wasn't there. ''Keely?'' When he didn't get an answer, he checked both bathrooms.

In her private bathroom he found the ribbon in the trash; that sent an uneasiness skittering along his nerve endings. He took out the ribbon and laid it beside the sink, then went through the bedroom into the hall.

''Keely, where are you?'' Only an eerie stillness greeted him.

Slipping on his sweatpants and jacket, he pushed out to the driveway. Her car was no longer next to the van. He stared at the empty spot, trying to think where she might have gone. He'd expected her to sleep most of the day.

"Hello, Coach McCandless," a voice said.

The elderly woman, whose little dog often ran with Keely in the mornings, waved to him from the neighboring yard. Her son was on a ladder stringing Christmas lights around the eaves of the house while she directed him.

Mac nodded to the man, then told her, "Your decorations are going to be the hit of the neighborhood, Mrs. Martin."

She smiled. "I hope so. I do love this time of year."

"Mrs. Martin…did you happen to see Keely earlier?"

"Yes, I did. She was leaving as I was coming home from church."

"Did she mention where she was going?"

"Well, no. I didn't actually talk to her, just noticed her as she walked to her car."

"Okay, thanks. I guess she drove to the store for something."

He started to push back through the gate, but her call stopped him. "Oh, Coach McCandless, I don't believe she's coming back for a while."

His heart pounded wildly. Turning, he asked, "Why would you think that, Mrs. Martin?"

"Because she took a suitcase."

THE DOORBELL RANG as Liz Wilson was coming down the stairs. "I'll get it, Louise," she called out to the housekeeper. Everett had promised to take her to the park to see the lighting of the Christmas tree, and afterward they were going shopping for gifts.

Her smile of expectation changed to surprise when she opened the door and found, not Everett, but a pale, gaunt Keely standing there with a suitcase in her hand and desperation on her face.

"Keely?"

"Please don't turn me away, Mother. I don't have anywhere else to go."

CHAPTER EIGHTEEN

KEELY WIPED HER BREATH from the windowpane with the hem of her nightgown. After sleeping more than twenty-four hours, she still felt terrible. Sore. Depressed. The antics of the squirrel outside would have lightened her mood on any other day, but now she knew nothing would ever make her feel better. She'd lost everything.

The squirrel again scampered down the tree until it had nearly reached the ground, then stopped and scouted the backyard with quick jerks of its head. The object of its attack—the bird feeder—sat atop a four-foot post in the center of the garden, an easy climb for the hungry squirrel, except for the metal guard that ballooned like a skirt from the base of the feeder.

Unable to climb under or over the guard, the squirrel had resorted to a series of well-planned attacks that Keely had been watching for several minutes. He'd tried jumping on top of the feeder from the oak tree, only to smack the ground because the limb didn't reach quite far enough. He'd tried jumping at it from the patio table, only to hit the rim of the guard and bounce off.

This time he was trying a sprint-and-leap attack. So far it hadn't landed him where he wanted to be, but he'd shaken loose so many sunflower seeds with each attempt, he no doubt thought he was making progress.

He raised his head and looked around, apparently satisfied that neither the cat nor the yard man was around. He ran again and launched himself, sending the feeding sparrows to the air in a panic and hitting the squirrel guard with a loud thud. Keely shook her head as he slid, spread-eagled, down the guard.

Stupid squirrel. He didn't have enough sense to know when the odds were stacked too high against him. *Just like you,* her inner voice nagged. Too stupid to know when her career was over. Too stupid to know when to quit.

Her throat clogged and her eyes watered. *Why me?* Because a driver had been in too much of a hurry, her dreams had been taken away. The man had ruined her life. In return, he'd only lost his driver's license for a year. The unfairness of it still rankled.

She thought of Mac, who had lost so much more than dreams, and wondered if he hated the man who had shot him. No, unlike her, Mac didn't have the capacity for hate. He'd made the best of his situation, had even managed to use his disability to be a better coach. In every way that was important, he was a stronger person than he'd been before.

I can't waste my life grieving over lost dreams any more than I can waste my life grieving over being in this chair, he had once told her.

If only she could be like that. She didn't want to spend her life grieving over something that was beyond her power to keep, but how did she let go of what had always been so much a part of her? Without her career, she was only a husk. There was nothing inside of any substance or importance.

The squirrel was getting into position for another attack on the feeder, but Keely had grown tired of his antics. She banged on the glass and yelled, "Get out of here!" sending him scurrying up the tree and out of sight.

"Who on earth are you talking to?" her mother asked from the doorway. She walked into the bedroom accompanied by a whisper of silk.

"No one. Just scaring away some crazy squirrel trying to get the bird seed."

"Oh, that pesky thing. He's been at it for weeks."

"Aren't squirrels supposed to hibernate or something in the winter?"

"I have no idea. If they do, someone obviously forgot to tell him."

Liz put a tray on the nightstand and took a seat on the bed, her back ramrod straight, her hands folded just so in her lap, like the proper lady Grandmother Bradshaw had raised her to be. Regal was how Keely had always thought of her mother. Elegant. Beautiful. Unbending.

Had she ever looked like normal people? Even now, at nine in the morning, her hair was swept up in some fancy twist and her face was perfect, right down to the soft coral of her lipstick. The emerald-green dress looked like something out of the pages of a fashion magazine.

"Come eat," she said. "Louise made you a nice big plate of fruit. The strawberries and peaches aren't fresh, but the oranges are. Or there's bacon and toast if you'd rather have that.''

"I don't eat bacon," Keely said automatically, then realized the ridiculousness of it and sighed. She wasn't in training, would never be in training again, and could eat anything—bacon, chocolate, pizza loaded with cheese. All the unhealthy things everyone else ate that she'd given up.

"At least eat the fruit and toast," her mother prodded. "You haven't eaten anything since you got here yesterday, and you know that's not good for you. You need to rebuild your strength."

"For what?"

"Sweetheart, I know things are very difficult for you right now, but if you don't eat and you get sick, it won't make your problems any easier to deal with, now will it?"

"I'm really not hungry."

"I know, but humor me, please?"

Stifling her natural urge to continue arguing, Keely walked to the bed and sat with a repressed groan of pain, tucking her sore legs underneath her.

Her mother had taken her in when she could rightfully have slammed the door in her face. If eating a couple of strawberries would make her happy, then she'd eat a couple of strawberries.

She was determined to be nice, no matter what. And that meant no arguing. No smart remarks when her mother criticized her or tried to tell her what to do. And definitely no mentioning old what's-his-name.

She'd apologized for her recent rude behavior, an apology her mother had stiffly accepted, but Keely wasn't going to press her luck by bringing up the subject again. If her mother wanted to spend her life with Everett Lathom, it was her life. Keely wasn't going to say another word against him.

"Come downstairs for a while," her mother suggested. "You could read or watch television."

"No, I don't feel like it. I haven't even been able to work up the energy to get in the shower yet."

"Do you feel well enough to talk to Mac? He was frantic yesterday when I called to tell him you were here, and he's called several times since wanting to speak to you. He's terribly worried."

Keely threw her half-eaten strawberry on the plate, no longer able to even pretend hunger. She hadn't meant to worry him. When she'd opened her eyes yesterday morning, her first thought had been, *Time to get up and run.* Then she'd remembered she didn't have running to look forward to.

Overwhelmed by the reality of that, and by Mac's out-of-the-blue proposal of marriage, she'd gone a little insane. She'd thrown clothes in a suitcase and left, with no idea where she was going or what she would do, only that she had do *something.* She'd surprised her mother and herself when she'd arrived on Liz's doorstep.

"Is Mac all right?" Keely asked softly.

"He's upset you left so abruptly and without telling him where you were going, but he'll be okay, I think, once he's talked to you."

"I was thoughtless. I should have written him a note so he wouldn't worry."

"You've been through a terrible ordeal, and you're

not thinking straight right now. Mac understands that.''

''Has he called this morning?''

''Four times. He wanted to drive up here, but I convinced him not to do anything until he's talked with you.''

Keely closed her eyes briefly and said a prayer of thanks. No way could she deal with him in person. Talking to him on the phone would be hard enough. He'd ask when she was coming back—and she didn't know. He'd ask what she was going to do with the rest of her miserable life—and she didn't know that, either.

''I feel so…'' She felt the sting of tears and lowered her gaze, chastising herself again for being such a mess.

''So what, sweetheart? Tell me what you feel.''

''You wouldn't understand.''

''Oh, I think I might.'' She smoothed Keely's hair from her face, a motherly gesture Keely normally disliked but endured. Today it felt almost…nice. ''You feel empty, like someone pulled the plug and all the important parts of you simply drained out. Your determination, your strength, your optimism, all the things that have always kept you going when life got tough suddenly don't seem to be there anymore, and it scares you.''

That was exactly how she felt, but how had her mother known? ''What do I do about it?'' she asked.

''You cry. You rail over the injustice of what's happened and wallow in self-pity for a few days because you've earned the right. Then, when your head's clearer and you realize you're *not* really empty, you'll be able to take the next step."

"What?"

"Deciding what makes you happy. And going after it with all your heart."

THE BOLT SLIPPED from Mac's hand and hit the concrete floor, bouncing under the workbench where he and Alan were trying to repair Alan's racer. Mac threw down the wrench, and in an uncharacteristic display of temper, vented his frustration over his separation from Keely by throwing the heavy roll of tape across the garage...then the spoke wrench...then the pry bar.

"Missed this one." Alan handed him the rubber mallet without so much as blinking. Mac threw it, too, hitting the waist-high rack where Alan had stored his lawn tools and garden hoses for the winter, making the hoses uncurl and writhe across the floor like snakes. A split second later, the rack itself crashed down. Tools flew everywhere.

Vicki appeared in the doorway before the echo of the clatter died down. "What is going on out here? I'd swear we're in the middle of a war zone." She surveyed the damage with a surprised, "Oh!"

"The rack fell," Alan said casually. "Go on back to the house and we'll take care of it. Too cold out here for you."

She looked at Alan with narrow-eyed suspicion, then at Mac, then back at Alan.

Mac waited for her to scold them both for the mess. But as if communicating with Alan by telepathy, she grasped that this wasn't the time to be scolding. With a quick compassionate glance at Mac but not a word, she walked back into the house.

"How many years does it take before you can read each other's minds like that?" Mac asked.

"More than I want to count." Alan took two beers from the cooler and handed them to Mac for opening, his dexterity limited to less difficult tasks. Alan could write, eat and do almost every other chore with the help of adaptive devices, but the simple ability to get his finger in a pull tab and manipulate it eluded him.

Mac opened the beers and handed one back, then took a swallow of his own and apologized for his lack of restraint. His anger had fizzled, but the dull throb of frustration remained. "I've been like dynamite ready to explode ever since Keely took off. I guess it's a miracle I haven't blown before now, the way I feel."

"You look bad, too."

Mac rubbed his jaw, darkened by a four-day growth of beard. "J.P. asked if I'd been eating dirt."

Alan chuckled. "That's because his face resembles that after he's been eating dirt. He recognized the look."

"You ought to feed the kid real food, Alan."

"Why, when it's so much cheaper for him to forage in the neighborhood and dig up his meals?"

Mac laughed despite his bad mood. This was what he'd needed for days, a heavy dose of Alan Sizemore and a chance to let off some steam.

They pushed to the wall and began picking up the fallen tools, deciding to wait until some other time to rehang the rack. "So tell me," Alan said, "did you get bad news from Keely or have you gotten all worked up like this just for fun?''

''*You* tell me if it's justified,'' Mac said, passing over the hedge trimmers. ''I've only talked to her directly once, and that was for about one minute. All the other times I've called, she's either been asleep or doesn't feel like coming to the phone. I've had more of a relationship with her mother the past four days than I have with Keely.''

''You going up there?''

''I want to, but she made me promise not to, says she needs some time alone to think and she can't think with me there. I don't even know what that means. How would I stop her from thinking?''

Alan offered no explanation.

''Then, and this really worries me, when I asked her when she thought she might be coming home, she started to cry. She wouldn't give me a straight answer about the plans we made to spend the holidays together, begged me not to press her, and right after that, she suddenly decided she had to get off the phone. She said talking to me only makes her feel worse.''

''Ah, man, I'm sorry.''

''See what I'm up against? I feel like I'm banging my head against a brick wall.''

He forced down the hot lump of pain beginning to rise in his throat. He'd really been looking forward to spending Christmas with Keely, had already told Christine and Megan not to expect him to fly to California this year because he had other plans.

Keely had been looking forward to it, too, or so he'd thought. ''We'll buy a tree and decorate your house and have a Christmas with all the trimmings," she'd suggested a few weeks ago.

Amazing how your life could go from terrific to desolate in a matter of hours.

"Has she given you any idea what she'll do now that she can't run?" Alan asked.

"No, and I'm afraid to push her about it, because she's so messed up right now. I don't want to urge her to finish school and coach if that's not what she really wants to do."

"But I thought you wanted her to coach. Wasn't that the whole idea of getting her back in school?"

"I *do* want her to coach, because I think she's got a natural talent for working with people, but as long as she's happy, it doesn't matter to me what she does. The decision is hers to make and I'll support her in whatever she decides."

"What if she decides on something that takes her out of Courtland? What will you do then?"

That was a question Mac had thought about constantly the last few days. He wanted to be part of her life, and if she wanted that, too, he would go wherever he had to go to be with her, even if it meant giving up his job.

"I'll deal with that problem when or if it happens. Right now I can't even get her to talk to me or return my phone calls. We don't seem to have a future." He took a ragged breath and ran a hand roughly through his hair. "I asked her to marry me the other day, Alan, and she just stared at me in horror like I'd lost my mind."

"Hell."

"Then she ran away in the middle of the night. I have to believe she loves me, but I can't understand why she wouldn't want to be with me when she's feeling so bad. Does it make sense to you?"

"She's a woman. Women aren't designed to make sense. I've been married to Vicki for seventeen years, and she still sometimes does the opposite of what I think she'll do. Women are built to confuse men. It's in their genes or something."

"I don't understand Keely at all. Our physical relationship is good. Her running isn't a barrier anymore to our being together. But the minute I proposed, she took off like a scalded cat. I don't get it. Have I fooled myself into believing she cares for me?"

"Nah, man, don't start thinking like that. She has a lot on her plate right now. Sounds to me like she just needs time to sort things out."

"I know, but I hate the idea of her up there in Atlanta, suffering. I should be there. Or she should be here where she belongs."

"I wouldn't worry. She's got her mom to help her if she needs it, and there still must be some feeling between the two of them, or Keely wouldn't have gone to her in the first place."

True. Maybe mother and daughter could find a way to resolve the years of pain that separated them.

"She's tough," Alan said. "If anybody can get through this, it's Keely."

Mac nodded, remembering how courageous she'd been during her running trial, the way she'd held on even when she was in so much pain and knew she couldn't make it. She'd given it everything she had, gone after her dream despite the incredible odds against her.

He almost felt shamed by her courage. She had so much of it. And he had so little.

"Alan, do you still get angry about what happened to you? Your accident, I mean."

His friend registered surprise at the question. Mulling it over a few seconds, he shrugged and said, "I guess so. Not as much as I used to, but yeah, I still get angry. I guess it comes with the wheels. You know, a package deal—wheelchair, anger, depression, insecurity."

"Insecurity? You? You're the most secure person I know. Nothing gets to you."

"Don't bet on it." He narrowed his gaze. "Why did you ask me that?"

"No particular reason." Taking a long swallow to finish his beer, he crumpled the can and sent it sailing toward the trash. "I hate to bug out on you, but if you don't need that racer right away, I think I'm going to head on home. I haven't slept much the last few days and I'm dead."

"I'm in no hurry."

"Then I'll see you later." Mac hesitated and added, "Thanks for letting me bend your ear tonight. Being able to talk helped."

"Sure. Anytime." As Mac rolled to the door, Alan called, "Cheer up, buddy. This thing with Keely will work out. And hey, shave in the morning, will ya? You're ugly enough without that all over your face."

Mac pushed across the street, smiling. The telephone was ringing as he got in and he snatched it up.

"Keely?" But it was only a salesman wanting him to switch long-distance telephone services.

He took a quick shower and went to bed, but the moment his head hit the pillow, he started feeling depressed again. He missed Keely's warmth, the way she held him and sighed contentedly in her sleep, the way she often awoke in the morning, her eyes heavy-lidded with desire. He loved to put that soft purr in her throat.

Although the sheets had been washed since she'd slept beside him and it had been weeks since she'd even been in his house, he imagined he could smell her sweet scent in the room.

He picked up the phone and called her, but Liz said she'd already gone to bed. "I'm sorry, Mac. She dropped off to sleep a couple of hours ago."

He muttered a curse under his breath, feeling both disappointment and anger. He had an overwhelming need to talk to her tonight, to reassure himself that everything between them was okay.

Okay? Who was he kidding? Nothing was okay. Nothing was even close to okay. She'd made that clear when she'd run away. She made it clear every time she refused to talk to him or return his calls. The last thing she wanted to do was spend her life with him.

"Let me wake her," Liz said.

He rubbed his tired eyes. "No, don't bother."

"Then let me give her a message first thing in the morning. What would you like to tell her?"

Tell her I'm going insane without her and I want her to come home. Tell her I love her.

"Just...that I won't call again. Obviously she

doesn't want to talk to me. If she decides she does, she knows where I am.''

''I'm so sorry, Mac.''

''Yeah, Liz, I'm sorry, too.''

After he'd hung up, he tried to sleep but couldn't. Was it possible for a man to be addicted to a woman? Because that was what this felt like. An addiction. And the pain of withdrawal was excruciating.

HIS WEEK WENT from bad to worse the next afternoon when Coach Stewart visited his office.

''Are you telling me Doug Crocker gave this kid Falcon tickets and spending money?'' he asked her, bile rising in his throat.

Laura Stewart turned her palms upward in a gesture of uncertainty. ''I don't know if it's true, but that's what I heard. This supposedly happened weeks ago, so maybe it's only a rumor. But I thought you should know before it got outside the department.''

He felt sweat pop out on his brow as he mentally weighed the consequences if these allegations were true.

Giving gifts to athletes you were trying to recruit was a violation of National Collegiate Athletic Association rules. The track program could face sanctions, probation, fines, a loss of scholarships. Mac would have ample reason to fire Crocker, but he himself might face a reprimand or be fired or demoted by the administration, even though he had no knowledge of Crocker's actions.

''Lack of Institutional Control,'' the NCAA called it, and he'd seen more than one good athletic director lose his job because of the improper actions of someone beneath him. If the association decided a violation was severe, it could result in the dreaded "Death Penalty," the termination of a program.

But he was getting ahead of himself here. As much as he disliked Crocker, he wouldn't judge him on gossip. He needed more information.

"Someone might be trying to cause trouble for Doug," Laura said, reflecting Mac's thoughts. "You know he's not the most popular person around here because of the way he acts and the things he says about…" She hesitated and flushed red.

"For the things he says about me behind my back?"

"Yes."

"I'm aware of what he says, Laura."

"I don't think a single person in the department would regret seeing him gone, but I hope he didn't do it. If he did, we're all going to suffer for it."

"I'll launch an internal investigation right away. I don't want to make any hasty judgments and ruin a man's career over some locker-room gossip. In the meantime, let's keep a lid on this. The staff doesn't need to be spreading it around."

"I'll do whatever I can to help you."

After getting all the information Laura had, he dismissed her and got on the intercom to Miriam. "Angel, I need you." She was in his office in an instant. "Where's Coach Crocker?"

"Left early. He'll be back Monday morning."

Monday. That was good. That gave Mac the weekend to check out the story and know what he was dealing with.

"What's on my schedule Monday?"

"You have a nine o'clock appointment with Mr. Hartselle from Hartselle Racers to discuss sponsoring the wheelers, but the rest of the day is open."

"I want Doug here waiting when I get out of that meeting. No excuses from him. Whatever else he has, tell him to cancel it."

Rusty Adair, responsible for the university's compliance with NCAA rules, also needed to be in on this, whatever it turned out to be. Mac told her to locate him immediately.

"I'll take care of it."

"Also, look up the number for a kid we're trying to recruit by the name of Willie Jackson, and see if you can get him on the phone for me. He lives with his grandmother in Carrolton. Ida Mae Jackson, I think her name is. The info should be in his file."

"Anything else?"

"Find me a couple of aspirins before my head falls off." He rubbed his throbbing temples and imagined his track program being destroyed because of the stupidity of Doug Crocker. Or maybe it was his *own* stupidity for not facing the demons that had haunted him since the shooting. "Hey, Miriam, better bring the aspirin bottle and leave it here."

CHAPTER NINETEEN

SOMETHING WOKE HER. Keely wasn't sure if it was the rain pounding on the window or something else. The erotic dream still clung to her like a mist, leaving her groggily aroused and her body damp with sweat. For a moment she lay suspended between the dream and reality, not understanding they were separate. She could feel his lips on her breasts and the excruciating pleasure of his hand between her legs, could smell the musky odor of sex on the sheets.

"Mac," she whispered to her phantom lover, but lightning suddenly illuminated the darkness and the empty bed beside her, thrusting her unwillingly toward reality. Mac wasn't here. She was alone.

Happiness gave way to emptiness.

Abruptly she sat up. She turned on the light next to the bed to make the frightening shadows in the room disappear. The clock showed eleven-forty. Mac would be asleep by now, his mouth a little open, a muscled forearm across his eyes. He snored slightly sometimes when he slept on his back, but she found odd comfort in the sound. She missed it now. Missed him.

Perhaps that was what had caused her to wake—the absence of that lulling snore and Mac's arm around her. With him she felt safe from the terror that skulked in the darkness, the one that wore the mask of death.

No, not death. The evil thing that disturbed her nights wasn't death, as she had once believed. Loneliness was its name. At night she was more vulnerable, and the loneliness closed in on her.

She picked up the telephone to call Mac, then quickly put it down. Picked it up again, only to put it back. With a cry of frustration she fell back on the bed.

This longing inside her was too much to bear. She'd never needed anyone like this, never *allowed* herself to need someone so badly. Even though she knew she had no choice but to give him up, she didn't want to.

She had deceived herself into believing she could make a life with Mac, but she was too much like her mother to succeed. Controlling. Self-centered. And Mac, dear sweet Mac, was an open generous person like her father had been. Marriage between them would be a grave mistake, just like marriage between her mother and father had been a mistake. Their differences would eventually tear them apart.

She had no skills, no talent. The invention of her InsuCare fabric, the only good thing she'd done outside of running, had been a fluke. She hadn't set out to create a medical product and save lives. Oh, no, she wasn't that noble. Her goal had been something as frivolous as exercise clothes.

She was worthless now that she couldn't run. What could she possibly offer Mac that some other woman couldn't? Nothing. Absolutely nothing.

Knowing sleep would elude her, she slipped on a

robe and quietly descended the stairs on her way to the kitchen for something to drink. It was quiet except for the occasional rumble of thunder and the ticking of the grandfather clock at the end of the hall. The housekeeper had retired hours earlier to her rooms at the back of the house. And Keely's mother had never been one to stay up late.

But someone was up. The doorway to the den expelled a pale flickering light. Keely walked toward it but stopped short at the sound of a feminine giggle and a man's voice.

"Mmm, that feels so good," the man said. "A little lower and to the… Hey, watch it. You promised no tickling."

"I lied. I love to watch you squirm."

"Oh, yeah? Well, let's see *you* squirm, Miss Prissy Pants."

The sound of a scuffle and more giggling echoed down the dark hall. Keely eased forward until she could see their reflections in the mirror just inside the den. Everett Lathom had her mother pinned to the couch and was tickling her unmercifully. Her hair, always up and tidy, was down and spilled over the cushion, and she had discarded her silk for a pair of jeans and a simple white shirt. Her feet were bare.

Jeans? Bare feet? Keely had never seen her dressed so casually. And the two of them were fooling around like a couple of giddy teenagers in love.

"No more, no more, please," her mother begged.

"Do you give?"

"I give." Instead of turning her loose, he kissed her long and hard. She put her arms around his neck.

"Yes, I definitely give. Have I told you today how much I love you?"

"About fifty times, but tell me again."

He laughed as she placed countless kisses across his face and told him she loved him with every one. "Promise me you'll tell me that every day of our married lives."

"That's an easy promise to keep, Everett. I only wish we were getting married tomorrow so I could start."

"We can, you know. All you have to do is say the word. I already have the marriage license and we've taken our blood tests."

"Very tempting, but I want to do this marriage right, with our children and our friends there to bless it. I've never had a real wedding. Spence and I eloped because we were young and foolish, and because my parents didn't approve of me marrying an insurance salesman. I want a real wedding with you. A long dress, flowers, someone singing 'Oh Promise Me.' A storybook wedding. I've dreamed of it."

"Then you'll get it, my love. Whatever makes you happy. I intend to spend the rest of my life pleasing you."

Keely stepped back where she could no longer see, feeling like a voyeur. The moment had been unmistakably tender. To see her mother as a woman with hopes and desires, to hear her dream of a special wedding with the man she loved—it made Keely feel strange, disoriented.

"Are you sure Keely's asleep?" Lathom asked. "She hates me enough without catching me making out with her mother.'' More kissing noises and murmurs of pleasure reached Keely's ears.

"She was when I peeked in on her a little while ago. And she doesn't hate you."

"She gives a pretty good imitation."

Her mother sighed loudly. "I know. At times I want to throttle her for the things she says and does, but she can't help herself. She sees our marriage as a betrayal of her father. If she accepted you, that would simply make the betrayal worse in her mind."

"You're making excuses for her again. She's a grown woman and she should be acting like one."

"I'm not making excuses. I know she behaves badly sometimes. But underneath that defensive exterior is a sweet generous woman with a great capacity for love. She's had a difficult life, Everett. All the fighting that went on in this house when she was growing up would have scarred any child. She's never had the emotional security your children had. She has a hard time expressing affection to me because of that."

Keely, touched by her mother's defense of her, felt a warmth spread through her body.

"Darling," Liz continued, "I'm positive that if the two of you got to know each other better, you'd be friends. You really have so much in common. Maybe if you'd spend some time with her while she's here, you—"

"No. We've already been through this. Every attempt I've made to get along with her she's thrown back in my face. For your sake I'll tolerate her, but I won't go out of my way to see her or be nice to her.

She's made it clear she doesn't want anything to do with me.''

With another huge sigh and acceptance of defeat, her mother said, ''All right. I can't say I blame you.''

''How's this week been with the two of you cooped up together? Every night when I get here, I expect to find one of you murdered.''

Every night? So that was why Keely hadn't seen him. He was waiting until she went to bed and then sneaking into the house.

''The week's been surprisingly nice,'' her mother told him. ''She's trying so hard not to get in the way or do anything to upset me.''

''Because she doesn't want to derail the gravy train and have you kick her out.''

''Now, that's not true. For the first time I believe she truly wants us to get along and put the past behind us.''

''You're kidding yourself, Liz. She treats you with contempt. If one of my daughters had talked to me the way yours talked to you the night we told her we were getting married, I'd have put her over my knee and spanked the living daylights out of her, regardless of how old she is.''

''She apologized.''

''Only because it was to her *advantage* to apologize so she could stay here,'' he said shortly. ''I'll bet you money it wasn't because she was really sorry about hurting your feelings. Has she even once wished you happiness? Has she even once said, 'Mother, I might not agree with your marriage, but I love you and I'll support your decision'? Whether or not she likes me, she should support your getting married again. But she's too busy thinking of herself to see how her attitude is ruining our plans.''

In the deafening silence that followed his speech, Keely raised a hand to her throat, feeling a tightness there. His words held a disturbing ring of truth. She'd never said those things to her mother, never even *thought* to say those things.

Guilty as charged.

''You don't think she loves me and wants me to be happy?'' A hitch in her mother's voice signaled that tears were imminent. ''Just because she doesn't say it doesn't mean—''

''Oh, honey, no, please don't cry. I didn't mean she doesn't love you. Of course she does. I guess it's like you said. She doesn't know how to tell you what she feels.''

''I love her so much. She means everything in the world to me.''

''I know she does. Please don't get upset.''

''I want the three of us to be a family.''

''We can. I promise I'll try again with her. Please don't cry.''

Lathom tried to quiet the flood without success. Keely's own tears coursed down her face, and she covered her mouth with her hand so the couple wouldn't hear her. She hadn't realized the hurt she'd caused her mother, not only over her impending marriage, but over so many things. As Lathom said, she'd been concerned only with her own feelings.

She backed away and fled to her room, burying her face in the pillow to muffle her tears.

How had things grown so out of whack? As a small child, she and her mother had been close. Nothing had been as comforting after a nightmare or a fall from the swing as putting her head in her mother's lap and feeling that soft hand on her back, to hear her mother say that everything was going to be all right. Her mother's attention had made her feel safe, cherished.

But as she'd grown older, she'd become increasingly less comfortable with Liz's mothering, seen it more as an attempt to orchestrate her life than an expression of love. She'd grown closer to her father. He had never tried to tether her independence, but told her to take risks and follow her heart. He'd encouraged her to resist her mother's control.

And she had. As *he* had resisted it.

She braced herself against the sudden storm of unpleasant memories—of lying awake in this very bed listening to her parents fight in the next room. The worst part had been waiting for the inevitable slamming of the bedroom door and the pounding of her father's footsteps as he angrily marched down the stairs and left the house. Each time she'd been afraid he wouldn't come back.

She'd tried to be good so that wouldn't happen. She'd openly adored her father, tried to be like him. But perhaps she'd taken her struggle for independence from her mother a little too far, needlessly alienating herself from someone who had once been very important to her.

The thought suddenly occurred to Keely that by coming here she might be seeking something she had once treasured, perhaps even needed in her life again—a close relationship with her mother. Only, to have that meant forgiving her mother for the anger and pain her sometimes overbearing ways had caused during the past twenty-five years. *Could* she forgive her? She wanted to so badly. Was it possible to wipe away all the hurt and all the bad memories?

Keely closed her eyes and tried to sort out her feelings, but dawn found her still awake and no closer to the answers she was seeking.

LIZ WALKED INTO THE KITCHEN the next morning to find Keely already dressed and eating one of Louise's orange muffins at the table. For the first time this week she hadn't had to physically pull her daughter out of bed and force her to get dressed.

"Are you all right?"

"Mmm-hmm."

"What are you doing up so early?"

Keely shrugged and slouched in the chair. "I just woke up early and couldn't go back to sleep."

She sounded normal enough, although she'd obviously been crying again. Her eyes were red, as was the tip of her nose. Liz longed to hug her but feared rejection. An occasional touch was all Keely ever allowed. Even then she sometimes stiffened.

"I'm on my way to Sunday School and church," Liz told her. "Would you like to come with me?"

"No, thanks."

"Please don't mope around all day. You've been here over a week and you haven't left the house. Take a walk or sit outside in the garden."

"Well, actually..." She straightened and picked

with nervous fingers at her muffin. Two bright spots of color appeared on her cheeks. "I thought I might get the Christmas stuff down from the attic. I could put up the tree and we could decorate it together when you get home. That is, if you want some help."

The offer made Liz stop in the middle of putting on her coat. Decorate the tree? Had she said *together*? That had always been Keely and Spence's job. After Spence moved out, Liz had done it alone because Keely either wasn't here for Christmas or avoided doing anything with her.

She slid the other arm into her coat and reached for her purse. "That would be wonderful," she told Keely, careful not to act too excited. If she made a fuss, she had no doubt her daughter would withdraw the offer. "I'll see you in a little while."

"Okay, I'll get everything ready while you're gone."

ACCESS TO THE ATTIC was through a set of narrow stairs in the closet of the master bedroom. An unusual place for stairs, Keely had always thought, but as a child she'd loved the idea of having a "secret" room with a hidden entrance. She'd often come here. Creaking noises and shadowed corners hadn't frightened her then, and only added to the room's appeal.

She opened the door at the top of the stairs. When she stepped into the unheated space, a blast of frigid air hit her and almost sent her scurrying back downstairs for a jacket.

She pulled the string to turn on the overhead bulb, revealing a junk lover's paradise of castaway furniture, toys, old hiking gear and boxes upon boxes of what turned out to be clothes sprinkled liberally with moth-balls.

Sorting through the clutter wasn't hard, but resisting the treasures among it proved impossible. Each piece of clothing she pulled out and examined brought back a memory: the boots she'd used hiking with Daddy in the mountains in north Georgia, the gown she'd worn to the only high-school dance she'd ever attended, an Easter bonnet from when she was six. She lingered over each article and each memory.

The wardrobe contained some of her father's old suit jackets, and she slipped one on against the chill. The fabric smelled faintly of cedar from the wardrobe and of the cigars her father had enjoyed. Pleasant smells. Pleasant memories.

The rhinestone tiara she'd worn for Halloween when she'd dressed as Cinderella's fairy godmother was lying on top of some costumes in a nearby box. She put it on, then picked up the accompanying magic wand and waved it in the air, in her mind's eye seeing a pumpkin turn into a coach. Foolishness, but it was nice to remember that not all of her childhood had been bad.

A stack of boxes next to the wardrobe had "Keely" written on the cardboard, and a peek inside the top carton revealed Barbie dolls, doll clothes, and the horse figurines she'd developed a passion for collecting one year.

Shaking off the dust from the cardboard flaps, she carried the box to the center of the room and sat down to go through it.

A wistful smile curved her lips when she took out one of the horses. She'd once so loved to play with these. But then she'd starting running and hadn't had time for play. Her father had said that if she wanted to be the best runner in the world, she needed to practice all the time and give up her silly horses. Because she wanted to be the best, because she wanted to please him, she had put the horses, her dolls, all her toys away.

No distractions, kitten. You have to put your whole heart into your running.

She was still on the floor, surrounded by the pieces of her childhood, when her mother climbed the stairs some time later.

"You're back early," Keely said, noticing she'd changed out of her dress and into a pair of slacks and matching sweater.

"The worship service was brief today." Liz rubbed her arms and shivered. "It's freezing up here! I see you got the tree put together in the den. Did you find the decorations?"

"Not yet. I found these and forgot about the decorations." She picked up one of the horses and showed it to her. "Remember when I went through that horse craze?"

Her mother took the horse and turned it over in her hands. "How could I forget? For a whole summer you lived in cowboy boots and jeans, and you wore that awful straw hat everywhere."

"And I begged for a real horse, thinking we could keep it in the backyard."

They both chuckled.

Her mother looked at the oversize jacket Keely was wearing. "Nice outfit, but I don't think the tiara is really you. A little too gaudy."

"I forgot I was wearing it," Keely said with a laugh, touching her head.

To her astonishment her mother sat down next to her, apparently unconcerned about the dirty floor, and together they looked through the figurines. Keely found one of polished wood and only about two inches tall, an intricately carved horse with a female rider. She held it up for her mother to see.

"This was always my favorite. I liked to pretend that was me on the back of the horse."

"It's beautiful."

"Maybe it's not too late for me to be a cowgirl."

Her mother smiled. "I'm glad to see your sense of humor returning. Being able to laugh at yourself will help you get past the hurt."

"I don't have much choice but to laugh at myself. Crying about it hasn't changed anything."

"You know, it might not be a bad idea for you to talk to Ross and tell him what's happened. He needs to know you're not going to be running so he can advise you on what to do."

"I already have an idea what he'll advise me to do. I've had some offers."

"Oh?"

"They came in after I got hurt, before I knew I'd have to retire. I didn't take them seriously at the time, but I'm sure Ross will want me to consider them now—if they're still available."

"What kind of offers?"

"A couple of endorsements for television commercials and print ads. One's for a soft-drink company. The other is modeling underwear. And a job with ABC Sports."

"Underwear?" Her mother's surprise turned to amusement. "Somebody wants *you* to model underwear? Do they realize you have an aversion to underwear?"

Keely's lips twitched. "I guess it is pretty ironic."

"What's the sports job?"

"Doing commentary and interviewing competitors for track events and for the Olympics in Sydney. The offer's good. Nice pay. I'd be traveling all over the world between now and then, visiting the athletes in their hometowns and putting together reports on their training. Most people would kill for the opportunity."

"Are you considering it?" Her mother's look said she hoped not.

"I probably should, but it's just not right for me. I'd planned to compete in the next Olympics, not sit in a commentator's booth and talk about who's competing. I'm not a broadcaster or an underwear model or a soft-drink hawker. I'm an athlete." With a humorless smile she added, "At least in my heart I still am."

"Have you given any thought to what you'll do?"

"A little bit but I haven't made any decisions yet."

"Why not get more involved in your company?"

"I've considered that, but I don't have any business experience. I balance my checkbook, and that's it. Ross handles everything else." She began putting the horses and dolls back in the box with her mother's help.

"It's never too late to learn, Keely."

"I suppose that's true."

"And what about Mac? The man's in love with you, and unless I've completely misread the situation, you're in love with him. You have to include him in any plans you make."

"Do I?"

"Yes, of course you do."

Keely just shrugged, not commenting.

"Sweetheart, it *is* possible for a man and woman to have a healthy lasting relationship. Just because your father and I couldn't make our marriage work doesn't mean that all marriages fail or that marriage brings unhappiness. You do understand that, don't you?"

"Yes."

"Do you? Then why are you here when the man who adores you is hundreds of miles away?"

Keely shook her head. "Maybe because I haven't figured out yet how our being together could work. We're such opposites."

Her mother squeezed her arm. "You'll figure it out. Stop looking at it with your head and see it with your heart."

"Okay, I'll try." Keely closed the box, had a thought and opened it again. She took out the miniature carved horse. "Can I keep this one? Gran gave it to me, and except for the jewelry she left me when she died, I don't have anything that reminds me of her."

"Of course you can keep it. It's yours. Keep all of

them if you want and the dolls, too, if you have a use for them.''

Keely put the horse in her pocket. Her hand touched paper, and she pulled it out and unfolded it.

''Maybe the children of that friend of yours would like them,'' her mother was saying. ''What's her name? Nicki something?''

''Vicki Sizemore.''

''Didn't you tell me she had two or three children? We could pack these up and send them to her.''

Her mother's voice seemed to come from far away. The blood had drained from Keely's head, making it impossible to think clearly or even respond. Her attention wasn't on the dolls but on the handwritten note she'd found in her father's jacket. She read it a second time, because her mind refused to accept what it said.

Spencer, darling, I can't wait another minute to see you. Eight tonight. I've reserved our usual room. The wine will be room temperature but I'll be very, very hot. I love you.

Your wicked Angela.

Stunned, Keely could only sit there and stare at the paper, trying to reconcile the apparent adulterer with the sweet loving man who was her father. Her heart said he could never have been so deceitful, yet reason told her she held the damning evidence in her hand.

''Sweetheart, what's wrong? You're white as a sheet.''

Keely's body began to shake uncontrollably. No, it was all a mistake. Her father wasn't capable of this.

"Keely?" Panic threaded her mother's voice. "What have you found?"

Keely looked up to find herself staring into a face as white as her own. "Nothing. Nothing…really." Her mother reached for the paper, but Keely crumpled it. "Only trash," she said, but her shaking, the warble of her voice, revealed the lie.

"Keely, give it to me."

"No, Mother. Don't read it."

"Give it to me." She pried the letter from Keely's fist.

"Please, don't read it."

But she did. And when she did, her eyes closed briefly and her body seemed to sag with the weight of the discovery. The letter slipped from her hand onto the floor. "Oh, no," she whispered so softly Keely had to strain to hear her. "I thought I'd burned all the letters years ago."

"You knew about his relationship with this woman?"

Then it had to be true. Her father had had an affair! In an instant, years of respect, love and pride for him turned to disillusionment.

No! *This* was what had broken apart their marriage. *He* had destroyed their family. Not her mother!

With painful clarity she remembered the many times she'd taken her father's side against her mother, times when he'd come in late from "working" and her mother had been furious. She remembered the many times she and her father had excluded her mother intentionally by choosing activities she didn't like—the ball games, the hiking trips—and left her to sit home alone. And Keely had let her mother know she preferred to be in her father's company.

How that must have hurt her.

A sob tore from her throat. The room began to spin and her breakfast started to come up. "I think I'm going to be sick."

Her mother was kneeling next to her in a second, pushing her head down. "Put your head as low as you can and take deep breaths."

"I didn't understand!" Keely cried, the tears pouring from her eyes. "I've been so hateful to you about the divorce because I thought it was your fault, but all the time it was him who wrecked everything. I'm so sorry. I'm so very sorry."

"Hush, now. Don't talk. Just close your eyes and take deep breaths."

Several minutes passed before Keely felt well enough to sit up. Unable to stand the touch of her father's jacket, she pulled it off and threw it on the floor. "I hate him!"

"No, you don't hate him. He was a human being who made mistakes. And regardless of how he felt about me or our marriage, he loved you."

"Was he in love with *her?*" The question took all of Keely's courage to ask.

"You don't want to know about this," her mother said, brushing the hair back from Keely's face. "Knowing will only hurt you. And it happened such a long time ago. The best thing is to accept that it happened and then put it behind you."

"I couldn't hurt any more than I'm hurting right now."

"Yes, you can, and I've tried so hard to protect you from it. You'd be better off not knowing the details."

"No, don't protect me anymore. I need to know what happened. All this time I believed the problems between you and Daddy were your fault. I've blamed you for everything. For the fights. The divorce."

Her mother's tears began to fall now, leaving streaks on her cheeks and dark mascara smudges under her eyes. "I know you have, and it ripped me apart."

"Please, tell me the truth. Did he love this woman?"

An ominous silence stretched between them and Keely held her breath. At last her mother spoke. "No, he didn't love her. I don't think he ever really loved any of them."

CHAPTER TWENTY

"IT'S WAY TOO QUIET in there," Alan said, straining to hear the muffled voices through the closed door of Mac's office. For the past forty-five minutes the level of the conversation had gone up and down. At the moment it was low, but Alan wasn't sure if that was a good sign or a bad one. He pushed to Miriam's desk. "Buzz him and pretend he has a call or something. Maybe you can hear what they're talking about."

She gave him one of her not-on-your-life looks.

"What'll it hurt? Buzz him and say I dropped by to take him to lunch. See if you can tell what kind of mood he's in, at least." Miriam didn't seem to be softening, so he leaned toward her and added with his most engaging grin, "Come on, beautiful, you know you're just as curious as I am about what's happening in there."

"Mac gave me strict instructions that he wasn't to be disturbed on the intercom or in person for any reason—so shoo." She waved him back. "And don't think you can bat those long eyelashes and get your way with me, Dr. Sizemore. I'm wise to your tricks."

"Oh, doll, you wound me. If only I *could* get my way with you, I'd be the happiest man on earth."

She scolded him for being an outrageous flirt but

couldn't quite hide her amusement. "I don't know how your wife puts up with your antics."

"I'm so cute she can't help herself." That made her chuckle so he pressed his advantage. "Okay, buzzing him is a bad idea, but can't you tell me what's going on and who the third person is? I recognize Crocker's voice but not the other guy's. Is Mac firing Crocker? What did he do?"

"What Mac wants you to know, I'm sure Mac will tell you."

"Aw, Miriam, you're killing me."

"Don't 'aw, Miriam' me. I honestly don't know what Coach Crocker did, and even if I did know, I couldn't say a word. Mac would have my hide."

"He didn't tell you anything?"

"Not a hint, but I've never seen him in such a black mood as he's been in during the past week."

"That's not all work-related."

"I guessed that, since I haven't seen a certain young lady around here lately, but I don't pry into Mac's personal life. There's enough gossip about the two of them in this department without me adding to it."

"Crocker-initiated gossip?"

"Uh-huh."

"Figures."

Alan scratched his jaw. What *was* going on? Mac had taken a mysterious business trip out of town on Saturday, canceling their plans to work out together. When Alan had asked him about the trip and if something other than Keely had him so on edge, he'd said it was a problem with one of his coaches and he'd tell him about it later.

Alan didn't have to wonder who the coach was, but he was curious about what that coach had done. And he was itching to know what Mac planned to do about him.

The volume of the voices on the other side of the door escalated again, this time to an alarming level. Crocker's angry voice rang out.

"You can't fire me! I've given seventeen years of my life to this place!"

Mac's calm response was too low to hear, but Crocker told Mac loudly what he thought of him, his speech sprinkled with expletives and accusations of unfair treatment. The verbal attack brought the third man into the dispute; he warned Crocker repeatedly to "back off and sit down."

Alan and Miriam looked at each other in concern. "This is getting way out of hand," Alan told her. He pushed toward the door.

Miriam jumped up and blocked his way with her considerable bulk. "Don't even *think* about going in there, buster."

"But Mac might need my help."

"He's capable of taking care of himself."

"Yeah, but—"

"No buts. You're not going in there."

From Mac's office they heard the sound of a scuffle. A split second later someone yelped in pain.

Miriam's confidence wavered and she whirled and reached for the knob. Before she could open the door, Crocker opened it from the other side and barreled out. Miriam, knocked backward by his hasty exit, landed in Alan's lap with the force of a cannonball being fired. She pressed the breath right out of him, along with his voice.

Mac pushed through the door right behind Crocker, followed by the third man from the office, Rusty Adair, Mac's rules-compliance officer. Both jolted to a stop at the sight of Miriam sprawled in Alan's lap.

"Miriam? Alan? What the…?" Mac asked.

Before Alan could answer, Miriam gasped in horror. "Mac, you're bleeding!" She leaped to her feet and rushed over, trying to find the source of the blood.

Alan saw big splotches of it down the front of Mac's white shirt, blood and red marks on his neck, but no wounds. "Buddy, you okay?"

"Yeah, I'm okay." Mac gently clasped Miriam's hands to stop their probing. "Angel, I'm okay. The blood's not mine—it's Doug's." He turned to Adair. "Rusty, see if you can find him and get him to the emergency room. I think I broke his nose."

THE TRACK at Keely's former high school was nearly deserted. Only three runners were dedicated enough to be out in the freezing weather. They puffed as they made their laps, their breath turning to steam in the frigid air.

Keely sat on the steps and watched them for a long time, remembering how this place had once been an important part of her life, as it probably was now for these young people. Here was where she'd come so many Saturdays with her father to train. Here was where she'd gained attention as a high-school runner.

She could almost hear her father as he coaxed her to work harder. *You can be the best in the whole world. Fight for it. C'mon. That's it. Faster. Keep going. Get tough. Show me you want it.*

She had wanted it more than anything, or so she'd believed back then. Now she wondered if maybe what she'd wanted most wasn't to be the best but to please her father. When she'd run well, it had made him happy, and when he was happy, it had eased the tension at home and given her a brief taste of what it felt like to be part of a loving family.

These many years after his death, maybe she was still trying to please him, or at least equating happiness with living up to his expectations.

After her failed running trial, she had looked at the good-luck ribbon her father had given her, and her first thought had been, *I've failed him. Now I'll never be happy.* She'd thrown the ribbon in the trash because it no longer represented her hope but her failure.

The loving father she'd adored and been so desperate to please hadn't been worth her adoration. Spencer Wilson. Cheater. Adulterer. She had spent most of her life believing he was a saint and blaming the unhappiness in her family on her mother.

The only time your mother's happy is when she's telling people what to do and how to act.

His words had been so easy to believe, growing up. Her mother had often seemed exactly as he described her, domineering and critical. She'd nagged about everything, found fault with every decision Keely had made from the clothes she'd bought to the few friends she'd chosen. She still nagged.

Was it like her father said, out of a need to control? Or was it merely a mother's way of showing concern?

Keely couldn't trust her memories to tell her the truth, because they were tainted by her father's deception.

Disturbed, she let out a long rattling breath. How could she put everything in perspective? She had too much pain to sift through, too many decision to make about her life.

A burst of wind danced across the track, reaching out to touch everything with its icy fingers. The force of it whirled bits of trash and sent the slender pines between the track and the baseball field swaying in an out-of-kilter rhythm. She shivered and slid her feet closer, tugging her jacket over her knees. She slipped her hands into the slash pockets. The night would be cold, perhaps the coldest of the season.

A bittersweet smile curved her lips as she thought of Mac and cold nights in front of the fire on his mother's quilt. They would talk and laugh and warm each other with hot sex. Oh, how she missed those times, missed the I-belong-here feeling she got when she was with him.

Those months she'd spent in Courtland had been good for her spirit, as well as her body, even though she hadn't saved her running career. For the first time in years she'd felt needed. By Mac. By the wheelers. By the students. The adrenaline high she'd experienced when a student suddenly understood a difficult problem was every bit as powerful as the high from winning a race.

But was a career in coaching and teaching really what she wanted?

No. With a heaviness of heart she had to admit it

wasn't. She liked working with the students, but she couldn't see herself doing it every day for the rest of her life.

Out on the track, one of the young men slowed to a jog to cool down, then did a few easy stretches. He walked to the edge where he'd left his gear bag and changed into tennis shoes, also swapping his woolen hat for a baseball cap. Covertly, he looked at her from beneath the bill.

Keely pulled up the collar on her jacket to bury as much of her face as she could, but he was openly staring now. He walked toward her. "Hey, aren't you Keely Wilson, the run—?"

"No, I'm not. I'm not her." She retreated up the steps and fled to the house, tired of being defined only by what she used to do. Mac was right. She could start over and do something else. She was bright. She had good ideas. She could learn to do anything she set her mind to. She was more than just a set of legs.

"MISS KEELY'S COMING UP the front walk," the housekeeper called from upstairs.

The fear that had risen in Liz with the passing hours melted to relief. "Thank you, Louise." She rushed from the den to the front door and ushered her daughter inside where it was warm. "I wish you'd told us you were going out. I got scared when I realized you weren't in the house."

"You were on the telephone and Louise was busy vacuuming." Keely coughed and cleared her throat. Her face looked frozen and she had nothing on her head or hands.

"Where on earth are your hat and gloves?"

"I forgot them." She slipped out of her lightweight jacket.

"Honestly, what were you thinking, going out with nothing on your head and only that flimsy thing when it's thirty-five degrees? Your system's already had a shock. Do you want to make yourself sick?"

"Mother, I'm not five anymore. Please don't nag me."

Liz's heart filled with regret. "You're right. I'm sorry." She took the jacket from Keely's arms and searched the foyer closet for a hanger. "I guess when I see you do something I think will hurt you, it's hard for me not to speak out. My concern for you didn't go away when you grew up."

When she didn't get a response, Liz glanced over her shoulder. Keely was staring at her as if she'd spoken in an unintelligible foreign tongue.

"You nag because you love me, don't you?" Keely asked.

The strange question surprised Liz. "Yes, of course. Because I love you very much."

Keely's face softened and one corner of her mouth eased upward into a soft smile. "Just checking."

Liz hung the jacket on the rod and closed the door. "How about a nice cup of hot tea to knock off the chill?"

She led the way to the den where a fire burned in the grate and a fresh pot of tea sat steeping on a silver tray on one of the end tables. The bare Christmas tree stood to one side of the fireplace, a visual reminder of things left unfinished.

When they were comfortably seated on the couch, Liz poured tea into a china cup and squeezed lemon into it. "Here, the lemon will soothe your throat."

Keely took the cup and saucer in her cold-reddened hands and inhaled the vapors. "Hot tea and lemon. How many times do you suppose you made my sore throats feel better with hot tea and lemon when I was little?"

"Oh, a few, as I recall." She shifted and tucked one leg under her so she could face Keely and not have to turn her head. Keely did the same. "You were never a sickly child, but you were prone to getting a tickle in cold weather."

"You always worried that the tickle would turn into something more serious, so you'd rub that menthol stuff on my throat and chest, then pin a washcloth to the inside of my nightgown so it wouldn't get greasy. I almost enjoyed getting sick because it felt so good when you fussed over me." Keely frowned suddenly. Her throat worked as if trying to handle something too large to swallow. "I'd forgotten that until this moment. I haven't thought about it in years."

"Sometimes the mind hides away memories, even good ones, until we're ready to face how they make us feel."

Keely nodded slowly. "Maybe that's true. This morning I've been flooded with memories of growing up in this house, of spending time with Daddy." She looked down into her cup. "And not being willing to spend time with you."

Her hand trembled, making the cup clatter on the saucer, so she set both on the coffee table. She hugged her arms tightly to keep them still, but they shook, anyway, as did her whole body. "I think my mind's trying to tell me it's time to face those memories, the good ones and the bad ones."

Liz prayed that was true. In the forty-eight hours since Keely had learned of her father's affairs, she'd done little but lie on the bed and gaze at the ceiling, tuning out everything around her. Liz, meanwhile, had spent those same hours torturing herself with questions. Would the revelation finally bring her daughter back to her? Or break the remaining threads holding their relationship together?

Guilt accompanied the questions, guilt for thinking about her own needs when her only child was dealing with two devastating events that had occurred in the past ten days.

"I'm sorry you found out about your father, especially now when you've already had so much other disappointment."

"I never thought anything could hurt me as much as not being able to run again, but finding that letter…"

"Oh, honey, I know. That's why I kept the truth from you when you were living at home. I thought it would be so much easier for you if you believed your father and I didn't get along because of our different personalities and backgrounds. That was the heart of the problem, yes, but not what finally ended the marriage."

"Why did you continue to keep the truth from me after I left to go to school? Or after you and Daddy separated? Even after he died and I so stupidly accused you of causing his heart attack, you never fought back. We've argued about the divorce a million times in the past eight years, and not one of those times did you tell me the real reason for it. Why?''

''Answer me truthfully. If I'd told you I filed for divorce because your father was unfaithful, would you have believed me?''

Keely's eyes provided the answer long before she spoke. ''No, I would never have believed that, not in a million years.''

''Of course not. You worshiped him. You would have resented me even more than you already did if I dared make an accusation like that. I couldn't risk alienating you further.''

''I'm sorry.'' Keely's bottom lip trembled. ''I never even gave you the chance to tell me the truth.''

''No, don't apologize. I don't blame you for anything that's happened. I know I'm often too rigid and you resent it. I suspect your father also set out to deliberately turn you against me. Am I right?''

Keely stood and walked to the fireplace to stare silently into the flames. Liz followed. She wanted to put her arms around her daughter, but years of rebuke had made her fearful. She stood a comfortable distance away, pretending to straighten a photograph on the mantel, and waited for Keely to decide if she truly was ready to face her memories.

''At the time,'' Keely finally said, her voice small and filled with hurt, ''I didn't understand that's what Daddy was doing, but I've been thinking about it, and yes, he did his best to make things worse between us. He said things, did things, to make sure I didn't trust your love. Finding ways to exclude you got to be a game between us.''

Liz had thought so, but whenever she confronted Spence, he'd denied it. He'd said she was too critical of Keely and only had herself to blame if her daughter didn't like being around her. For a while Liz was too occupied with trying to keep her marriage together to even see that Keely had started to withdraw from her. When she did finally notice something was wrong, it was already too late to repair the damage.

"I suspected it. When you were small we were so close. You used to throw those sweet little arms around me and hug me as tightly as you could and say, 'I love you, Lis-bet,' trying to imitate your grandmother.''

"I didn't have any front teeth and I couldn't pronounce Elizabeth.''

"Then, suddenly, I became 'Mother' and you didn't even want me touching you. I know the fighting between me and your father didn't help, and that your running was something you and he shared that we couldn't. But I always sensed there was more to your sudden aversion to me.''

"He warned me that I'd gotten too close to you and that you would use that to hurt me. He said...no matter what I did or how hard I tried to please you, it would never be enough, that you were cold and could never love me as much as he did.''

"Dear God!''

"So I stopped trying to win your approval. Only his.''

The tears that had pooled in Keely's eyes when they started this conversation began to fall quietly now. Liz, too, felt the sting of tears; the depth of Spence's deceit was like a knife to the heart.

"Why, Mother? Why did he do it?"

"I'm not sure I know. His desire to hurt me. Fear of losing you in a custody battle if we divorced. He seemed to have a constant need for validation, to see proof that people loved him, yet even when he had proof, he wouldn't believe it. He wasn't treated well as a child. His mother showed him little affection, and his father left them when he was very small. I can only guess that had something to do with his affairs and his lies."

Keely swiped at her tears. "I thought I hated him, but all I feel is this dull empty ache where my feelings for him used to be. I don't feel hate or love, just...nothing."

"Perhaps one day you can feel love again. Or at least forgiveness. Despite his faults, he was your father and he loved you very much."

Keely turned her head. "Do *you* forgive him?"

Liz wanted to answer honestly but wasn't sure how. The affairs, the years of lies, had devastated not only her marriage but her self-esteem. She'd been a carefree trusting girl when she married Spence, but he'd quickly changed her into a hard suspicious woman. Only with Everett's love had that carefree girl come to life again.

And yet, for most of the years of her marriage to Spence, she had to admit she loved him desperately. She'd clung stubbornly to the ideal of commitment and to her vows, despite every horrible thing he said and every woman he'd thrown in her face. Even now, even when she no longer loved him, she wanted to believe that something good had come from their marriage, something other than this child who stood next to her.

Could she forgive him? She had to. For Keely's chance at a happy future and for her own.

"Yes, I forgive him," she said. "I forgive him because that's the only way I can free myself of him. I want to go forward without regret, to wake up every morning without having the pain of the past influence my every thought, my every decision."

"I wish I could find the same peace of mind, and not only over this thing with Daddy but the accident and the other problems in my life."

"You can. Take one step forward. Then another. And another."

"Kind of like running a race."

"Yes, I suppose it is."

"Do you think that approach would work for mending a relationship? I've badly hurt someone I love."

Mac, Liz thought. *She's talking about Mac.*

"I don't see why not. You can damage love, but it isn't easily destroyed. Take the first step and let Mac know you love him. See what happens."

Keely's face, always an open reflection of the emotion that lay underneath, was a dark canvas of sadness, regret and pain; but also held the paler colors of resolution and hope.

To Liz's surprise, she took a step closer. Her heart stilled as her daughter reached out her arms, asking to be held for the first time in more than fifteen years.

"I meant you," Keely said softly, her chin quivering. "I love you, Liz-bet."

CHAPTER TWENTY-ONE

CHRISTMAS EVE had turned the athletic complex into a catacomb of eerily empty rooms. Reporters wanting a comment kept the telephones ringing all afternoon, but the calls finally died off at about eight. The two souls, besides Mac, who'd been foolish enough to come in today had long ago gone home to be with their families. Mac had no one waiting at home, so he lingered, the silence here somehow easier to bear than the silence of his little house.

He could go to Alan's or catch a flight out to spend the holiday with his sisters or brother, but the idea of kissing someone else's wife under the mistletoe and playing with someone else's children after Christmas dinner didn't appeal to him this year. He preferred, instead, the mindless act of updating files, of rearranging the books in his office according to subject.

His written report on the now-infamous nose-breaking incident was typed and ready to deliver to the university president after Christmas, a follow-up to his oral report, already given. Neither he nor the university had yet released an official statement on Doug Crocker's dismissal, but the story had shot through the staff, then the college community, like wildfire. The news had hit the Associated Press sports wire that afternoon.

A cold. A stupid cold had saved the track program from sanctions. Mac shook his head, still unable to believe it. The kid, Willie Jackson, hadn't used the tickets Crocker had improperly given him. He'd caught a cold and his grandmother had made him stay home from the game.

Willie also claimed Crocker hadn't given him any money. Mac was certain that was a lie, although he couldn't prove it. But neither could anyone else.

Because the kid hadn't used the tickets and because no evidence of a gift of money existed, technically Crocker hadn't violated NCAA rules. The track program was safe from sanctions.

But Crocker *had* killed his career at Courtland. The university supported Mac, both in his investigation of the alleged violation and in his subsequent firing of Crocker for unethical recruiting practices. If the broken nose became an issue, Rusty Adair could testify that Mac had only defended himself against an unprovoked physical attack. The bruises on Mac's throat, where Crocker had tried to choke him, were evidence enough.

Still…the situation should never have gotten to the point of physical violence. Mac had screwed up. Maybe not in the eyes of his superiors or staff, but in his own eyes.

He'd done the right thing in firing Doug. He was comfortable with his decision. If he was going to be honest, he'd even admit he'd *enjoyed* popping him in the nose. But Mac knew he'd definitely done the wrong thing in letting his disability interfere with doing his job. By failing to deal with Doug Crocker's improper behavior months ago, he'd created an explosive situation. He'd turned Doug into the living, breathing personification of the fears Mac still had about being in a wheelchair.

Pretty stupid, McCandless.

Down the hall a drink machine burped as if in agreement.

Never again would he let self-doubt keep him from doing what was right. Never again would he allow this wheelchair to keep him from going after what he wanted in his professional—or personal—life.

He was giving Keely twenty-four hours to get her feelings straightened out. Let her spend Christmas with her mom, but then he was going to Atlanta to bring her home. Never mind his promise to stay away. If she loved him, she had to tell him so. If she didn't love him, she had to tell him that, too. And to his face.

With no filing left to be done and the books arranged in a long colorful row, he decided it was foolish to hang around any longer. He locked up the office and headed home.

The streets of downtown were deserted, the stores dark. The garlands of green that looped in intervals along the utility wires swayed in the cold wind as he passed underneath them.

At the Sizemores' house, the multicolored lights on a tree in the window blinked on and off in cheery welcome, and a lighted Santa in the yard waved hello. But at Mac's house…

He stopped the van in the street and stared.

His front window also had a tree.

"Vicki," he grumbled. He wished she hadn't bothered. Sometimes women had a hard time understanding that men need their own unviolated space.

He punched the remote to open the garage door, then parked. The soft light of the Christmas tree spilled into the kitchen to guide him to the living room. Beneath the tree he recognized the packages he'd wrapped for Alan, Vicki and the kids, but the others had been put there by a different hand.

Shrugging out of his jacket, he tossed it toward a nearby chair. He picked up a red-foil package with an elaborate bow and read the name tag. "To Mac, from Keely."

Keely?

"I was beginning to think you were never coming home."

Startled by the voice, he dropped the package, sending it sliding across the hardwood floor. He whirled the chair around. His heart beat in double time as he saw what he couldn't see before. Keely lay on her side on his mother's quilt before the fireplace watching him, her head resting in one hand.

She sat up and tucked her jean-clad legs under her. "I was afraid you might run the other way if you saw my car, so Alan let me park it in his garage," she said, as if that explained everything. It didn't. Not by a long shot. "I heard about your fight with Crocker. Are you okay?"

She'd momentarily stunned him, but he found his voice quickly now. "Is that why you came back?"

"No, Alan only just told me about it."

"Then what are you doing here?"

"Getting cozy. I hear it's going to be a cold night." She patted the quilt. "Come down here with me? We can start a fire. I'd love to hear one of your family stories." When he didn't move, uncertainty clouded her face. She retracted her hand. "I was hoping you'd be at least a little glad to see me."

"Glad? I'm angry as hell at you! You ran out on me without a word, and the worry from that alone took a good ten years off my life. Then you gave the knife a couple of extra twists by acting like I wasn't important enough to talk to when I called your mother's. Do you have any idea how that made me feel?"

"Foolish. Abused. Unloved."

"You've got that straight!"

She blew out a troubled breath. "Okay, that's fair. I hurt you deeply and you have every right to be angry. But do you think you might put your anger aside for a few minutes and give me the chance to talk to you, to apologize?"

He didn't answer immediately.

"Mac, please don't be hardheaded. That's *my* job."

Begrudgingly he agreed. "Okay, I'm listening."

"I'm sorry I hurt you. I wish I could say I was only running away from the pain of losing what I thought was the most important thing in my life. But the truth is…I was running away from you, too. You're the first man to tell me he loved me and truly mean it. And then on top of everything else I was dealing with at the moment, you said you wanted to marry me. Pretty serious stuff to throw at me right then."

"My timing was lousy," he said stiffly.

"Yes, it was. But I'm not telling you this to make you feel bad for what you said, only to try and explain why I ran away. Failing my running test and having you propose was way too much for me to handle at one time. You know the old saying—Out of sight, out of mind. I thought getting away would make my problems disappear."

"Denying your problems doesn't solve them. I've learned that lesson the hard way."

"No, you're right. But leaving did turn out to be good for me in one way. Mother and I cleared up the misunderstandings that have been keeping us apart. We talked and got everything out in the open, and I feel really good about our relationship now. It still needs work, but the hard part is behind us. She and Everett even agreed to let me be part of the wedding."

"You're okay now with them getting married?"

She nodded. "Daddy made her miserable for years. Everett is a nice man who's very much in love with her. He'll be good to her. With him she can finally be happy."

"So old what's-his-name isn't such a bad guy, after all?"

"No, old what's-his-name is pretty okay. I invited him to the house to help decorate the Christmas tree, and I actually enjoyed talking with him. Having a stepfather will take some getting used to, but it might be nice."

"And you'll be getting the sisters you always wanted."

"Sisters?"

"Remember the pictures he showed us of his two

daughters when he was here? They'll be your stepsisters."

"Oh, I hadn't thought of that," she said, her eyes shining. "Sisters. I got sisters for Christmas, just like I asked."

"I'm glad for you, Keely. Sounds like the time spent at your mother's was pretty special."

A sudden shadow of pain crossed her face. "Yes, mostly. Something not so special happened, too, something I won't go into right now. But the result of it was like finding the missing piece in a big puzzle. Once I had that piece, I was able to step back and see the complete picture of my life. For the first time I could put running, and why it meant so much to me, into perspective. Finding that piece also helped me come to terms with some hard truths about myself."

"Like what?"

"Like understanding that I'm very much like my mother. For years I've tried to convince myself it isn't true. But it *is*, and I'm not ashamed to admit it. I'm even proud of it, because I've discovered she's a very strong woman."

"You inherited her strength."

"I hope so. I also inherited some of her faults, like the need to always feel in control. That, too, has bothered me for a long time. But I've come to accept that being like my mother doesn't automatically mean I'm going to make the same mistakes she did."

Keely moved forward and knelt in front of him, but thankfully not so close that he could reach out and touch her. The temptation to draw her into his arms and try to soothe the tired lines around her eyes with his lips was overwhelming. Only distance saved him from the humiliation of letting her know how easily he could forgive her.

"Mac, when I realized I could never compete professionally again, it devastated me. Running has always been a major part of who I am. It doesn't have to be the only part, though. You've forced me to understand that. You've made me peel back all the outside layers to find a person inside me that I had no idea was even there. And you know what? I can learn to like that person. She's not as worthless as she thought she was."

"I've been telling her that for months."

"I know," she conceded. "But...the next thing I'm going to say will disappoint you, I'm afraid. She also doesn't want to be a coach. I know you hoped that by getting me back in school, I'd come to love coaching as much as you do, but I'm sorry, I don't. Getting my master's degree in Health and Human Performance is a waste of my time."

Hope shattered. She was dropping out of school and leaving town permanently. Leaving him. He tried to keep his voice level when he asked, "What will you do?"

"I've decided Coxwell Industries needs a working president rather than one who only playacts. I enjoy being in the chemistry lab a great deal, and I have hundreds of ideas for products I'd like to develop, so I've told Ross I'm going into full commercial production with the InsulCare fabric. I'm going to run my own business."

For her sake he tamped down the sorrow of losing her. He would deal with it when he was alone.

"Keely Wilson, corporate bigwig. Sounds pretty good."

He tried to smile, but couldn't. The thought of her living hundreds of miles away in Miami was as awful a thing as he could imagine.

"That description isn't at all what I had in mind," she said. "I want to be Keely *McCandless,* corporate bigwig."

He wasn't sure he heard her correctly. "Run that by me again?"

"What I'm clumsily trying to tell you is that I've realized no career alone can make me happy. Running my own business appeals to me very much. I'm even looking forward to finishing school once I change my major to chemistry. But if I woke up tomorrow and discovered by some miracle I could race and compete professionally again, even that couldn't make me happy. Only you can do that."

Something warm and beautiful filled her eyes. She seemed to glow in the twinkling lights from the tree.

"Mac, the instant you walked across that track eleven years ago and introduced yourself, my life changed. I've spent years caring for you in one way or another. You've been my mentor, my teacher and my coach. Eventually, you became my friend and my lover. But I panicked when you said you loved me. My parents failed miserably at their relationship, and I convinced myself the same thing would happen to us. I didn't believe I had enough substance to truly make you happy."

He opened his mouth to tell her that wasn't true, but she held up her hand and stopped him.

"No, let me finish. You need to hear this and I need to say it. I've never been thoughtful enough of other people. Lord knows, you deserve to spend your life with someone who's a lot smarter and a lot less emotional than I am. Ever since you proposed, I've racked my brain trying to come up with even one thing I have to offer you that no other woman can. Now, finally, I've done it. I know what makes me perfect for you and why we have to get married."

"And that is?"

"No other woman on this earth could possibly love you as much as I do."

He closed his eyes for a moment and thanked God. "I thought you came here to tell me you were leaving me for good."

"Leaving you? No, my love, I'm not leaving you. You're the best thing in my life, and I want the chance to prove I can be the best thing in yours. I intend to spend the next sixty years making you glad to wake up every morning beside me. If you'll have me." She held out her arms to him. "Will you grow old with me?"

He wasn't sure how he got from the wheelchair to the floor so fast, but suddenly he was holding her, and she was laughing and crying at the same time.

"Is this a yes?" she asked. He kissed her hard, then more slowly with passion, again and again, until the familiar catlike purr of desire started in her throat and her body hummed with desire. "Mmm. John Patrick McCandless, I do love the way you say yes."

CHAPTER TWENTY-TWO

October 2000
Sydney, Australia

THE MARATHON was the longest of Keely's life, two hours and thirty minutes of torture that had her insides churning and her heart beating so fast it threatened to explode from her chest.

She tried taking deep breaths. She tried shallow ones, but neither made her feel better. Every passing minute brought a new agony and reinforced doubt. Had attempting this race been a terrible mistake?

Just when she thought she might pass out from the stress, the race leaders entered the Olympic stadium. Torture turned to sheer terror. Mac and a member of the Canadian team were in front of their division, side by side, racing their wheelchairs for the finish line. Even on the huge video screens overhead it was impossible to tell who was leading.

One man would take home the gold medal; the other would take home the silver.

"Please," Keely prayed out loud, but the cheering of the crowd behind her obliterated her words.

More than 125 nations were represented here in Sydney, but international boundaries dissolved the moment the announcer said Mac's name. He was a hero. His and Keely's story, leaked by his staff to *The Atlanta Journal* and broadcast by the wire services, had endeared him to people all over the world. They knew he was trying to win a gold medal for her. Now, 110,000 fans let him know by their screams and waving arms that they supported him.

Amid the chaos, Keely continued to stand in the trainers' area and pray. Mac had worked so hard to make the U.S. team. He'd raced on weekends and trained every night after work for more than two years. This moment meant everything to him, to both of them.

The marathon wasn't his usual event. He was so much stronger in the four hundred and eight hundred meters. But he'd insisted that with her help he had a chance.

"I have to try the marathon," he'd told her. "For my dreams and for yours."

Now he was only seconds away from either capturing their dreams or losing them forever, and the crowd, the millions of people around the world watching live on television, knew what was at stake.

Thirty yards to go.

Fifteen yards to go.

"You can do it," she whispered, as if he could hear her. Before the race, she'd pinned her father's faded ribbon to Mac's jersey for luck. But it would take more than luck now. Everything was up to Mac. He had to *want* to win, not for her, but for himself.

He seemed to surge. He crossed the finish line half a wheel in front of the Canadian, and the victory sent the spectators and the U.S. team into a frenzy.

People began hugging and kissing Keely. Television reporters tried to snag her for a comment, but she fought her way through the gate and onto the track where Mac was about to take his victory lap.

He scanned the track apron for her. She raced forward and dropped to her knees. His arms were already open to receive her.

A teammate handed him an American flag and he tried to pass it to Keely. "Run alongside me, Coach," he said to her over the noise. "You earned this gold as much as I did."

Keely's heart swelled with emotion. She had wanted for a lifetime to do this, to hear the cheers of the crowd and experience the thrill of a gold-medal win. He was offering her the chance.

She kissed him. "I love you more than anything," she said.

And then she stepped back into the crowd and let him take the victory lap without her.

EPILOGUE

Three years later...

"PLEASE, PLEASE, let me ride you. I'll try not to squeal this time."

Mac groaned. "Aw, Linda, not tonight. We still have a ton of inventory to take."

"Please? One little ride? You rode Roberta and Miriam last night, but I didn't get a turn."

He was about to give in to the secretary's pleading when he looked down the hall.

"Sorry, Linda, but you know my wife gets mad if I let anyone have her seat." He smiled at Keely and pushed forward to meet her. "Hey, Sport Model."

"Hey, handsome." She bent down and brushed his lips with hers.

"You're off early," he said.

"I finished the prototype for the portable trainer ahead of schedule. Do you think I can ask the wheelers to field-test it next weekend when Dean takes them to Augusta? I could use some feedback."

"Sure. He'd love to test it."

A runner could warm up or cool down off the track, but an athlete in a wheelchair needed track space. When the wheelers traveled, they often didn't have that space. Keely had come up with an idea for light-weight portable trainer they could take with them.

Her ability to see a problem and find a solution continued to astound Mac. Her company produced a range of equipment used by able-bodied and disabled athletes and held several patents for medical equipment. The commercial application of her InsulCare fabric alone had made a tidy profit.

With a plant in Miami and now a second one in Courtland, she had expanded Coxwell and increased profits ten percent. But what mattered most to both of them was that she loved what she was doing.

"I brought a picnic supper and put it in your office," she said. "I was hoping you could take thirty minutes to eat with me. We've hardly talked all week."

"I know, and something's got to give. I feel like I never see you anymore, and I don't spend enough time with my students, either. That bothers me."

"Dean's doing a good job with them, isn't he?"

After his graduation, Dean had joined the staff as an assistant coach. Mac had put him in charge of the wheelers.

"Dean's doing a great job. The problem isn't him, baby, it's me. I miss you. And I miss not having the time to coach. What if I told you I've been thinking about retiring from racing? What would you say?"

She cocked her head. "Seriously?"

"I wouldn't trade these past three years for anything, but I've accomplished what I set out to do. Now I want to coach again. I want to be with my students. That's where I belong."

"I can't say I'm surprised."

"Do you have any problems with it?"

"No, not if that's what you want."

"Are you sure you won't be disappointed? I know you enjoy the races as much as I do."

"I'd miss it, but to be honest, I've been thinking I might start staying home on the weekends, anyway, if you could manage without me. There's a quilting class I want to take Saturday mornings, and I've also got a big project coming up that's not the kind of thing I want to be carrying around to races every weekend."

"What kind of project?"

"Oh, something very special. Actually, you initiated it, so I'm going to need your help. You can coach me."

Coach her? Doing what?

He patted his lap. "Hop on. I'll ride you to the office. We can have our picnic and talk about this coaching thing. I've got news about Ginny Sasser and Dean you'll want to hear, too."

"Can you ride both of us?" she asked.

"Both?"

He glanced past her to see if he had overlooked J.P. or one of the other Sizemore kids. The hall was empty.

Then he had another thought, a crazy one, and his insides turned to mush. He looked at Keely's stomach. She'd been putting her hand there a lot lately, the way she did when she felt queasy.

He was afraid to hope. They had only recently started trying again for a child.

The first year he'd been so sure he could impregnate Keely. Every couple of months she'd undergone intrauterine insemination with sperm they'd taken from him through electro ejaculation. They'd pooled and specially processed the sperm to increase its effectiveness, but still Keely hadn't gotten pregnant.

Time after time the news was the same: no baby. Mac finally accepted there never would be.

Keely, though, had refused to give up on the idea and she'd talked him into trying again. He'd indulged her, but he hadn't allowed himself to hope for success.

He looked up to find her beaming down at him.

She patted her stomach. "Instead of Sport Model, you're going to have to start calling me Family Sedan. You may even have to put a bumper sticker on my behind that says 'Wide Load.'"

"A baby?" he asked, his voice cracking.

She nodded. "I've suspected since last week. But I didn't want to get your hopes up and then find out it wasn't true. The fertility clinic confirmed it a little while ago."

"But it's only been a couple of months. How...?"

"Haven't you heard? I'm terribly impatient. And I never quit until I get what I want."

An image flashed into his head. A little girl. Big blue eyes. Dimples. Strong-willed like her mother.

He smiled, and then his smile turned into a chuckle. His chuckle turned into laughter. He pulled Keely onto his lap, needing to touch her, to hold her.

"A baby," he said with wonder.

"I'm going to need a birthing coach. Want the job?"

"What does it pay?"

"Oh, let's see. Hugs. Kisses. Your back scratched

whenever you want.'' Her expression softened. ''Love for a lifetime.''

''Sounds like a great deal. I'll take it.''

She kissed him and caressed his cheek. ''My beautiful perfect husband, you've given me a miracle, after all.''